WHERE TIME STANDS STILL

N.S. PERKINS

Book Cover Design by Murphy Rae

Editing by Jacqueline Hritz

Formatting by Champagne Book Design

To my love.

The memories I have with you are my most prized possession.

WHERE TIME
STANDS STILL

AUTHOR'S NOTE

My dear readers,

Before beginning, I wanted to address the fact that while this book is a romance, it deals with heavy topics, including chronic illness, debilitating accidents, death, and dying. There are also instances where the protagonist has ableist views and discourses about herself and her condition. While the narrative, just like myself, condemns this self-taught ableism, some parts of this book might be triggering to read for some of you. I have tried to handle these themes with the utmost care, respect, and love, but I still I want you all to take care of yourselves.

Love,
N.S. Perkins

PROLOGUE

I ALWAYS WEAR A RING WHEN I GO OUT.

Not that I go out often—far from it—but when I do, I want to keep the drunk men looking for someone to warm their beds at bay. It usually works.

Except for tonight.

The man sits down on the stool next to mine before I can say anything. I wouldn't have hesitated to tell him this seat was taken before he sat down, but now it feels a little rude. Especially since he's already sprawled on the bar, his head draped on top of his arms.

Wow. I didn't know it was possible to get this plastered on a Tuesday night.

And *this* is why I don't go out.

I shake my head and take a sip of my vodka soda. It's not like I had much of a large selection of places to visit tonight. I needed to get out of my apartment. Do something—anything—that could take my mind away from my problems for at least an hour or two. This bar seemed as good a place as any to do just that. The ceilings are high, the light is dim, and the jazz music that's playing from the built-in speakers is not too loud. Plus, the alcohol they're serving is useful to take the edge off. All in all, this place is helping. So the guy can sit there if he likes. I'll just ignore him.

Except it's hard to ignore a person when they keep mumbling things that are incomprehensible half of the time. I keep thinking he's talking to me, but apparently, he's only talking to himself.

"...can't believe this."

I turn to my right and once again find that he wasn't addressing me, but I do a double take when I realize he's opened his eyes. They're a light brown, droopy and red rimmed. But that's not what's most noticeable about them; they look so very *sad*. In fact, they don't fit with the rest of him. Even when hunched, I can see he's tall and has a muscular build. His dark-brown hair is curly and ruffled, as if he's dragged his hands through it more than once. The skin of his forearms is sun-kissed, a nice gold shade. His lips are plump, too big for a man's face, really, but somehow, it all works.

He's stunning.

And he's also deeply unhappy.

In my experience, gorgeous people always seem happy, or maybe they only hide their pain to let it out once they're alone, but there's no mistaking his state of mind. It's easy to conceal the truth with words, but eyes don't lie. That's something my mom used to tell me over and over again. Before forgetting about me, that is.

I take another sip of my drink as I keep looking at him. Thankfully, his gaze is lost in space, so he doesn't see me. Funny how I was complaining about him sitting next to me a few minutes ago, yet I'm the one acting like a stalker now. It's not for the same reason guys usually look at girls, though. I don't want to get in his pants—not by a long shot. What I do want is to know what's wrong with him. Something's eating at him, and it's got my attention. Maybe if I learn about someone else's real problems, it will make mine feel smaller. It might seem selfish, but after today, I need it.

Before I can overthink it, I turn to him and ask, "Are you all right?"

His gaze climbs to mine as if it's completely natural for a total stranger to ask how you're doing. Maybe this guy goes out more than I do and it's actually a normal practice. Who knows.

His eyes are glassy. I can see it even better when he straightens and blinks at me. The beer he takes a chug of is definitely not his first or second of the night. With a voice deeper than what I would've imagined, he says, "I will be, but right now, I'd say life could go fuck itself."

I can't help it. I snort. I wasn't expecting such blunt honesty, but somehow, that's the most perfect answer he could've given me.

"Cheers to that," I say before downing the rest of my drink. Coughing a little, I lift my hand and signal to the bartender for another one. Since I don't drink often, I'll probably regret it once I get to the office tomorrow morning, but right now, I'd say I deserve it.

"I'll take it your life sucks too?" Tall Guy asks as he leans his head on his hand.

"That's one way to put it."

"What happened to you?"

Creases form on my forehead as I lift my brows. I know I was about to ask him the same thing, but it feels like a pretty intrusive question for someone I met five minutes ago. Plus, it's not a simple one to answer. Too much has happened—and will happen—for me to be able to narrow it done to one thing.

So instead, I narrow my gaze and reply, "What happened to *you*?"

"That's cheating," he says, as if we're playing some kind of game. Maybe we are. *Who's the worse off between the two of us?* No matter what he tells me, I know I'll win.

Goodness, I sound like a whiny, broken record tonight.

Sighing, he picks up the beer the bartender brought him a second ago, after he finished the previous one, and takes a long swig. "I just proposed to the girl I've been with for the past ten months, and she said no."

I wince. "Ouch. I'm sorry."

His shoulders lift in the most half-assed shrug I've ever seen. "'s all right. Guess I shouldn't have expected anything different."

I don't ask him what he means by this. Instead, I take another sip of my newly served drink and say, "So are you still going to stay together?" I don't know who I am at the moment. The real Wren

Lawson would never involve herself in someone else's personal life like this. She'd never even have tried to engage in a conversation with a stranger in the first place. Must be the alcohol, or the fact that asking him about his problems takes my mind somewhere else.

He blinks slowly, his gaze getting lost for a moment. "Nah. What's the point in staying with someone who doesn't see herself with you in the long run?"

I don't answer because he has a point. One I've lived by my whole life. The reason why I'm single and plan on staying that way forever. I lift my glass in my second toast of the night.

The music around us becomes slightly louder, and I close my eyes, slowly moving my body left and right. Drunk Wren really is a different person. The AC is cold against my skin, which feels amazing compared to the sticky June air of downtown Boston. My hair was starting to curl out of my tight bun as I walked here.

"What about you?" Tall Guy asks, head tilting.

"Hm?"

"Why are you drinking?"

My eyes drift down to the glass I'm holding.

"I told you my reason. It's your turn now," he adds, and even though he's drunk, he makes a fair point. And if there's one thing I care about in life, it's fairness. I didn't become a lawyer for nothing, after all.

"My genes suck," I answer simply, the test results I received today flashing in my mind, all those letters I could barely decipher sticking a punch to my jaw.

While this might not be the kind of detailed answer he'd expected, it's more than I would've given anyone in normal circumstances. It's surprising that I've even given him that. Apparently, there's something about this guy that makes me be honest. Maybe it's the small wrinkles around his mouth that tell me this man smiles more often than not, or maybe it's the warmth in his gaze, the color of a flickering fireplace. Or maybe it's the fact that I know I'll never see him again after tonight, so why not?

Tall Guy nods like he understands exactly what I mean. He probably doesn't, but I appreciate the fact that he acts like it.

"Life always finds a way to screw us," he answers after a while. "But you know what helps?"

"What?"

With a lift of his half-empty pint, he says, "Alcohol." Then, for the first time tonight, he smiles. It's small, but it's explosive. It's not exactly symmetrical either, yet somehow, that makes it even more charming.

I'm not a big smiler. Anyone at the firm would tell you. Focused? Yes. Hardworking? Absolutely. But a smiling person? Not really. It's not that I don't like it. It's that the majority of the time, I don't see a reason to smile. Not like I'm sad or depressed, just constantly neutral. Things are the way they are, and I accept that. Doesn't mean I need to celebrate it by expressing a happiness I don't feel.

But his grin triggers something in me. It's almost like a bumper car. He hits me with it, and the only thing I can do in response is to grin back.

Tonight really is the strangest night I've spent in a while.

After we both take a large gulp of our drinks, I say, "So what's next for you then?"

He puffs his cheeks, then slowly releases the air. "I don't know. Figuring out how to be alone, I guess."

Before I can control it, a snicker comes out of me.

"What's so funny?" he asks.

"Nothing. It's just that I'm an expert in that."

"Being alone?"

"Uh-huh."

He smirks. "Maybe I'll call you for advice then."

The strangest thing happens then. Something in the air

changes. Or maybe it's something in me that shifts. But one second we're joking about our shitty lives, and the next, I'd swear he's about to kiss me. He doesn't utter a word, yet I feel it everywhere. It's like a bubble surrounds us, the air warmer, the chatter of patrons softer. His gaze dips to my lips, lightning fast, and I'm hit with mixed feelings. A part of me wants to get up and run away, but another part wants to stay here and learn what this stranger tastes like, how he could make me forget. Maybe it wouldn't be so bad to let go for once. His tongue darts out, wetting his rosy lips. I swallow, the alcohol in my veins making everything fuzzy. Or is it him?

But before either of us can move, the bubble is burst by a hairy arm placing two bar tabs in front of us, the leather smacking against the granite bar. I jump, my heart beating way too fast all of a sudden.

What the heck was that? Did I imagine it?

I look down at my phone and see it's close to midnight.

"I should probably get going," I say, looking everywhere but at him. Not waiting for his answer, I get up to pay my tab. Once I'm done and the bartender has wished me a good night, I put my wallet back in my purse and look over my shoulder at the guy I most likely will never see again in my life. His eyes are a little less glossy than before, and he sits straighter. Smiling softly, he lifts a hand and gives me a quick wave.

"It was nice meeting you, stranger," he says. No awkwardness.

Yeah, I definitely imagined things.

With a nod, I wave back, then walk toward the door.

I know nothing about this guy. He knows nothing about me. In the past half hour, we haven't even exchanged names. But somehow, as I walk out of the bar into the warm summer night, I feel lighter than I did coming in.

A miracle.

CHAPTER 1

Five months later
Wren

MEMORY IS A STRANGE THING.

In fact, even scientists haven't completely mastered it. A network of neurons in your hippocampus conserving moments and experiences, down to the tastes and smells associated with them, is a wild thing to wrap your head around. And no one has been able to explain without a doubt why we remember certain things but not others. We do know that vivid emotions associated with a moment will help us remember it better, but really, there's no saying what we will remember in five minutes, or five years, or five decades. Some things, like the day you got your first dog or the last time you hugged your mother, you would like to remember but can't. And other things, you remember for no specific reason. For example, the face of the man who you thought was going to kiss you in a bar months ago.

Which is a bad thing, considering it's the first thing I see as I climb out of my car at the Evermore Christmas Tree Farm.

What in the world?

I stand frozen as I try but fail to catch my breath. Today has already become one of the weirdest days I've ever lived, and it's only ten in the morning. First, I've been forced to throw my usual schedule out the window to get here. Selina, my boss, told me a few days ago that a new client had requested to work with me specifically on a medical malpractice case and that I'd meet them on Monday. But last night, she called to say they couldn't come to Boston after all and would need me to drive to their place in Vermont to meet with them.

I'd only heard of a few rare occasions when Silver & Prescott had agreed to meet a client away from our offices. However, she didn't leave me much choice to say no, so I agreed, only mentally biting my nails. Because of that, instead of walking across town and entering the office at 8:00 a.m. on the dot this morning, I got up earlier than usual and made the almost two-hour drive to get to this place I'd never heard of. For a person who literally never does anything different, that sudden change to my schedule should've been the only strange thing to happen to me.

But of course, I should've anticipated that one bad surprise never comes alone.

Tall Guy looks exactly as I remember him, except his hair is shorter than when I last saw him, the waves a little tamer. Other than that, he has the same light-brown eyes that look like molten gold in the sunlight, the same large build that would make any man jealous, and the same golden-brown skin that has no right looking this good in late November. He's also dressed in a completely different style. This summer he wore a dress shirt and nice pants, but here, it's a flannel shirt and lumberjack boots.

What could he possibly be doing here, almost two hours away from the place where we first met?

Next to him stands a short lady who has the same brown complexion, dark hair, and warm-honey eyes. Beside her is a pale man with white hair and a bright blue gaze, standing up with a walker. The reason I'm here, I assume.

"You must be Ms. Lawson," the lady says with a light accent—Spanish, maybe—which finally brings me out of my staring trance. Right. I'm here for a job. It doesn't matter whether I've met Tall Guy before. Besides, he was so wasted that night, he probably doesn't even remember me or the weird moment we shared.

"Yes, I am. And you must be the Scott-Perez family," I say, closing the door of my sedan behind me and approaching them. The heels of my knee-high leather boots dig into the fresh snow as I look around, a literal winter wonderland of large evergreens covered in white powder surrounding me. I've never been to a Christmas tree farm before, and I had no idea a place could look so magical. The view is almost worth the long drive and the disruption of my usual habits. *Almost.*

Once I stand in front of them, I take a better look at the two older adults before quickly meeting Tall Guy's eyes. It's the first time I get to see him upright, and while I knew he seemed tall, it's nothing compared to standing next to him. I'm five eight, and I almost need to tilt my head back to look at him. Thankfully, his face doesn't show any signs of recognition—not that I would've expected it to. We didn't speak much that night months ago. I don't even know why *I* remember him. Again, memory is a strange, strange thing.

"I'm Aaron," Tall Guy says as he steps forward, hand extended.

Aaron. After all these months, I finally know his name. It suits him.

"Wren," I answer as I grab his large hand and shake it. It feels so surreal, to be here, acting professional with him as if I didn't meet him while in a state so unlike my real self. If he'd remembered, I would've been humiliated to my core.

He takes a step back, then gestures toward the tiny woman. "This is my mom, Martina." I shake her hand too as he says, "And this is my dad, Dennis."

The man's handshake is weak. Too weak for someone of his stature. Still, he maintains my gaze the whole time.

After taking a step back, I say, "Nice to meet you all. Shall we?"

Tall Guy—Aaron—nods once, then leads the way toward a large rustic house made of chestnut-colored wooden logs, smoke billowing out of a chimney. The place fits with the whole winter cottagecore vibe they have going on here. I walk behind Martina, who keeps a hand on Dennis's back as he pushes his walker through the not-so-practical gravel entryway. The air is crisp and cold, and I hug my thin suede wrap-up coat tighter around me.

Once we get inside, the smell of firewood and fresh cookies fills my nose, and I can't help but hum low. Christmas carols play softly in the background. From the foyer, we can see all the way through the kitchen to a large living room housing a woodstove and brown leather couches covered in throw blankets.

I can't imagine this place during summer. It's like it must be inhabited by a perpetual Christmas spirit.

Aaron leads us through the kitchen, with pots hung to the ceiling over a square wooden island, then turns to his left and stops once we reach what I assume is the dining room, a gigantic table made of a big slab of tree in the middle. I take a seat facing the three of them, then grab a notepad and my favorite black-ink pen out of my leather briefcase.

I clear my throat at the sight of the three members of the family staring at me. "So, why don't you start by telling me about your situation and what you need a lawyer for."

Aaron automatically looks at his dad, then exchanges a look with his mom. She nods and pats his hand, giving him a warm smile.

Her expression falters as she swallows, then looks at me. "My husband was the victim of a medical error at the local hospital three months ago, and we would like to seek legal counsel regarding our options here."

Sounds like what Selina had told me. Twirling the pen

between my fingers, I say, "I understand. Can you tell me a bit more about what happened?"

Martina opens her mouth, but no word comes out, and somehow, I can feel her pain, deep and sharp, just by looking at her. It's written all over her face.

"He had a stroke," Aaron says after grabbing his mother's hand. "It was apparently an atypical presentation, but instead of doing any investigation or whatever it is they're supposed to do, the ER doctor sent my dad back home, saying he probably had the stomach flu and to just wait until it went away. We brought him to bed once we got home, and when we went to wake him up hours later, he was..." He drags a hand over the short bristles of his beard. "He was in a much worse state."

Dennis's eyes follow the conversation, but despite his seeming understanding of the situation, he doesn't say a word.

I place my hands on the table and slowly lean forward. "I know this is difficult, and I'm so sorry about it, but I have to ask. What complications are we talking about here?"

Aaron turns to his father, grabbing his hand just like he did his mom's minutes ago. "He lost the ability to speak. He lost control over some of the right side of his body. He, um... He understands everything, you know? But he can't tell us what he needs. And the doctor we saw when we went to another hospital told us that some of these problems might've been avoided if he'd received treatment right away."

I write down all of what they've told me, my mind working double speed. This is going to be a big and long case. It's a medical mistake that's resulted in severe disability. They might want to sue the hospital as well as the doctor. They'll ask for a big compensation. It's going to be tedious. Something that would require me to disrupt my whole life for weeks, possibly months. I get shivers just thinking about everything I would need to adapt. Plus, the reason for which they're seeking legal counsel makes sense, but why did they want to work with me specifically? That part doesn't make any sense. No one's ever asked for my services in particular, especially not for a case of this size.

Once I'm done with my notes, I put my pen down and link my fingers in front of me. "First, I'd like to say I'm very sorry that happened to you, and I'll be happy to talk to you about your options going forward after today. From what you've told me, I think you have enough here to build a strong case." I look up to find Martina and Dennis gazing at each other, but Aaron's eyes are straight on me. They look so much more alive than the first time we met, but still so sad.

It causes something in my chest to pinch. His life hasn't gotten any better since the bar this summer—far from it. For some reason, it makes me uneasy.

I toy with my bracelet.

"But I'm actually not the most experienced at Silver & Prescott for medical liability cases, so I will—" I lean down to grab my bag, then pull out a card from the pocket where I leave them, "—give you the names of some of the best attorneys we have who specialize in cases like these."

I hand the card to Martina, who takes it with a shaky hand, her eyebrows high.

"There's a number on this card from the branch of the firm that's located in Windsor, which is also going to be much closer for you. Just ask for Randall Stevenson. He's the best." I realize all this probably sounded dry, so I add a tight smile.

I wish I could help them more, but I didn't lie. This isn't my specialty. Sure, I've done a few medical liability cases over the past two years, but I'd rather they be with the best. They look like good people, and they deserve to win this. And that's without taking into account all the personal reasons why working all the way up here would be less than ideal for me.

Aaron's eyes are narrowed, an emotion I can't quite pinpoint in them. He's still holding his father's hand, grip tight.

Beside him, Martina reads what's written on the card, then says, "But...are you sure?" Something in her voice sounds disappointed. She probably hoped the first lawyer they met with would be the right one. I wish I had been.

Straightening the papers in front of me, I say, "I'm quite sure. This is what will be best for you." Best for everyone, really. "Now, let's discuss what options you'll have with your attorney going forward."

CHAPTER 2

Aaron

SHIT.

Shit, shit, shit.

She can't leave.

She's spent the past hour and a half going over the possible avenues we can pursue to get some kind of compensation for what happened to my dad—as if any amount of money could ever make up for what he's been through. And through it all, she's been fantastic. She knows her stuff. She doesn't look the tiniest bit uncomfortable with explaining things to a client who can't answer back. Her voice is soft but clear, not babying. Dad's happy about it. I can see it in his eyes. And while she's not a particularly warm person, there's something about her that's comforting. Like she's got her shit together and can handle anything life throws at her.

But now she's getting ready to leave, and I can't let that happen. We're winning this case, and she's our best shot. Everyone here knows it—except for her, maybe.

"Well," she says as she stands and puts her notepad and computer back in her bag, "it's been a pleasure meeting you all, and I truly wish you the best of luck going forward."

Ma gives her a smile that is nowhere close to happy. "Thank you. You've been very helpful."

Before thinking about it, I get up, my chair scraping the floor. "Ms. Lawson—"

"Wren, please," she says.

I nod. "Wren." The name comes out of my mouth smoothly,

and I can't help but be happy I finally know it. "Would you mind stepping outside so we can have a word?"

Please say yes.

I can feel rather than see Ma's gaze burn a hole in the back of my head, probably wondering what the hell I'm doing, but this is my last chance to convince her, and I'm not wasting it. Maybe my mother was too polite to fight for her, but I'm not.

Wren's eyes widen a second. They're a dark-blue shade, almost indigo. In the dark, they could pass for black, but in the sunlight of the dining room, the color is unmistakable.

She quickly regains a neutral expression and says, "Sure."

I lead her away from my parents, then make the trek to the front door, where I stop and steal another glance at her. She doesn't look like she belongs in this outdoorsy scene. At all. Her coat is thinner than the flannel shirt I'm wearing.

"The wind's pretty harsh on the farm. Would you like something warmer to wear?" I say as I grab my fleece-lined jacket.

She shakes her head. "Thank you, but I'm fine."

Sure.

"All right," I say anyway as I open the door, then lead her out so we can talk away from my parents' sneaky ears. Once we're finally alone, though, all the words die down in my throat.

I can't believe *she*'s here. Of all the people in the world, the lawyer we wanted had to be the woman I met on one of the worst days of my life, who I probably traumatized. The one I've had to stop myself from thinking a time or three.

She looks exactly the same as she did that night, except maybe less relaxed. Her back is ramrod straight, half of her dark, shoulder-length hair pinned behind her head. Her lips are painted a light red, although I do everything not to look in that direction. No need for a reenactment of that night.

Does she remember me? I hope to God not.

Definitely should've looked for a photo of attorney Wren

Lawson online before today. I could've prepared myself to see her again, at least.

"I wanted to, uh..." I clear my throat. These nerves are unusual for me. Then again, I rarely have to deal with anything this serious. I'm not doing this for me. It's for Dad.

Two dark eyebrows climb on her forehead. "You wanted...?"

Get it together, Aaron.

Wind carries white powder from the trees, flying around our heads as I say, "I wanted to know what it would take for you to take this case." There. Wasn't so hard.

"Oh. Um." Her fingers' grip tightens around the handles of her bag. "As I explained before, I truly think transferring the case to the branch closest to here is for the best."

"Yeah, I got that." The snow crunches under my boots as I take a step forward. This is the time to be convincing. "Now I want to know what it would take for you to keep it."

Her lips pull to the side. Bad sign.

"Aaron, I—"

"Do you know why we asked for you specifically?" My throat is dry, but I try to sound confident.

She blinks. "Honestly? Not really, no."

My question has piqued her interest. Something in her stance has changed, as if I've gained a slight upper hand. I don't know how law firms work specifically, but if it's anything like the graphic design field, it must not occur that often that clients request to work with one of the younger professionals. She's probably in the second half of her twenties, max thirty. That doesn't mean a thing, though. She's good, and she's who I—who *we*—want.

"I saw your name in the *Boston Globe*, a few months back," I say.

The slight part of her lips tells me she knows what I'm talking about, but I continue anyway. "You won the case for that dementia patient who lost her legs because of a medical mistake. Refused to settle. Got those bastards to pay."

"That..." She exhales slowly, then looks back at me. "That was an exception. There was a lot of luck involved. We have lawyers much more experienced who—"

"I don't care about that. What I care about is finding someone who will fight for my dad as much as a family member would. And what I saw in those media reports and court transcripts? It was someone who fought and someone who cared. That's what we want." I'm a little breathless as I stop talking. Ever since Dad's stroke three months ago, I haven't been able to stop thinking about much else, and now that I have a chance to do this for him, I can't imagine not succeeding in keeping her with us.

"I..." Her gaze drifts to her left, where row after row of fir trees stand, soon to be chopped, sold, and decorated. Something's still bothering her, but I can see her resolve slowly fading. I hate being this insistent, but right now, I don't have a choice.

"Is it the distance?" I ask, trying to meet her gaze. "Because if it is, we can make sure to get adapted transport for my dad to get to you, or we can pay for a hotel for you to stay close to here." I take another step forward, twisting the fabric lining the inside of my coat pockets between my fingers. "Is it a money problem? Because if it is, just name your price."

She jerks back, brows furrowing. "No, of course it's not that."

"Then what is it? What will it take?"

She doesn't answer, making my pulse increase even more. This situation feels like it's slipping through my hands, and I don't know what else to say. So I go with the only thing left. "Is it because of that night?"

Her head jerks up so fast, it almost makes me jump. "You..."

"What?" I say in a low voice.

"Nothing, I just..." She shakes her head. "I wasn't sure you remembered."

I almost laugh at that. How could I not remember the person who made one of the shittiest nights of my life...well, less shitty? The whole sequence of events is crystal clear in my mind.

It wasn't so much that I was sad about Amber. I got shitfaced mostly because I had no idea where my life was headed from there. And then all of a sudden, there was this stranger who made that moment a little easier to get through. Sure, I'd noticed how gorgeous she was—I wasn't blind—but that wasn't important at that point. I could feel that she was going through some shit too, and for a few minutes, she made me feel less alone.

And then, of course, I went ahead and almost kissed her like the drunk dumbass I was. Thank God I stopped myself from doing it. It wouldn't have been right, and it probably would've ruined all our chances of working with her. I'm not even sure if she noticed I was about to do that, but I'm praying she didn't. I can't imagine the guilt I'd have to live through if she dumped us because of it.

"Yeah, I remember," I say nonchalantly.

She doesn't speak for a moment, busy looking at the house behind me. Her face is so hard to read. I remember thinking the same thing that night, maybe because it's something I'm not used to. I have a family of expressive people. Anyone can tell whether we're mad or sad or happy by the look on our faces. I can't do that with her, not then and not now. And right this moment, there's not much I wouldn't give to know what she's thinking.

"Is that it?" I ask. "Is it because of that night? Because if I'm the problem, then I can make sure never to be there when you are." I'll just go back to my place in Boston and let Ma handle it. It wouldn't be ideal, but we'd make it work.

"No, you didn't do anything wrong." Her eyelids flutter as she looks down at her boots. "Quite the opposite, really."

Pressure eases off my chest. *I didn't ruin everything.*

"Okay. Good." I pull one side of my lips up. "Then what's the problem here?"

Hands clasped tightly together, she says, "I get your point about this, but I still don't think—"

"Wren." *Please forgive me for interrupting you again,* I think to myself, but I can't let her list all the reasons why this isn't the best option again. I know for a fact no middle-aged white guy parading around in a Brooks Brothers suit would care as much as her. Just the way she interacted with my parents for an hour told me that.

Her eyes lift to mine, softer than before. Her mouth opens, but she lets me speak.

Just like that summer night, I let myself be completely honest with her.

"You remember when we said that life sucks sometimes? Well, life has sucked pretty bad for me—for all of us—recently." Dad, Ma, Callie... They've gone through the wringer. In the snap of a finger, everyone's life changed. "We really, really need a win right now. And you're the one who can get us there. I know it."

She swallows.

"I know I'm being persistent," I say, my whole body leaned forward, pleading, "but what if this was your parent? Wouldn't you do everything to help them?"

She stills. The heavy silence of the forest smothers me for a second, then another.

Please, please, please.

Finally, she looks at me and tells me the four most beautiful words in the world. "Okay. I'll do it."

CHAPTER 3

Wren

THIS IS BAD.

This is really bad.

I've been driving for close to two hours, and I still haven't wrapped my head around what happened exactly. How is it possible to be such a sucker?

I lean an elbow against my window as I stop at the red light closest to my place, the red-bricked buildings of the South End neighborhood welcoming me. My back hurts from driving this long back and forth, and apparently, that's not going to be a rare occurrence from now on. I should've stood my ground and said I truly couldn't take such a big and semi-long-term project so far from my home.

But when he brought up the fact that this was his father and he'd do just about anything for him, I already knew I'd say yes.

The light turns green, and I finish the drive back to the triplex unit I'm renting. It's nothing big or fancy—the black paint around the windows is chipped, which irks me to no end—but it has parking and is within walking distance from work, so I can't complain.

Once my car is parked, I climb the three sets of stairs to reach my floor, then open my door.

The moment I step inside, a chorus of barking fills the space. It immediately makes me smile, some of the tension I've been harboring for the past hours leaving my shoulders. After removing my boots in a hurry and placing them neatly to the left of the mat, next to my pair of running shoes, I make sure to put my keys on the hanger, then walk to the crates holding the two little beasts that own my heart.

"Hi, baby," I say as I open the biggest crate and let Molly out. Her long scruffy tail hits my thighs as she starts running and jumps on the couch. I'd never let her remain free in the apartment because while she's a sweetheart, she can become a real nightmare when I'm not looking.

The high-pitched bark becomes louder as I make my way to the smaller crate sitting next to my suede couch. Maybelle's small, fluffy body spins in circles, her nails clicking against the bottom of the crate. Once I open the door, she doesn't immediately come out. She waits for me to pet her head a time of two and pull her out. With two of the biggest cataracts I have ever seen in my entire life, she's had her fair share of running into walls and closed doors.

"You're okay, sweetheart," I whisper above her head before pecking two kisses on her ears.

While I carefully place my little bundle of love in her tiny bed on the floor, my crazy, much larger beast jumps off the couch and lands on my back, almost making me fall forward.

"Molly!" I shout as I turn around. "You better calm down right now!"

That's what happens when we don't go on our run together in the morning. She needs to spend her energy almost as soon as we wake up or else she's unstoppable for the rest of the day.

And if I need to wake up two hours earlier every day for the duration of this project, then there's no way we'll be able to do that.

I quickly bring the dogs out, and when I come back in, I deflate like a balloon, letting myself drop onto my couch, where Molly comes to cuddle next to me almost instantly. I let my hand roam up and down her wiry brown, black, and beige fur. I've had her for five years, and I'm still not sure what type of mixed-breed she is. There's probably some Labrador and some German Shepard in there, but otherwise, I don't know. She's honestly pretty ugly; I love her with all my heart.

"What am I going to do, Moll?"

As if in response, she drops her muzzle on my thigh. Not that helpful, but I'll take it. It's not like I have anyone to call who could give me advice. There's always my cousin Aqidah, but I don't think she'd give me advice I'd want to follow.

With a sigh, I grab my phone and google my own name. I read the article in the *Globe* when it came out, but I want to go through it again and try to analyze it from Aaron's perspective.

Goodness, I still can't believe it's him.

He was different today from the man I met at the bar. This summer, he seemed like a person who'd stopped giving a care. But now? Now, he's ready to fight. Which is exactly what got me to say yes. Because I know I would've been just as argumentative if it had been my mom. In fact, I was that person at some point.

When my mom got sick, I fought like hell for her to get her the services she deserved. I wasn't a lawyer yet, but I made the calls, sent the emails, and argued with what seemed like every person on planet Earth. I was nineteen when her mind started fading, so I was at least old enough to take care of everything for her. Not everyone is that lucky.

It was for that same reason I took the case of Lilian Miller close to a year ago. She reminded me so much of my mother in all the ways that mattered, except that she had no one by her side. And when she got hurt, no one cared to make sure she got the compensation she was due. The people at fault assumed a patient with Lewy body dementia could not blame them for everything, but when I'd read in the news about what had happened to that poor old lady, I felt like something wasn't right, and only a little investigation was enough to tell me there had clearly been a mistake made. If someone had admitted it, I would've laid it to rest, but no one came forward, so I made sure she got her justice. I took the case pro bono—thank goodness Selina, my boss, let me—and I won it for her. Because if this had been my mom, I'd have wanted someone to do it for her.

And now here I am again, involved in a case I have no interest in taking because Aaron's words struck a chord in me. He said they needed a fighter in their corner, but that wasn't true. They already have one.

Just as I'm about to get up to go make the green smoothie I skipped drinking this morning, my phone rings in my hands.

"Hello?" I say as I answer.

"Wren, hi!" Selina says. "How's it going?"

"Great, you?" I'm not about to tell her I'm two seconds away from having a panic attack at the idea that I'll need to disrupt my life for the next few months.

"I'm great! Busy, but good." I can hear the smile in her voice. She's exactly what you'd want for in a boss. Whip-smart, direct, instructive, but also so nice and caring. People who say women need to act heartless to succeed in high-end jobs have never met Selina. "I was wondering how this morning went?"

See? The best.

"It went okay." Two of my fingers slide to my temple, where I feel the start of a headache building. "To be fully transparent with you, I tried leading them toward someone more experienced with healthcare litigation, like Randall or Assem, but they'd read about the Miller case and really wanted to stick with me."

"Oh, Wren, that's wonderful!" she says, having a reaction opposite from mine. "You're making a name for yourself out there."

"Yeah." I can't even muster fake enthusiasm. If that success were in Boston, where I'd be able to go on my run at 6:15 with

Molly and eat breakfast in a kitchen where I know the location of every item and be close to my mom, then yeah, I'd be ecstatic. But that's not the case.

I wish I didn't need the kind of reassurance that steadiness brings me, yet there's no way I can change it. I am the way I am.

"I'm proud of you," she says, making me feel bad for my lack of excitement. This *is* big. I'm twenty-six. I've been working for barely two years as a lawyer. Getting recognized for my work at this point in time is a huge honor. Still, being honored doesn't ease the sick feeling in my chest.

"Thank you." Clearing my throat, I redirect the conversation by saying, "But it's going to be a big project. Weeks, months, possibly. Are you sure you can spare me that long?" I don't usually take cases by myself. The only one I did was Ms. Miller's, and that was because I had no choice. It was me or no one.

"Of course I'm sure! Don't take this the wrong way, but we'll be fine without you." She chuckles, then hisses. "But I don't think we'll be able to spare any paralegals to work with you. You'll have to do it mostly on your own. Are you all right with that?"

I want to say no. This would be the perfect excuse. Blame my lack of experience and give the case to someone else.

But I told Aaron I'd do it. And while it isn't ideal, I never break my word.

"Yeah, it shouldn't be a problem. If you give me permission to work mostly on that for a while, then I should be fine."

"Permission granted," she says like she's my fairy godmother.

"Good, thank you." Something pushes my leg, and I look down to find Molly nudging me with her muzzle. I'll probably need to squeeze in a run with her before starting to work again. "Was there anything else?

"Oh, actually, yes!" The sound of papers crinkling and

drawers being opened and closed comes through the receiver. As good an attorney as Selina is, her office is always a mess. "The girls at the front invited me and Jenna to go for drinks at this new place on Boylston. I'm trying to find the name but..." More papers crunching. "Oh, got it! At Bubbly's. Want to come with us?"

I don't even need to think about it before saying, "I'm pretty busy tonight, but thanks for the invitation."

"You sure?"

Always the same thing. She offers. I decline. She asks if I'm certain.

"Yeah, I'm sure, but you girls have fun."

"All right, then. Bye Wren!"

After saying goodbye and hanging up, I go grab my planner, an eraser, and a pencil. If I can't back out of this plan, then the only thing I can do is create a new routine for myself. My eyelid twitches as I read over the carefully planned schedule I'd written for the next month.

Relax, Wren.

My hands are tight around the eraser as I go through the pages one last time. Realistically, I know that changing the schedule won't have an impact on the state of my brain. It's not like the acetylcholine release between my neurons will decrease all of a sudden because of it.

It still feels like removing a safety net from under me, though.

Dropping my agenda on the coffee table, I go to my room and change into running clothes, then clip the leash to Molly's collar. Running will help take my mind off things. Maybelle stays behind, sleeping soundly in her small bed. With her old age, small frame, and damaged eyes, she much prefers staying inside to exercising, especially in this frigid New England weather.

As I leave the apartment, I find myself thinking maybe I

should've said yes to going out. Talking to other people about the weird coincidence of working for the family of the man I met in a strange way last summer might've helped.

But then I would've created a precedent.

"Going to be just you and me, I guess," I say as I pet the head of one of my two best friends and start running. It has to be. Because to have someone to talk to, you need to let someone in. And that's not happening anytime soon.

CHAPTER 4

Aaron

"CALLIE, COME ON, YOU'RE GOING TO BE LATE!" I shout from the kitchen as I finish packing my little sister's lunch. I'll never understand how it can take this long for a ten-year-old girl to get ready in the morning.

"Coming!" she answers from upstairs, which I know is a complete lie. It always is when she says that.

A loud sigh makes me turn around. Ma is standing next to the coffee pot, the dark circles under her eyes even bigger than usual.

I walk toward her. "Morning," I say before pressing a kiss to her cheek.

She grumbles a response.

"You okay?"

"Sí."

I raise an eyebrow.

Spanish rolls off her tongue quicker than she speaks in English. "Stephanie called in sick this morning, so I've had to help your dad with his exercises instead, but my back is killing me now."

"*Mamá*..." Pressure builds in my chest. Even though he's been able to regain a lot of mobility in his rehab center, he still needs daily therapy to get as much autonomy as he can, and helping him with it requires heavy physical work.

It's hard seeing her like this. Some days, like today, she reminds me of a robot. Functioning instead of living. It's been weeks since I've seen her be her usual carefree self. I try helping out with Callie and the farm as much as I can to ease some weight off her shoulders, but it's not enough. And that's one of the reasons why Wren's work means that much to me; someone needs to pay for what we're going through.

After looking at the time again, I shout, "Callie, come on now!"

"It's okay, I'll make sure she has everything before she leaves," Ma says, pushing me out of the way. "You should go have breakfast with your dad. He's in the living room."

I scratch my head, looking down. "Actually, I really need to start my work in the farm, but tell him I'll see him later."

"**¿Estás seguro?**" *Are you sure?*

I nod. We've fallen behind a lot in the past weeks, and Christmas season is literally right around the corner. I need to be out there *yesterday*. Plus, working outside will keep my mind busy. Patting her hand, I give her a reassuring smile, then go put my fleece-lined coat and boots and walk out the door.

The farm used to be synonymous with comfort for me. The fresh air and the seemingly infinite forest allowed me the quiet I needed to think when the house was loud, filled with friends and family and my parents singing to Juan Luis Guerra.

However, the moment I start walking through the rows of trees, it becomes obvious that Evermore doesn't bring me what it used to. The only thing I see as I look around is not the peacefulness of the place, but the work it needs. We—well, my parents—have close to forty acres of land, most of it covered in conifers we eventually cut down and ship all across the United States during the Christmas season. Our trees are known for their quality, so making sure that we export them in pristine condition every year requires much more work than anyone might think. If I'm being honest, even I didn't know the extent of the work that's needed on the farm every year. I came to face the hard truth when I became the one responsible for overseeing it all.

Which means I need to get started if I want to be able to end my day before nightfall.

"Hey!" a voice I've known since I was in diapers calls behind me an hour later, as I finish cutting down what must be my twentieth tree of the day. Wiping a gloved hand over my sweaty forehead, I turn around and find Finn coming my way.

I've asked him a few weeks ago if he'd be willing to come help out, at least for the Christmas season. We have a few part-time employees on the farm, but I'm not used to overseeing everything yet, and Ma is way too busy dealing with Dad's recovery, Callie, and the coming lawsuit to help. She would if I asked, but I never will. I can take care of this, and if I need to ask my best friend for help while he's in between jobs to make sure our biggest period of the year runs smoothly, then I will.

"Hey, how's it going?" I move closer to give him a quick hug and a pat on the back, then get back to work.

"Looking good, man," Finn says with a chuckle. "Much manlier than in your little office."

I roll my eyes, my lips curving just a little. As much as I like physical work from time to time, I miss my little office quite a lot right about now. No amount of nature and quiet will bring me the same amount of peace that working on a new design with my headphones on, lost in my own world, can.

"Kidding," he says before tapping my back. "Where do you need me today?"

I tip my head toward the trees I've laid down in the past hour. "We need to prepare the truck for tomorrow's delivery, so you can start packing those."

"All right, captain."

Working with Finn is easy. He always does what he's asked without complaining, works efficiently, and stays quiet when I need him to.

Jesus, what kind of man am I becoming, appreciating his quietness? I'm no longer sure I recognize myself these days. I shake my head, pushing the thought away. *Right now isn't about you.* Dad needs the help. That's the only thing I need to be focusing on, and if it means I can't be the same fun guy I used to be, then so be it.

I finish cutting down another tree, then throw it into the pile. Maybe I use a little too much force as I do so because Finn, who's coming back from a trip to the truck, looks at me with wide eyes and says, "What did this tree do to you, man?"

I throw him a look, then get back to work.

"Hey, everything okay?" he asks, stopping next to me.

"Course," I lie. It's not like I can't talk to Finn. I just don't see the use in it.

"Uh-huh, sure."

I guess that's the biggest disadvantage—or advantage, depending on how you see it—of having a best friend who you've known forever: they always know when you're bullshitting.

"It's complicated," I add.

"Yeah, I get it." The sad smile he gives me tells me he truly does. Shelli, his mom and Ma's best friend, must've filled in the blanks of things I haven't shared with him. They met when Mom moved to the States and Shelli became her next-door neighbor, and they've been inseparable ever since. I'm thankful for it. Ma needs her support, and it's good to have Finn around. Having someone who understands is worth a lot.

We both do a few hauls to the truck in silence before Finn asks, "So, how long are you planning on staying here?"

"Not sure yet." It's not exactly the truth, but I'm not ready to talk about what will happen in the future. Although with the way he's looking at me, he probably knows what I'm thinking. This place is Dad's most precious possession. It has to continue being run by someone in the family.

"And what does your boss say about that?" the sneaky ass asks.

I shrug. "I can do some work from here. I brought all I need from the office." No need to mention that I barely have had the time to sleep more than five hours a night since I got here, much less work forty hours a week on my designs on top of the work I do on the land.

"And is that a viable option for you?" Finn asks, seeing straight through me.

"Sure."

We both know it's not. At least he's a good enough friend not to call me out on it.

"What about you?" I ask. "You know what you're gonna do next?"

"Nice deflection."

I narrow my eyes.

Grinning as if he's got me good, he says, "I don't know, man. Haven't heard another calling yet. Guess I'll stick around here for now."

"Good to know."

Finn has spent his twenties as nomad as can be. He's traveled the world a few times—spent a year couch-surfing in Australia while working in some kind of ranch, even at some point went to live with a German girl he met on Instagram, just to learn the language. I don't know if he actually likes working here or if he's just staying to help me, but I'm grateful for it either way.

We return to our silent work—well, I'm silent while Finn sings through what seems like the complete album of some rock band, his voice so off-key it's almost painful—until we hear gravel crunching from the driveway that leads to the house. I recognize the car immediately.

We're far enough in the field that Wren probably can't see us, or at least doesn't know to look for us, but we see her. She gets out of her car, dressed in a black suit and heels, the same thin beige coat on her shoulders I saw her freezing in yesterday. She looks so put together, she could be in a TV show. Her spine is straight as she walks toward the house, her dark hair pulled tight in a bun. It's hard to look away from her. She's the kind of person who commands attention, no matter what she does. I've known that since the moment I sat beside her at that bar, like a gravitational pull from one large planet to a smaller one.

"Who. Is. That?" Finn asks, practically drooling as he looks at her while she knocks at my parents' front door.

I hit his stomach with the back of my hand. "No one you should be looking at."

I love Finn. He's one of the best guys I've ever had the chance to meet. He's also the biggest playboy I know, so there's no way I'll let him approach our lawyer.

He turns to me, mouth gaping. "Really, who is it?"

"No. One." I point to one of the trees. "Now get back to work."

"Oh, come on, man," he says as I turn around and walk to another tree we need to cut down. "You can't keep all the hot ones for yourself."

I give him the finger over my shoulder, and his laughter resonates behind me. But this is no joking matter. I worked hard enough to get her to take on our case. He can do whatever he wants once she's done here, but in the meantime, there's no way I'm letting Finn—or anyone—mess it up.

CHAPTER 5

Wren

I learned about early onset familial Alzheimer's disease when I was eighteen.

I knew what regular Alzheimer's was much before, though.

I was four when my grandpa Landon started mixing up his days of the week and got his driver's license taken away. Mom told me right away that grandpa had some trouble with his memory and was starting to need help at home. We lived in a small apartment, and Mom couldn't take care of him by herself, so we had to have him placed. It was strange for him to develop it at 57, but we didn't think too much of it.

However, when my mom came to my eighteenth birthday party with two left shoes on, I felt in my gut that grandpa Landon's diagnosis wasn't the end of it.

I brought her to the doctor a few days later, and sure enough, they said she had early signs of dementia. And while one person in the family developing Alzheimer's disease before the age of sixty-five was possible, two was very unlikely. Gene panels were run, confirming it wasn't regular Alzheimer's my mom had, but rather a subtype of it that gets transmitted through family lines and causes an early onset of the disease. Doctors consider anything before the age of sixty-five an early diagnosis, but since my mom started deteriorating at forty-five and her younger brother, my uncle Bryan, at forty-six, I always knew it was more severe in our family.

Having everyone around you start to forget who you are is its own kind of hell. Sure, your mind is technically intact, but most of the time, you wish it wasn't. Every day I woke up, I saw my mom lose a bit more of herself. I saw the proud lady who had raised me on her own forget to shower. I saw my wicked-smart grandfather who had taught me how to play chess forget the rules of the game. I saw my uncle cry almost every day for the last two years of his life for no particular reason, and no one could make him stop. In truth, it would've been better to not be myself in those moments.

So when I see Martina's grip on her husband's hand as he tries to speak but is unable to get the proper words out, I understand her pain. Watching someone you love struggle through a new disability is probably one of the hardest things anyone could ever go through.

Dennis's condition is, in a way, the total opposite of my mother's. She could speak all she wanted, but nothing she said made any sense. He has all the right thoughts, but can't get them out. I'm not sure which one is worse.

It's something I've become used to in the past two weeks, working with the Scott-Perez family every few days. One of the first steps in a medical liability case is to investigate what happened and find as much information as one can from the people involved and from experts, so I've had to conduct a lot of interviews to get my facts straight.

"It's okay, Dennis," I tell him as I finish writing down what daily living tasks he can't do anymore, mostly provided by Martina. "I think I got all that I need for the moment."

Still, he opens his mouth and produces a few sounds followed by a couple of unrelated words. With the frustration in his face, they're clearly not the ones he's trying to express.

"I think he's trying to add something I missed," Martina says, eyes narrowed as she rubs Dennis's arm. "It's okay, *mi amor*."

His left hand balled into a fist on the table, he purses his lips, then tries again, to no avail. It breaks my heart through and through.

"If it's okay with you, I could go over today's questions with your son too. Maybe he'll find that missing detail, Dennis."

I don't know where Aaron is today. In fact, I haven't seen him much in the times I've been here, and I've worked from the office in the past two days.

It was good to go back to my usual schedule, like sliding into an old pair of slippers. I could rely on muscle memory to go through the motions. However, I have to admit that it hasn't been too bad to come here from time to time. On the first days, it was destabilizing, to say the least, but I got used to it quickly enough, and I haven't seen any change in my functioning as of yet, so I'd say it's been overall better than expected.

"That's a good idea," Martina says, her face brightening for the first time since Dennis started to show disagreement with what she was saying. "He went to pick Callie up after his work, but he should be back soon, I think."

Callie. Is that Aaron's girlfriend? I've heard that name here before, but I don't remember in what context. For all I know, it could be the girl he proposed to this summer. He'd told me he wouldn't stay with her, but he could've changed his mind. I haven't asked him about what happened after that night. To be honest, neither one of us has brought up the day we met since I agreed to take the job. Not like we've talked all that much anyway.

I look down at my watch, realizing it's almost 4:00 p.m. I've asked my dog-loving neighbor if she could take Molly for a walk during lunchtime while I'm here, but I still need to get going soon if I don't want her to be going out of her mind by the time I get home. "Actually, if you don't mind, I was thinking we could continue this tomorrow?"

"Oh, of course, honey," Martina says.

I almost jump at the sound of the pet name rolling over me. I don't remember the last time someone called me by anything other than my name. Even when my mom was alive, it never happened. She wasn't the affectionate type, which is the total opposite of Martina. When she opened the door for me this morning, the first thing she did was hug me as if we were old-time friends. I froze for a second before patting her back in return.

I don't know what to think of it. It's not a bad thing to be this open and caring, just a little jarring.

"Okay, well, I'll see you then."

I get up to pack my stuff, and just then, we hear the sound of the front door opening, followed by a pair of feet running around and another walking behind.

"Hey, hey, hey," comes Aaron's voice from somewhere I still can't see. "Shoes off! You know this."

"They're clean," a high-pitched voice answers. Then, a head full of thick black curls pops through the door. The girl looks to be around nine or ten, with large brown eyes and thick lashes. "¿Mami, puedo ir a la casa de Zoe esta noche? Aarón me dijo que no." She's pouting, only looking at Martina, as if asking her for something.

"Callie!" Aaron bellows as he enters the room. His gaze finds mine first, and he does a double take before saying, "Sorry, guys. Callie, come on."

Huh. So not a girlfriend, after all.

"Hola, mija," Martina says before pressing a kiss on Callie's head. The young girl rolls her eyes, but at the same time, sinks deeper into Martina's embrace. "It's okay, Aarón," she tells him before tipping her head toward my packed work bag. "Ms. Lawson was just finishing."

He stares at me in question, so I tip my head in agreement. His gaze doesn't go anywhere, though, which makes my cheeks burn. Being under someone's spotlight has never been something I enjoy. Ironic for an attorney, I guess, but it's different when I receive attention while I work. Here, I feel more vulnerable.

With a small wave, I tell Martina and Dennis, "Okay, well, I'll see you both tomorrow." I give Aaron and Callie a tight-lipped dip of the head, then walk outside.

Snow crunches as I head to my car; it's melted a little from the warmer temperature of the past week but still covering most of the ground. It's rare that we have this much snow in November. In the city, I'm not a fan of it. Molly has made a mess every single day after our runs in the past month. But here, it gives an even more magical element to this place. Like we're truly in another world. The view is one of my favorite things about coming here.

Because of the milder temperature, some parts of the gravel driveway have melted while others are still icy, creating a dangerous path for me and my pretty-but-horribly-useless boots. Thankfully, I get to my car in one piece.

Today was a heavy day of work, more emotionally than mentally. I'll enjoy doing nothing while petting May's little head tonight.

Once I've put my bag at the foot of the passenger seat, I start the engine.

Except nothing happens.

I try, then try again, but despite all my best efforts, the sound of my motor drowning remains the only thing I hear.

Crap.

How will I get back to my girls?

I remove the key, then put it back in and try again for what must be the tenth time. No luck. Slowly, I move my hands to my lips, exhaling through my nose. Shit.

This is so embarrassing. I need someone to help me, but then again, the last thing I want is to go back there and ask for it when *I'm* supposed to be helping *them*.

Luck is seemingly on my side tonight because just as the thought appears, a knock comes from my car window. Jumping, I turn and find Aaron there, hunched. He motions for me to open the door.

"You okay?" he asks once I've obliged, his five-o'clock shadow darker in the fading daylight.

"Sure," I say, only half sarcastic.

Ignoring me, Aaron says, "Heard some not-so-great noises

from the house, so thought I'd come see." He dips his head toward my hood. "Need a hand?"

Do I want to crawl into a hole right now? Absolutely. But what choice do I have?

With a small nod, I get out of the car.

"Be right back," Aaron says before he jogs to his car and drives it next to mine.

He's not dressed in his usual outdoor clothes. With a long black wool coat, a navy crewneck sweater and chinos, he looks more like the man I met this summer than the lumberjack I've seen around the place in the past two weeks.

"What do you think it is?" I ask once he's back. My arms are wrapped around my torso, the air suddenly much colder. It's not like I can help Aaron in any way. I should've asked one of my mother's boyfriends to show me how to do basic car work while I had the chance.

Hood popped, Aaron leans over my car and says, "Not sure, but I guess we can try to jump it."

"Sure," I say as if I have an opinion on the matter. Shifting from foot to foot, I add, "Is there anything I can do?"

Aaron walks back to his SUV and dips inside the trunk, coming back with a bundle of cables in his arms.

"You can help me untangle these," he says.

The thing's a mess, but if it can help me get back home, I'll break every one of my nails to do it. I hold out my hands, and he gives me one part of the bundle.

"So," Aaron asks as we get to work, "how's the case going?" The nonchalance of his voice doesn't reach his eyes, which are burning with questions.

"Good," I say. "I might need to ask you a couple more questions before I can write the subpoena so I have all the information I need, but we're making good progress, I think."

"Good. That's good," he says, seemingly more to himself than to me.

With a grunt, I finish untangling the last of the cables, then hand them to Aaron.

"Thanks," he says as he walks to his car and clamps two of them to what I'm guessing is his battery.

"Thank you again for doing this," Aaron says as he unfurls from his position.

"Doing what?" Letting my car break down in his driveway?

"My dad's case." He walks to my car, then clamps the two others ends of the cables. Not looking at me, he says, "I hope you know how grateful we all are."

I lean against the side of my car, arms crossed. "Of course. And no need to thank me, really." Even though I hesitated at first, I don't see how I could've said no to this case. "Your parents are great."

Straightening, he smiles, a sight that makes something in my chest feel weird. I've never seen him look so...*bright* before. Even this summer, when he grinned, it didn't feel genuine. Not like now. This expression transforms him. "Yeah, they really are," he says.

After a moment of staring that lasts a tad too long, he claps his hands, then says, "All right. I'll start my car, then it's your turn."

I listen to him and head inside my car. After a few seconds, I hear the rumble of Aaron's engine being started, which makes me jealous.

Please, please, please.

I turn the key in my ignition, eyes screwed shut.

Aaaaaand—

Nothing.

I don't even bother cursing my car in my head this time. The sound of its grumbling makes me think it's already laughing at me.

I try again, just for luck, but no such thing.

My door opens a few seconds later. "I don't think you're leaving in this one tonight."

I look at him blandly. Great sense of observation.

"Want a ride?" he asks.

"What do you mean?"

He snickers, that smile appearing once again. "I mean, want a ride?" When I lift an eyebrow, he says, "I was already going back to Boston to pick up some stuff and sleep in my bed for once. I can give you a ride and bring you back here tomorrow." He gives my car a quick once-over. "We can call the local mechanic to come tow it in the meantime."

I wring my fingers a little longer before saying, "Are you sure?"

"Very sure."

I only hesitate for about a second before making my decision. My dogs are waiting for me at home. I'm not letting them down, even if it means getting into a car with a near stranger for a two-hour drive. With a little huff at the Universe, I grab my stuff and follow him to his small SUV. After getting into the passenger seat, I put my bag at my feet.

"You can put that on the backseat," Aaron says as he puts his seatbelt on.

I shake my head. "That's fine. I like having it here."

He looks at me but doesn't say anything else before turning his car on—successfully. Lucky him.

We get out the long driveway surrounded by tall trees, and in a light clearing, I notice a small wooden house that looks right out of a Nordic town, with its log walls and small chimney on top of the roof. It almost looks like a miniature replica of the Scott-Perez home. It's cute.

As soon as we get onto the long road that leads to the highway, Aaron tells me to look through his phone for the number of the garage. I do, then call and explain to the mechanic, who explains what the problem seems to be.

"Crap," I say as I hang up the phone.

"What?" Aaron asks.

"They said they can come tow the car today, but they're booked for the next few days, so it might take a while for them to get to it." My fingers tighten around Aaron's phone.

His lips twist to the side before he says, "There's a cabin."

"Huh?"

"We rent it sometimes to tourists who want to live the full Christmas experience, or whatever that means. You could stay there until your car is ready or until the case is done, if you want."

Going to live in a completely new place? That's more than just changing some parts of a routine. It sounds like a nightmare. Anyway, it's not an option. "I couldn't do that to my babies," I say, looking out. Maybelle and Molly are so petty, they would probably pee on my carpets for weeks if I left them with a dog sitter.

"Hm," he says.

Sonder Hill's main road reaches the I-91 with a sign that says *Boston, 140.*

"I was wondering about Boston," I say while wringing my fingers in my lap.

"Huh?"

"If you actually lived there. You know, since that's where we met."

A short but thick silence falls between us.

"Right." He clears his throat. "Yeah, I do."

"So do you always work at the farm?" I can't imagine he'd want to do that kind of commute every day, no matter how nice the city is.

He shakes his head vigorously. "No. Well, not before. I just came back to help out after my dad's accident."

"Oh."

Accident. Funny, how we keep referring to the stroke as an accident. As if it's easier to accept that it was a mistake rather than his body working against him. I've learned a while back that it's much easier to refer to disease as something that is random. Not necessarily the truth, but easier.

A moment passes before I ask, "And what did you do before?"

I don't know what's making me ask all these questions. It must be the stress of my car situation. I'm usually comfortable in silence, and I'm definitely not known for being a talkative person, both with strangers and with the few people I do know. It's like that summer night all over again.

"I'm a graphic designer for a video game company."

"So you make the drawings that become the games?"

"Something like that, yeah."

"Hm. Interesting." I don't think I've ever heard of someone actually doing that for a living.

He turns to me, then smiles. "Yeah, it is." When he turns back to the road, his happy expression leaves. "I'm kinda sad about leaving it, if I'm being honest."

I adjust my body so I'm angled in his direction. "Why do you have to quit?"

A long sigh leaves his mouth. "The farm's been in my family for four generations. Dad can't take care of it anymore, and my mom is overwhelmed with his health. I'll keep it running, at least until Callie can take over, if she ever wants to."

A frown takes over my face before I can help it. "Are you sure that's what they'd want?" From the conversations I've had with Aaron's parents, the last thing they currently have on their mind is the land.

"Dad's life has always revolved around the farm. He's always said it's his legacy." He raises his eyebrows. "And legacy matters more than my job."

I frown. "How?"

"What do you mean, how?"

"Well, you entertain people. Make them happy." I shrug. "To me, that's important all right."

He turns to me and stares for a second too long. When I feel my neck start to warm, I tip my chin and say, "Eyes on the road."

He chuckles before following the command.

We spend a few minutes in silence with only the soft folk music playing from his radio before he asks, "So how long have you worked as a lawyer?"

"Almost two years now."

His eyebrows furrow. "Aren't you young to have worked that long?"

"I'm twenty-six, not thirteen," I huff.

"Still."

I shrug. "I skipped third grade."

"Smart even then," he says.

Thank God it's dark inside the car. He can't see the slight curl of my lips.

We continue talking about my career and his, small talk that is safe, until we enter Boston and I lead him to my neighborhood. By then, I'm pretty much an expert in all things graphic design.

"Right here," I say, pointing to my building, where snow drifts from the roof, as if some fell here today. He stops in front of the entryway.

"Thank you for the ride." I open my door.

"No problem."

Just as I'm about to close the door, he leans over and says, "Hey, why don't you give me your number? You know, so I can text you tomorrow when I'm here."

I eye him for a second before chastising myself. *He doesn't care about you like that.* This is work related. And work related, I can do. "Sure."

I tell him my number, and he texts me a smiley face to give me his.

"Got it," I say. "Hopefully, we won't need to do that too much."

"Texting?"

My gaze narrows in on him. "The carpooling."

"Oh." He chuckles. "Yeah. Well, the offer for the cabin still stands, if ever you change your mind."

I nod.

"All right, then." He throws a finger salute my way. "Good night, Wren."

A shiver runs through my body. It's so cold outside.

"Good night, Aaron." His eyes don't leave mine, even after I've stopped speaking. They're intimidating. As if they could read me if he tried.

I get out of the car and close the door before he can.

CHAPTER 6

Aaron

I'M OUT FRONT, I TEXT HER AFTER I'VE PARKED MY CAR THE next morning, fog blanching my windshield in the chilly November morning.

Coming down now, she answers a few seconds later.

Eyes on the front door of her building, I lean back in my seat. My corduroy-clad legs are restless, and I put my palms on them to stop bouncing. I've been fidgety all morning. I don't know if it's because I'm scared she won't want to return to Sonder Hill knowing she might not be able to come back home tonight, or maybe it's because I've been running through our conversation from yesterday over and over again ever since she left my car.

She struck a chord, that's for sure, saying my job was important, a few simple words that made me toss and turn in bed all night. It had been a long time since I'd felt this *seen*. And then she mentioned her babies, and I felt like a jackass for not asking before. She probably has a family here. A partner and kids. Meanwhile I'm here, asking her to drive hours every day or to stay back in Sonder Hill until her car is repaired.

Last night, just as I got into my apartment after dropping her off, I received a text from her asking if I would be coming back to Boston at the end of the day today. I almost said I would even if I wasn't planning to, but Dad has physical therapy tonight, so Mom needs me to stay with Callie. I can't just drop everything and drive to Boston, so I had to tell her no.

Where does that leave her? If she can't come back home after work and needs to work in person with clients, she might decide it's not worth it to work with us anymore.

I'm not sure what I'm going to do if she tells me she wants to drop the case. Do whatever it takes to accommodate her and her work, probably. Also, fall to my knees and beg her to keep us as clients. Even though he can't tell me in words, I can see that Dad is pleased with the progress they've made together and the plan she's built for him. That alone is worth all the begging in the world.

At the same time that thought crosses my mind, her building's black door finally opens, and out comes Wren with two large bags on her shoulder and two dogs, one tall and nearly obese, the other tiny and frail. They seem excited, their leashes tangling in front of Wren as she tries to balance her bags. Hand already on the door handle, I get out of my car and rush to help her.

"Hey, thanks," she says as I take two of the bags off her shoulder.

"What's all this?" I ask, even though the one thing I'm truly thinking is, *thank God you're still here.*

"Stuff for us for the next few days," she answers as I drop the bags in the trunk of my SUV. She keeps her purse with her. When I look back up at her, she's playing with a loose thread on the smaller dog's leash. "If the offer to use the cabin still stands, obviously."

"O-of course," I stutter like an idiot. Then, I look down at the two hyperactive dogs on the ground, and a light turns on in my head. "Are *these* your babies?"

She bobs her head, a small but obviously happy smile coloring her lips. The tightness in my chest is gone with my next breath, though I'm not sure why.

She continues looking at me, not moving as the big dog walks forward to lick my hand, large snout damp. I wait for a moment, but when I realize she's not going back to her apartment, I ask, "Are the babies coming with us?"

That gets her grin to grow a little. "The babies can't stay alone while I'm there."

I don't know if Ma and Dad accept dogs in the cabin, but what am I going to tell that usually stoic woman who just smiled while talking about her dogs? No, they can't come? Fuck that.

"All right, hop in, guys," I tell the two pups as I open the back door of the car.

"It's *girls,*" Wren tells me as she gets the dogs inside, going as far as buckling them with their own little belts she pulled out from God knows where.

"Pardon?"

She throws me a look over her shoulder. "Molly's the big one. Maybelle's the small one. They're girls."

I fight hard to keep my amusement in check. She's cute when she talks about them. Wren comes off as someone who's got her shit together, which makes her appear older than she actually is. But now, she looks her age.

"Girls. My sincerest apologies."

"They forgive you," she says, a hint of humor in her voice as she goes to sit in the passenger seat.

Before closing the door of the backseat, I steal a glance at the two dogs, who look much calmer now that they're inside, then at the figure who's turned around to look at them. I shake my head, then head to the driver's seat, allowing myself a little incredulous chuckle. That's quite literally the last thing I was expecting coming here this morning.

I can't say I'm disappointed.

* * *

"I think that's the last of it," I say as I hoist one of Wren's bags out of the trunk. Jesus, what did she put in here? Her entire house?

As I swing it over my shoulder, a book falls out. No wonder it's so heavy, if she's carrying books in it.

"Thanks," Wren's voice calls from inside the car, where she's grabbing the dogs.

I lean down to pick up the book, which is titled *When She Disappeared*. The cover shows a woman's face half-hidden by a door, blood dripping on her cheek. I snicker.

"What?" Wren says, now standing in front of me.

"You read thrillers?"

She crosses her arms over her chest, not giving a single crap about the dogs spinning in circles at her feet. "So what?"

"Nothing, I just...wasn't expecting this."

The lift of her brows is a question in itself.

"I pegged you more of a romance type."

She huffs a laugh with a slight roll of her eyes. "I'd rather be scared or thrilled than read fairytales, thank you very much." In a quick move, she steals the book from my grip.

I grin, though I'm sure I must look puzzled.

Starting to walk in front of me, Wren twists the conversation 180 degrees. "I promise I won't be in the way. You won't even notice I'm here."

I hurry behind her. "I told you it's no problem. You're welcome to stay as long as you want."

"Thank you, but still. We'll be discreet, and I want you to send me the bill for—"

"Wren," I deadpan. "Stop it."

She only stares in response, the dogs never stopping their jiggling at her feet while none of her muscles twitch.

"It's the least we can do," I add.

She opens her mouth—to argue, I'm sure—but the sound of a door slamming shut makes us turn toward my parents' home.

"Whose dogs are these?" my little sister shouts as she comes running toward us.

"Mine," Wren answers, her carefree expression from this morning gone, but a small smile still succeeds in pushing through.

"Callie, what are you doing here?" I ask as she reaches us and drops to her knees in front of the white dog. It's close to 10:00 a.m. on a weekday.

Not bothering to look up, she says, "Huh?" As if she doesn't know what I'm talking about. The little girl I knew as my sister is gone and has been replaced by a preteen in a matter of weeks.

"School, Callie," I say.

Beside me, Wren tries to take a step back toward the cabin, but the dogs don't budge, only bothered with Callie.

Still avoiding my eyes, Callie says, "Dad had his speech-language-something this morning, and Mamá had forgotten about it, so they had to leave in a hurry."

Fuck.

"Why didn't you take the bus?"

"It was too late by then. Ma was supposed to drop me off."

Double fuck.

"I think we'll…go," Wren says softly, pulling harder on the leashes.

Callie looks up then, pouting dramatically. "Can you stay a little longer? Or maybe I could babysit them sometimes?"

"Not now, Callie. You're going to school," I state.

She frowns. "But it's too late now."

Eye twitching, I say, "Go get your stuff. I'll bring you and say you didn't feel well this morning, okay?"

Instead of answering, she returns her attention to Wren, whose lips are pinched as she looks back and forth between the two of us.

"You should probably go to school, but you can come see them whenever you want, okay?"

Callie lights up. "For real?"

One side of Wren's lips twitches up for a moment. "For real."

"All right. Thank you, Ms. Wren."

"Just Wren is fine."

"Come on, now," I tell Callie as a thousand emotions bubble in my chest. "You're already late."

"Bye!" she says to Wren in a sing-songy tone before running back toward the house.

"Okay, well, I'll leave you to your stuff," Wren says once we're alone.

"Thank you for that," I tell her while cocking my head in the direction my sister went.

"No worries. See you later." She bends down to pick two of her bags, then starts walking toward the cabin. She asked for the keys before even exiting the car, so she doesn't need me. Still, I have the urge to go help her with all of her bags and the dogs' leashes. I can't, though. Not now.

This whole thing is a mess. I should've been here this morning. There was no real obligation for me to go back to the city in the first place, except that I wanted the peace and quiet for one night. And now, because I wasn't there, Callie is hanging out alone at the house instead of being at school.

Thank God she didn't look too bothered by it. I don't know how I could've forgiven myself if I'd found a way to hurt her even more than she already is.

In my periphery, Callie comes out of the house and starts walking toward my car with her too-large backpack and purple lunchbox. At least Ma had the time to pack that.

I can't be selfish anymore. This was a clear reminder of it. Ma can't do everything by herself, and me dicking around can't lead to anything good. They need me.

If twenty-four seven is what it takes, then that's what I'll give.

***

I wake up in a panic as the loudest scream I've ever heard rings in my ears.

What the hell?

I wait to hear more noise in the house, something like other people shouting or an object breaking, but nothing comes. It's eerily quiet.

In a heartbeat, I'm on my feet, jogging to Callie's room, which sits right next to mine, but when I open the door, I find her sleeping tight. Weird. It really sounded like a girl's scream.

I pad down to my parents' room next but find a similar scene—Dad in the mechanical bed we got him after his stroke and Ma in the twin bed next to him, both fast asleep.

Did I dream it? Maybe I'm going crazy. That's probably what happens when you work two jobs at once and survive on coffee, energy bars, and sleep deprivation.

I'm not even sure why I'm keeping the job at Arcade Games. I was planning on quitting as soon as I was settled at the farm and knew for sure I'd be staying in Sonder Hill, but I've been stalling. And since I talked about it with Wren yesterday, I've been second-guessing my choice even more. What if moving here is a mistake? Or what if quitting this job I love bites me in the ass one day? Everything in my life is a mess. I have no clue what I'm doing with any of it, but I guess I can stall a little longer while I figure it out.

Making sure once again that everything is good in my parents' room, I close the door and head back to bed. My parents had converted my childhood bedroom into a neutral guest room for when people like my cousin Will and his family come to visit, so the place is decorated simply. A queen-sized bed covered with a cream comforter sits in the middle, surrounded by two bedside tables, and that's it. Different from my room at my place, but whatever. It's not like I spend much time here anyway.

Sitting on the plush covers, I try to convince myself that the high-pitched scream I heard was nothing. But right before I can lie down, I hear it again. Except now, I'm awake and can tell it's not coming from inside.

And there's only one girl I know who's not sleeping inside this house right now.

Shit.

Just as fast as I got up earlier, I run down the stairs, slide into my boots, and rush toward the cabin that sits right next to the house. Thank God I'd gone to sleep with pants on. Another scream pierces the air once I'm halfway there, making me run even faster. A thousand scenarios run into my head, from a man attacking her all the way to a wild bear crushing her between its teeth. I don't think about anything as I knock once, then try to open the door. It's locked. Fuck.

I knock again, shouting, "Wren! Open up!"

The door opens wide a second later, allowing me to take a breath for the first time in a minute.

"Aaron?" Wren asks, out of breath. "What are you doing here?"

She looks so different than usual, I almost take a step back. Her hair is falling over her shoulders, strands all over the place. She doesn't have a stitch of makeup on. The black lines she usually has over her eyelids are gone, which softens her traits even more. At her feet, a tiny ball of white fluff pokes its head out.

"I..." My eyes drift from the dog to where her short nightgown ends, long, naked legs coming into view. *Not your business, Aaron.* I clear my throat. "I heard you scream. Thought something had happened to you."

"Oh, something happened to me all right," she huffs, looking over her shoulder then back to me. "Almost had a heart attack."

"What happened?"

"Oh, only my worst nightma-AAAAAH!"

I don't have the time to understand what's happening. One second she's talking to me, the next she's standing on the couch, tearing through my eardrums like a knife.

"What the hell?" I say as I cross the threshold.

"You couldn't tell me that the cabin was infested with rats

before you invited me?" Her thin, delicate hands are balled into fists in front of her chest, as if she will single-handedly destroy anyone who dares come close to her. Behind her on the vintage brown couch sit the two dogs who look almost as scared as her.

"Rats? What do you mean rats?"

Her eyes almost pop out of their socket. "What do you think I mean? The little disgusting things with pointy teeth that roam around in sewers and live in this place, apparently!"

"We don't have rats."

"Yeah, you do! I may not have the best functioning brain, but I do have two perfectly working eyes, and there's a freaking rat that walked around this place. Even Molly saw it."

"So that's what's got you screaming like that?" I ask, my worry rapidly fading away and giving its place to humor. "A rat?"

She narrows in on me. "What's so funny about that?"

I let out a small chuckle. "Nothing, just..." I give a shake of my head. "You look like you're absolutely fearless, but you're afraid of a tiny animal?"

She huffs. "What makes you think I'm fearless? I'm afraid of literally so many things." Her gaze moves to the floor, as if she's looking for the culprit of her panic. "And I fucking *hate* rats."

My mouth twitches. I fight really, really hard to keep it under control, but in the end, I'm only human, and I can't resist. The chuckle bursts out of me.

"Stop laughing and find the beast instead!" she hisses, which makes me laugh even harder. God, who would've thought that girl had it in her?

Still fighting hard to control my amusement, I lean down and start looking under the bed, then the couch and the dining table. The cabin is far from big, a kitchen, living room, and bedroom all in one. At the end sits a large wooden bedpost, next to which are the small oven and fridge. Closer to the door, the couch rests against the wall and faces a retro TV box. The curtains are heavy and a deep burgundy, allowing people to drift off in the dark for hours on end without waking up. In the cabin is always where I get the best sleep.

"Where did you see it last?" I ask as I look in the cupboard under the sink of the kitchenette.

"Literally crossing the room like the sneaky bastard it is. Right in front of our eyes!"

I pinch my lips harder. Wren usually speaks in an even, composed tone, and I don't think I've ever heard her curse once. Apparently, that was hiding under her sweet cover.

"I don't see a rat anywhere." My head bangs the top of the tiny kitchen counter as I get back up. I bite my tongue to drown my curse. "Are you even sure it was a rat? A mouse, I could believe, but—"

"I don't care what type of rodent it is, Aaron," she states as if I'm a total idiot. Usually I'd find it irritating, but right now it only amuses me more. "If it has a long leathery tail and tiny teeth that can come gnaw on my bones while I'm sleeping, I want it out."

Don't laugh. Don't laugh. Don't laugh. She already looks like a bomb halfway ready to blow. No need to give her more ammunition.

I do another complete tour of the cabin, but still find nothing. Hands lifted in front of me, I turn to her and say, "I'm not saying you imagined something, but I can't find a mouse or a rat anywhere here."

"It was there," she almost growls.

"I believe you, but…" I shrug. "I'm not sure what else to tell you."

She looks down at the two dogs huddled on the couch with her, then back to me. "You're not going to leave us alone with that rat, are you?"

I smile as I look at her face, which I can finally read for once. Even scared looks good on her. She looks more alive, her whole body more vibrant. My eyes drift down again to the legs she curled under her, but I force them away.

Goddammit, get a grip.

"I can invite you in and give you my bed in the main house if you don't want to stay here, or I can sleep on the couch," I say, pointing to where she's sitting.

Her mouth moves to the side as she studies me. Again, I thank whoever's looking up on me that I wore actual clothes before going to bed. It's already weird enough that I'm in our lawyer's room at night and watching her naked legs for a second too long.

"Would you mind?" she asks in a smaller voice, much shier all of a sudden. "That way if I see it again, I won't have to have to choose who to sacrifice between Moll and May."

"Sure." It's because of me she's here, after all.

She only seems to hesitate for an extra moment before she jumps off the couch and runs to her bed, the white dog in her arms, the brown one following her there. Meanwhile, I go to the small closet beside the couch to grab a heavy wool blanket. Once she looks comfortable in bed, I turn the lights off, then head over to lie on the couch.

Even though the cabin is completely silent, I would bet a kidney she's not asleep. Five minutes later, she confirms my suspicions by saying, "Are you sure you don't mind?"

"I'm sure, Wren. Go to sleep. You're fine."

"Okay. Thank you."

She's been so good to us. If sleeping on an uncomfortable couch is the one thing I can do for her, you can be sure I'd never pass on the opportunity.

I wait until I can't hear the sheets rustling before I allow myself to fall asleep. And I'm pretty sure it's the first time in a long while there are no tension lines on my face when I do.

CHAPTER 7

Wren

RUNNING IS ONE OF THE ONLY THINGS PROVEN TO BE ABLE to hold off dementia.

I say hold off because nothing can actually prevent it. Not every form, at least. If someone has the PSEN1 mutation on their fourteenth chromosome, no amount of running will keep them from losing themselves one memory at a time. However, even with the abnormal changes in one's DNA strands, it's been hypothesized that running could delay the process. So I run. A lot.

It's not actually just running. Any physical activity can do. But running is far superior in my opinion. Nothing beats it in terms of taking your mind off things. And this morning, keeping my mind busy is the principal factor that keeps my feet pouncing on the cold ground of the Sonder Hill Main Road.

I still can't believe last night actually happened. When I woke up this morning, I thought for a second that perhaps I'd dreamed it all, but that hope only lasted for a sweet, short second. Then I remembered everything in too many details, which told me it couldn't be a figment of my imagination.

How I'd let myself scream so loud because of some tiny animal that it woke up one of the people who hired me is beyond me.

At least I hope it's only one of the people. If I woke the whole house with my stupid cries, I'll start looking for ways to subtly disappear.

And not only did I wake him up, I screamed loud enough that he thought I was in danger, which made him come out of his house to check if I was doing all right. When I opened the door to the cabin, I couldn't quite believe what I was seeing. Aaron was there, clad in gray sweat pants and a white T-shirt that hugged every single muscle in his chest. It was truly something out of a dream.

The fact that I noticed those muscles is another reason why I needed this morning's run; what was I doing, ogling his body like that? Something dumb, that's what. I've never had any problem keeping my eyes off men before. I can appreciate good-looking guys, sure, but I never stare at them like a desperate lioness.

It's those freaking rats' fault.

Molly's paws hit the ground at the same pace as mine as we turn around. As much as I'd like to keep running from my problems, both figuratively and literally, I can't do it forever.

It's brisk and misty this morning, the cold seeping through my bones. However, there's nothing like breathing in the pure air of the forest, with its smell of pine and musk. The road I'm on is long enough that for miles there's nothing around it but trees and sparse, long driveways.

Molly seems to have more energy than ever this morning. We've been running for close to an hour, and she's not showing any signs of fatigue. She probably likes not having to stop at red lights every two minutes.

I tried bringing Maybelle with us once, but she whined as soon as we started, and after five minutes, I had to stop and carry her home because the little miss had decided to stop moving. I've learned the hard way that she would much rather sleep in.

My feet too soon lead me back to the farm, where I start slowing down.

"Good girl," I tell Molly, who snuggles her head against my hand as our jogging turns into a speed walk, her big chest panting almost as fast as mine.

"Hey!" a voice calls behind us as I start climbing the steps to the cabin. A voice I recognize.

No. Please no. Couldn't I at least have the time to take a proper shower before having to face him again? He was gone by the time I woke up this morning. I thought I'd been blessed by the gods and had been given a free pass for yesterday, but apparently not.

I let out a tight breath through my nose. At least it'll be done. Trying not to look as embarrassed as I feel, I spin on my heels. "Hey."

Aaron is dressed the same way he was when I got here the first time, with a fleece-lined plaid coat, khakis, and work boots. His dark brown locks are covered with a simple black beanie, mischief in his gaze. "Sleep well?"

I purse my lips, which makes him laugh.

"Hope the bed was more comfortable than the couch," he says, still smirking.

"Look, I'm sorry about all that," I say, arms crossed. "I shouldn't have asked you to stay. I just really, um..."

"Hate rats?"

"Yes. That."

His eyes twinkle in amusement.

"All that a few hours after saying you wouldn't realize I'm here," I grunt. "I swear I'm not usually so..."

One of his hands shoots forward and pats my shoulder. "Hey, Wren, stop it. I'm just messing with you." His skin is warm, burning me even through my thermal shirt. He removes it fast.

Why am I even noticing the warmth of his hands? Something's wrong with me.

"Okay, well—"

"Let me show you around," he interrupts.

"Huh?"

"You've only seen the bad bits—not that I believe we have rats," he says, making me roll my eyes. With a laugh, he adds, "You haven't been given a proper tour. Let me show you the good parts of this place."

My lips pull to one side. I have a lot of work to do. I need to call the garage to ask what's going on with my car and whether I'll be able to use it again soon. There are a bunch of phone calls I need to return. But something in my brain must not be working properly because I say, "Okay, why not." And it's the truth. I've been wondering for a while what the whole place looks like and what a Christmas tree farm owner does for a living. Still, my answer has surprised even me. "You owe me for the rats anyway."

He snickers, nudging his head to the side. "Come on now."

"Just give me a sec," I say before rushing inside. There, I feed Molly, change into a warmer coat, and at the last second, grab Maybelle, not wanting to leave her alone for too long. I place her in the special backpack that allows me to carry her everywhere while allowing her to look outside and stay warm, even in winter. I think the thing was built for cats, but she fits in perfectly, so we adopted the thing for our walks.

"Okay, I'm ready," I say as I walk back out.

He nods, then leads the way toward the evergreen forest.

"She looks cozy in there," he says, pointing at May on my back.

"Yeah, she loves it."

"I'm sure she does."

I narrow my eyes. "Was that sarcastic?"

"Of course, not," he says with a smile, which might also be sarcastic. I can't be sure, though. I'm starting to realize Aaron smiles a lot, no matter what he says. When we met, he looked more serious, but in the past few days, I've seen a more jovial side of him. If I had to guess, I'd say it's his natural one.

"My dog doesn't like to walk on cold ground. Sue me."

He laughs. "I'd never dare."

We exchange a look before we continue to walk, passing the main house and heading toward the forest. Meanwhile, Aaron starts explaining to me the process of getting trees to maturation and then making sure they stay in good shape until they reach people's homes for Christmas time. I had no idea it took that much work for people to get a nicely shaped Christmas tree every year, but the farm definitely needs employees to work full time all year, between the weeding, the planting, the disease preventing, and the cultivating.

"So I guess you have a lot of work set up for you here," I say.

He chuckles, though there's no humor left in his voice. "You could say that, yeah."

His pace accelerates, and I observe his back for a moment. This isn't just a second-choice job for him. It's a burden. His words might not have told me that, but the change in his attitude just did.

Aaron looks over his shoulder, unfreezing me. I hurry to him.

We continue walking, with the sound of crows cawing in the background, until Aaron slows and says, "Want to go for a ride?" To our right is a large garage—or a small barn—in front of which are parked a black pickup truck and two ATVs.

"Uh, I think I'll pass."

He quirks an eyebrow. "You going to tour the sixty acres of land on foot?"

"Sure," I say with a lift of my chin.

"You scared?" he asks, amused.

"No, I'm not scared." But seriously, who would want to go on one of these just for the sake of it?

"It's okay if you are." His light-brown eyes shine as he smirks. "It's not like I haven't seen it all before."

"You're the worst." With a sharp exhale, I walk past him and climb onto the ATV.

He stands in place, half gawking, half smiling.

"You coming?" I ask over my shoulder.

With a shake of his head, he joins me on the ATV. The side of his thigh touches mine as he inserts himself between my legs, the position putting me in the running for Most Inappropriate Lawyer, but you gotta do what you gotta do. Careful to touch him the least possible, I lean backward, but the seat is barely large enough to fit two people, and with Maybelle on my back, I can't pull away much. My groin stays seated against his butt, my efforts useless.

"You okay back there?" he asks as he turns the engine on.

"Peachy."

I feel his back shake as he flicks his wrist and jerks us forward. The movement is so sudden, I reflexively put my arms around his torso and squeeze my legs around him to hold on.

So much for keeping my distance.

Aaron drives us slowly at first, then gains speed as we move through the forest with trees of all sizes, most covered with fluffy white snow that twinkles in the early morning sunlight. The land is incredibly vast, pines and firs covering the space in front of me as far as my eyes can see. He was right, there was no way to see it all on foot. I would've missed out on something. Except for our engine, the whole space is quiet. So peaceful.

"Do you have siblings?" Aaron asks after a while, slowing the ATV down as we come close to a small pond, the surface frozen and shining a bright silver, like a million tiny diamonds.

"What?" I ask, jerking back.

"You were good with Callie yesterday," he explains. "She can have a little bit of an attitude sometimes, but not with you."

"Oh. I don't know. She's great." She did come to the cabin after school to pet the dogs. I gladly let her play with them while I finished working on Dennis's statement of claim. Aaron hasn't brought it up, so maybe he doesn't even know.

"Yeah, she is." He grins. "When she's not being a little shit, that is."

I snort at that.

The silence reappears as we round the pond, and I realize I never answered his previous question. I don't know why I got so shaken. It wasn't intrusive in the slightest. In fact, it's probably one of the first questions anyone who is trying to get to know someone else would ask. But that's the thing: I can't say when was the last time I've allowed someone to try and get to know me.

And since he's someone I won't see again after a short while, isn't he the perfect person to talk to?

Plus, his back is to me. It's always easier to open up when you don't have the pressure of someone's eyes on you.

My gaze lands on a mole on the back of his neck, exposed to the frigid air above his coat. His light-brown skin shouldn't fit in this winter paradise, but somehow, it does.

"No, I don't have siblings," I say.

He doesn't ask anything else, but his silence invites me to continue.

"My father had already left by the time I was born, and my mother was so busy with my grandpa when he got sick that I don't think she ever thought of having more kids."

"So it's just you and your mom?"

"It was, yeah."

"I'm so sorry," he says in a soft voice, still facing forward.

I frown for a second before realizing how that sounded. Oh. He thinks she's dead.

Hesitation lingers for a few moments, but in the end, for some reason, I don't correct him. It's not like the situation Mom and I are in now is much better than what he assumed. In fact, some days, I find myself thinking maybe it'd be less painful if she had in fact died. It's a horrible, shame-inducing thought, but I can't help it. If I had lost her—*really* lost her—when I was eighteen, then I could reminisce only on the nice moments we spent together and not on the hurt I feel every time we see each other. It's not like we were ever that close, but we still shared good times. Now, though, the pain outweighs all of it.

I clear my throat. "What about you? Is Callie your only sibling?"

"Yeah."

"You have a big age gap," I say. Probably something like fifteen years, if I had to guess.

"My parents adopted her when I was seventeen. Mom had a niece in the Dominican Republic who got pregnant at sixteen and couldn't keep her, so they took her in."

"Wow. That's something." I can't imagine having a seventeen-year-old kid, almost an adult, then starting the whole process all over again. "They seem like great people, your parents."

He turns to me, emotion written all over his face. "The best." His smile slowly fades, and I can tell where his mind has gone.

I never make any promises as an attorney. I can't swear on my life that we will win a case. I would eventually have to break my word, so I'd rather not promise anything. But today, I allow myself to break that rule. Hand on his forearm, I say, "I'll win that case for you. For them."

His eyes gleam as they meet mine, so solemn a shiver runs down my spine. "I know you will, Wren."

Never have I seen anyone have so much faith in me. My clients always put some trust in me, yes, but I've never felt anything like that. Like there isn't one doubt in his mind that I will do the right thing for them.

One thing's for sure: I'll do whatever it takes not to let him down.

CHAPTER 8

Aaron

MY PEN SLIDES AGAINST THE SCREEN OF THE TABLET in front of me, something so intuitive I could do it with my eyes closed.

I'm at peace for the first time in a while. It's like my brain has left the building, which is what happens every time I get enthralled with a project. If I'm in the zone, I can spend hours without thinking about a single thing. It's like the art flows directly from my fingers to the page, not even needing a thought process behind it. There's no feeling quite like it.

I haven't been able to create in a while. I've answered emails here and there, but sit down and truly focus only on my designs? It feels like it's been ages. Today, though, I needed to do it. Craig, my boss, has called me a few times in the past days to ask me if I'd gotten started on the primary sketch of the background design for the next game Arcade Games will release. I should've told him right then and there I wouldn't be able to do it because I'm quitting, but I couldn't make myself do it. It's too painful to leave a job that makes me happy, no matter how much I need to do it. And I will do it. Just not now. Not when this project has lit me up inside like a firecracker.

I've never been an expert in character drawings, but designs of foreign—or not-so-foreign—lands are my thing. The creation team has been having meetings recently about the theme we want to go for, and even though I had to miss the last few, they sent me a list of ideas I needed to work with. Inspiration automatically hit.

Ideas have been flowing through my mind for weeks. However, between managing the farm, making sure Callie has everything she needs when Ma is busy, helping out as best I can inside the house, and installing mouse traps inside the cabin, I haven't had much time on hand.

But today, I arranged all my schedule so I would be able to work on this. I woke up at 4:00 a.m. to make sure I'd be done with what needed to be done on the farm by noon, and I've been locked in the office-turned-art-studio since then.

It's been nothing short of a blessing.

The team decided the new game could possibly take place in a Highlands-like setting, and after a little more research, I've created a land of tall cliffs bordered by infinite bodies of water, the grass green and the sky stormy. The sketches on my tablet almost look lifelike. That's not me showing off. I'm not good at a lot of stuff, but that's my gift.

The pen in my left hand glides against the screen as I touch up the gray in one of the rocks. I hope Craig's happy with my work. If he's not, with the time I'm spending away from the office, he'd have a reason to fire me. That would probably be useful, considering it'd save me from having to resign, but I wouldn't want to leave like that.

The simple thought of not doing this ever again makes me drop my pen and lean my head between my shoulders. Here goes the momentum I'd built. I need to get a grip. Soon. Just not yet.

As if on cue, my phone rings next to my hand. It's Craig.

After clearing my throat of the emotion that might still be there, I answer and say, "Hey, boss."

"Aaron! My man," he shouts through the phone. I can almost see him leaned back in his plush office chair, throwing his stress ball in the air as he holds his phone with the other hand. "How's that design going?"

Thank God I started working on it today. I'd have looked like a real asshole if I still hadn't sketched anything three weeks after he sent me the ideas I needed to work with.

"Good, good." I look back down at my drawing. It's nowhere near perfect, but at least if he wants to see it, I'll have something pretty good to show him.

"Ah, you have no idea how happy I am to hear that, because guess what?"

Oh fuck. I'm pretty sure I don't want to hear what's about to come.

"What?" I get out, semi-cringing.

"We have new investors coming to the office in two months, and if they like the game, we might get an even bigger financing than we expected! Which would be huge for us before a new release."

And there goes all the calm I built during my drafting session.

Craig continues talking about the opportunity with so much excitement, and I understand. If it had been three months ago, I would've been ecstatic. I started working at Arcade when they were only a start-up, believing that the company would go far. And apparently, that's what's happening now. Except I'm nowhere near able to work all the hours it will take prior to a meeting of that importance. I drag a hand through my hair, sighing softly so he won't hear me. This is the worst timing they could've picked.

"That's great, Craig," I end up saying, my voice not even remotely excited, "but I—"

"You'll have a proper primary design ready for us by then, Aaron, won't you?"

Double fuck. Craig was one of the first people to believe in me in this industry. Wanting to work in the video game field is a lot of people's dreams, and there aren't that many jobs to begin with, especially in the design departments. He's never made me regret my choice to work there. I couldn't have wished for a better boss.

Which also means that I can't disappoint him.

Plus, this project is rapidly becoming a favorite of mine.

There's a lot of new designs I want to draft for specific challenges the players will need to do in pubs and old churches and fairy pools. I need to tell him I can't do it. I also one hundred percent need to do this project.

"Sure, no problem," I lie. I know for sure I'll regret the shit out of this promise in a few weeks, but saying no to Craig about this is impossible. I'll find a way to make it work. There's no other choice.

"Ah, I knew I could count on you. This is going to be fucking fantastic!"

Nervous laughter comes out of my mouth. "Sure will."

"I'll let you get back to it, then. Bye, Ron!"

"Bye." After putting the phone down, I try to get back to my drawing, but my head isn't in it anymore.

It'll be okay, I keep repeating to myself. I'll find a way. I always do. And after this project, I'll drop Arcade and move here full time. The transition can wait a couple months. In the meantime, I'll keep doing both.

Once I've succeeded in convincing myself of the feasibility of this plan, I get back to drawing, and this time, I'm able to focus. That is, until three faint knocks come from the door behind my desk.

"Yes?" I say, turning in my chair.

The door opens slowly, revealing the tall woman with dark brown hair and bright blue eyes I've come to see almost every day.

"Sorry to bother you," Wren whispers. "Can I come in?"

I stand fast to my feet. "Of course."

It's the first time I've seen her today, even though she's still living in the cabin. Her engine is officially dead, and the garage needed to order pieces to be able to make the proper repairs, so she's been here for three days and counting. Not that I'm complaining. She usually stays with us for dinner—Ma practically forces her to—and she's brought some much-needed change to our meal times. Ever since Dad's accident, we'd been eating in near silence. Our dinner tables used to be so lively, with everyone adding their two cents to the conversation, but now that Dad can't contribute like he used to, we all feel the need to stop speaking. It's strange, if I'm being honest. He probably doesn't want that for us. It's not like it's a rule for us to keep quiet, but it's what came naturally for everyone.

Yet ever since Wren has been around, our meals have become lively again. She's been able to make Callie and Ma smile while talking about "the girls," as she calls them, or about why she's so scared of rats. Everyone ended up learning about Wren's little event during the night two days ago because the morning after, Ma was sitting in the kitchen when I came back inside, and I had to spill the beans. She, of course, then told the entire family.

It's not even like Wren makes an effort to be funny or lovable; she simply is.

"It's just…" She points her thumb to something over her shoulder. "I think your father wants to tell you something. I'm done working with him for the day, and he's been motioning toward this room for the past ten minutes."

My stomach drops. I feel like shit for avoiding spending time alone with him, but I can't help it. It's too hard. I try to stay strong for the family, to take on his work like it's no big deal, without ever complaining, but seeing him trying to talk without succeeding is something that hurts too much, even for me.

"Uh, yeah, sure," I say, turning my back to her as if something incredibly interesting just appeared on my desk.

I wait for her to go, but she doesn't. Instead, she says in a low voice, "It won't get better just because you ignore it, you know."

When I look back her way, her face is focused, as usual. Neutral.

"How do you know I'm avoiding it?" I ask. It's like she can always read my mind, while I spend my time trying to decipher what she's thinking. It's frustrating, but also fascinating. Like she's a puzzle with more pieces than I can deal with.

She swallows. "Because I did the same."

It doesn't take long for me to figure out she's not talking about my dad. Ever since she got here, she has been comfortable discussing his case with him even though she knew he wouldn't be able to answer her. Which means she's talking about somebody else.

She knows so much about my family, yet I barely know anything about hers. The only hints I've received are the ones she offered for some reason during our ATV ride two days ago. Is she talking about her mother, before she passed? Wren didn't even say how she died. Maybe she had a stroke at some point too, or maybe she had something else. I can't imagine anything as bad as a parent wanting to say something but their muscles not being able to get the words out, but by the way she's blinking fast, I'd say maybe there *is* something just as bad, if not worse.

"How?" I ask, trying to get something more. Anything. *How did you move on? How did you survive this?*

Her mouth opens, then closes. I stare at her intently, waiting. I don't know why it's so important that she tells me. I just know there's something inside me that wants to get her. Fully get her.

Something in her is burning. Her gaze is alive, trying to communicate something with me. But no word comes out.

Taking a step forward, I say, "Are you talking about—"

"She's not here!" a voice screams down the hallway. A voice I'd recognize anywhere. "Aarón!" Ma shouts, panic lacing her voice. "I can't find her!"

I'm out of the room in a second, Wren right beside me. I find Ma a few feet away, her eyes red, face blotchy.

"Whoa, whoa, whoa," I say, grabbing her arms. "What's going on?"

"Callie," she says, panting. "I can't find her anywhere. She wasn't there when school finished, and she's not at Sylvia's, and she's not in the yard, and—"

"Okay, Ma, calm down," I say, even though my own heartbeat is through the roof. "I'll take care of it."

"Mi bebé," my mother wails, fat tears starting to roll down her cheeks.

Fuck. Fuck, fuck, fuck.

"Ma, it's going to be fine, okay? I'll find her. Just… Can you go with Dad and take a breath?" The words barely come out of my mouth. Air seems scarce all of a sudden. Thankfully, she listens to me. She can't see that I'm panicking.

I head up the stairs—for what, I don't know—and as soon as I have some space to freak out, I do. Big time.

Focus, Aaron.

I can't. Not when my little sister is missing, and I'm the one who's supposed to find her.

I put my hands behind my head and start walking around, but my lungs don't expand as much as I want them to. This is too much. For Ma, for Dad, for me.

"Hey," a soft voice says behind me. I turn the moment I realize Wren followed me up the stairs. "It's going to be okay." She has her serious work face on. It's reassuring. It reminds me precisely of why I wanted to hire her in the first place.

"I'm responsible for them. For her," I breathe, my eyes stinging. "What if she's lying in a ditch somewhere?" All that while I was fucking working on some stupid project. I should've been there. I should've quit even before today. Maybe Ma was late to pick her up, and if I'd been there, she'd be safe and sound at home.

"Aaron, stop it." Her voice is harsh. It takes me out of my panic, at least a little. "I'll help you find her. And we *will* find her, okay?"

It feels so good to hear her say it. Like someone actually believes it. I nod.

Eyes right on mine, she says, "Take a deep breath." I do. "Another." I follow her instructions. "Good. You're okay," she says, so convincing.

And suddenly, I'm not so bad.

"I'll figure a plan with you, okay? You're not alone in this," she says.

I don't know how she does it. She's not a clairvoyant. She doesn't know what will happen. But somehow, I believe every single word that's coming out of her mouth.

If Wren says it'll be okay, then it'll be okay.

CHAPTER 9

Wren

"FOLLOW ME," I TELL AARON AS I GRAB HIS ARM AND drag him downstairs.

Do I know what I'm doing? Not really. But someone needed to take control of the situation, and with the deer-in-the-headlights face Aaron was making seconds ago, I knew I had to be that person. Plus, I can think clearly in situations of distress. Kind of an ironic gift considering my future condition, but right now, I'm thankful for it.

Aaron follows me blindly as I tell a panicked Martina and a distressed Dennis that we'll be back with Callie, then head out the door, my thin coat quickly thrown over my shoulders. Aaron stays silent, and when I turn to him, I find him flushed and breathing fast, gaze lost in space.

"Do you have any friends who could help us look for her?" I ask him, which makes him focus on me. Good. As long as I keep him busy, I'm pretty sure I can keep him in a functional state of mind.

He acquiesces. "Yeah, I have, um, a friend who can help."

"Good. Call them."

Following my order, he grabs his phone and calls this friend. After uttering a few words in a low voice, he hangs up. "He's coming," Aaron says, body angled toward the tree farm. One of his feet is tapping the ground repeatedly. "He was working today."

"Okay." *Keep his mind busy.* "Now I need you to think about all the places she could possibly be. Things she likes to do, places she likes to visit, friends she might have mentioned in the past…"

"Ma already looked everywhere. If she's not anywhere, then…" He bites his inner cheek, gaze drifting again.

"Aaron," I say sternly, a hand reaching for his wrist. "I need you to focus. You won't get anywhere by worrying."

He swallows.

More softly, I say, "She's okay. She probably just decided to be a kid and do something stupid like go somewhere new without telling her parents."

His eyes are on me, listening to my words like he needs to believe them. Good.

"She's okay," he repeats in a low voice.

I give his wrist a squeeze.

A pair of boots hitting the ground makes me turn around. The guy, who I assume is Aaron's friend, looks to be in his late twenties, with a buzz cut and a strong build.

"Hear anything?" he asks as he reaches us, sounding out of breath.

Aaron shakes his head.

"I'm Wren, the family's lawyer," I tell him, not bothering to shake his hand. We have more important things to do right now.

"Finn," he answers, giving me a curt dip of the head before he gives Aaron a worried look.

"Okay, Finn," I say, "I need you to go back to Callie's school and try to find people who might know where she went. Kids, teachers, parents, whoever you can find. Some people might still be there." Martina probably left in a hurry after she didn't see her, so it's a good idea to return there. "Aaron and I will drive around town and try to look in other places we might've missed."

"On it," Finn says before disappearing toward one of the trucks parked in front of the large garage.

Now alone, I turn to Aaron and ask, "Okay?"

He nods. "Thank you." The two words hang heavy between us in the air.

"Of course," I answer, meaning it completely. Aaron's a good one. His *family's* a good one. They deserve all the help they can get.

"All right," I say as I start walking toward Aaron's SUV. "I'll drive, you'll look."

He doesn't argue with me, instead handing me his set of keys. I climb in the driver's seat, then take a second to adjust it to my height before I start the car and drive into town.

Sonder Hill is small, thank goodness. If this had happened in Boston, my panic level would've been much higher. At least here, it's easier to look for her everywhere before calling the cops.

With Aaron's guidance, we drive to the only grocery store in town, to the few playgrounds, to the ice cream shop, and to the indoor swimming pool. Nothing.

Aaron's knee is jumping beside me, his eyes fixated outside. The sky is gray, sunrays barely passing through, which adds an ominous feel to the day.

"Do you have any other ideas?" I ask softly while making a U-turn so we can examine the route a second time.

"I don't know." He drags a hand through his hair, exhaling slowly. "Wren, I can't—"

"Does she like to read?" I interrupt while I narrow in on one of the buildings I missed while driving in the opposite direction. When I was young, my mother had to work two jobs to make ends meet. As a single mom who didn't have the opportunity to get higher education, she didn't have the choice. My grandpa's dementia had already started to progress by the time I was ten, so Mom couldn't rely on him, considering all his money had to go for the care he needed. Having support at home, or in a care facility, is extremely expensive, but also indispensable for someone with advanced Alzheimer's—one of the reasons I picked a high-paying job and am careful with my savings. So with a mother who worked so much and no one else to hang out with, reading became my main entertainment.

"She does. Why?"

Sonder Hill's library is located inside a small brick building, easy to miss. The insignia on the front door is the only thing that tipped me off. Instead of answering Aaron's question, I turn into the parking lot of the library and stop the car.

"Let's go in," I tell him while unbuckling my seat belt. He follows.

"This is a long walk from the school," he says as we head toward the front door.

"She seems like a persistent kid."

This has to be it. Otherwise, we're lost. I'm coming up short of ideas, and if she's not here, then I'm not sure what we'll do. Call the police? Aaron will start panicking, for real this time. Maybe I'll be right there with him.

We walk inside the small space that brings us straight back to the seventies, with vertical wood panels on the walls and popcorn ceilings. I head to the single clerk manning the front desk.

"Good afternoon," she says.

"Hi. Have you seen a little girl this big? Black hair, brown eyes?"

"Actually, yes, I did. I think I saw her heading toward the back," she says.

"Thank you," I answer, then run after Aaron, who didn't wait for the clerk to finish speaking before going to look for his sister.

And there she is.

"Callie!" Aaron shouts before starting to run toward his little sister, who's seated at a table with a small book in front of her. A few heads turn his way, but from the look of relief on Aaron's face as he drops to his knees and wraps his arms around his sister, I'd say he couldn't give less of a crap. "You scared the hell out of us!"

"What's going on?" she says, looking confused, both at her

brother's strong reaction and his tight hug. Large headphones hang around her neck, plugged into an old device that doesn't look like a phone.

"What's going on?" he repeats, voice still loud. "We couldn't find you! You almost gave all of us a heart attack."

She shrugs, an eyebrow up like she still doesn't understand why Aaron's so upset. "Mom wasn't there to pick me up, so I thought I'd just come here instead of waiting outside."

He closes his eyes. "Christ, Callie, you can't do that kind of thing without warning us."

As much as she tries to keep her bored expression on, I catch her lips tilting downward. "I'm sorry, I guess."

"It's okay," he says, hugging her tight again. "Let's just bring you home."

For the first time in the last hour, I think I feel Aaron exhale. I'd be lying if I said I don't feel equally relieved

* * *

"Oh, mi corazón," Martina wails into Callie's hair, tears streaming down her cheeks.

"I'm okay, Mami," Callie answers, though I can see she's shaken. She didn't expect to have unnerved her family this much.

Aaron and Finn are speaking quietly next to Finn's pickup truck as Martina talks to Callie in Spanish. She's still hugging her tighter than ever. Behind them stands Dennis, his eyes watery. He approaches them slowly, his walker dragging in the snow on the driveway before he drapes his left arm around Martina and Callie.

The love everyone in this family shares is palpable.

A knot forms in my throat. I turn around and start walking toward the cabin before it can worsen. I hate when I get like this. I shouldn't be jealous of a ten-year-old girl. It's embarrassing.

I'm halfway to the cabin when a deep voice calls, "Hey, wait up!"

Aaron is jogging my way, his demeanor a 180 from how it was thirty minutes ago. I force my face into a small smile. Who the hell would be scowling in this happy situation? I'm so messed up.

He slows in front of me, then buries his hands in the pockets of his coat. "I need to thank you again. For everything." He inhales deeply. "I don't know what I—what *we*—would've done today without you."

"I told you we'd find her."

He grins. "You did."

I shift on my feet. I could really use a cuddle with Molly or Maybelle right now.

"We're just all a little on edge right now, with everything..."

"I get it," I say. "Really."

His lips twitch.

"Well—"

"Would you like to come have a drink?" Aaron blurts out. "I mean, with me and Finn. We were supposed to go tonight, but you should come."

"Oh no, I wouldn't want to impose." Plus, I really need that cuddle with my dogs.

"Come on," he says. "I owe you."

I open my mouth to answer, but leave it hanging when I study his face. He's not just suggesting this to be polite. He looks like he actually wants me to say yes. I don't remember the last time this has happened. Even when the girls at work invite me to come with them, it always feels a little like a pity invite.

Remember, you won't see him again in a few months.

Plus, after the day he's had, I'd hate to disappoint him.

"Okay," I answer, which makes him smile as bright as the lights in the tall pine tree behind him.

* * *

"So, Wren, tell me about yourself."

Finn is lounging next to Aaron in the brown leather booth of the local pub, both of them facing me. His arms are spread wide over the top of their seat, one hand around Aaron's neck. He's good-looking. Not as good as the guy who slept on my couch four days ago, but still cute. He's funny too. I like him.

His question, though, I don't like. My chest feels tight with the next breath I take. It's been so long since I've been out with people like this. The last time was with Aaron last summer, if that even counts.

"You don't have to answer any of his stupid questions," Aaron tells me, although his eyes are fixed on his friend, who has a smug grin on his lips.

"Ah, come on now, I didn't even say anything," Finn answers, a hand on his heart.

Aaron's gaze stays narrowed.

I clear my throat. "How about you tell me about you two instead?"

"Diverting the conversation away from herself. Smart girl." He winks. "I've known this little shit since he was just a wee baby."

Aaron rolls his eyes, then says, "You're the little shit. And you were a baby too, don't forget to say that."

My lips twitch. There's definitely history there. It's cute.

Finn turns to me, the wicked grin still present. "Your turn. You gotta give me something here, darling."

Aaron scowls. He's been in a pissy mood ever since Finn met us at the bar fifteen minutes after we got there and joined the conversation. I don't know why. Maybe he's still shaken by what happened today and realized he didn't want to be away from his family tonight, or maybe they got into an argument. Either way, I don't care about it; it's funny to see him like this. He's never been in a foul mood in front of me before. Sad or anxious, sure, but never properly annoyed.

I lift my glass of sparkling water to my lips while I think about Finn's question. He's another person who'll stop thinking about me the second I drive away from this town, so answering him is no big deal. After putting the glass back down, I say, "What do you want to know?"

"Well, first, how did you get so pretty?"

"Are you serious?" Aaron mutters.

Finn laughs at his reaction. "I'm just messing with you both, man, calm down."

The two men exchange a look, and for a second, I feel like I'm missing something. But as fast as it happened, Finn turns back to me and says, "Okay, seriously, though, where are you from?"

"Boston," I answer, my eyes flitting to Aaron. He's already looking at me. He could've given that answer to Finn already, which means they never talked about me together. Good. "You?"

"Originally from here, but I've been living all over the place. Maybe Boston will be next." He adds another wink, making me laugh. God, this guy. If he was a real stranger in a bar, I'd have chased him away already, but he's obviously just teasing.

Aaron exhales loudly before lifting a hand for the waitress to come to our table. "Another beer, please," he asks her.

"Me too, darling. Thanks," the tease adds. She gives him a thumbs-up, then turns around.

"And what do you do, Finn?" I ask.

"Oh, you know, this and that." He nudges Aaron with his elbow. "Currently I'm helping this guy out."

"On the farm?"

Finn nods. I glance at Aaron, eyebrows drawn. "So you're still officially in charge?" Guess he still hasn't found a way to keep doing what he likes.

"Yep," he says as the waitress comes in with their drinks. He doesn't quite meet my eye after answering.

"Huh," I say. That gets him to look up, but he doesn't say anything else.

"And do you like it?" I ask Finn.

"It's great. Being outdoor all the time is fucking fantastic."

"Yeah, not my thing," I say.

"But you always run outside," Aaron interjects.

"Someone's been looking," Finn says under his breath before taking a large sip of his beer. I ignore him.

"Yeah, because I need to, not because I want to," I tell Aaron.

"You could just let Molly run by herself outside," he says.

"Not for her. I need it for me."

He looks at me questioningly, but before he can ask anything else, Finn calls out to me. "Okay, one question to determine whether I really like you or not. If you could travel anywhere right now, where would it be?"

I frown. "What kind of question is that?"

"Just answer it," Finn says.

I shrug. "Home, I guess. I don't travel much."

Aaron's friend's jaw falls, as if I've just said something crazy like dogs aren't the Universe's greatest creation. "But…how? Why?"

I can't answer his question honestly when he doesn't have the full story. He wouldn't understand if I said I don't see the point of discovering new places when I know I won't remember them in a few years. So instead, I say, "I'm comfortable in my stuff."

While Finn gives me the stink eye, Aaron studies me silently. I feel rather than see his gaze.

"Okayyy," Finn says, "but let's say you need to choose somewhere. Where would you go."

With my index finger, I trace the circle of condensation my glass has made on the sticky table. I haven't thought about traveling in so long. Not since my uncle got sick. Grandpa could've been a one-time thing. Mom could've been really unlucky. But three in a row? I didn't need superpowers to know I'd be next. Most of my life plans went up in flames then.

There used to be a time when I had a bucket list of places I wanted to visit. Back when I was a young girl who dreamed of doing grand things with my life. I still remember the place I'd written at the top of that imaginary list.

"Australia," I answer.

Finn grins. "And why's that?"

I shrug again, this time for another reason. There's probably never been a stupider explanation. "I've always wanted to see koalas in their natural habitat." It's not the same seeing animals in a zoo. Anyway, I don't like seeing wild animals trapped in a cage.

"Really?" Aaron says, crinkles lining his forehead.

"Yeah, really. They look super soft."

He clearly tries to hold it in, but his grin only grows at my answer. A corner of my lips rises in return.

"Well, I know some people Down Under, so if ever you decide to go, just let me know, and I'll show you all the things you've been missing," Finn says, smirking.

Aaron jumps to his feet, putting both hands on Finn's shoulders. "All right, lover boy. Time to go back home."

Finn frowns jokingly. "Really? But Wren and I just started building our friendship."

With the fakest smile I've ever seen, Aaron leans forward and murmurs something to Finn, which sounds a lot like, "Too fucking bad."

I laugh at that, deep and loud.

Never thought there'd come a day when I'd have a good time looking at two men bickering, and yet.

CHAPTER 10

Aaron

"MAMÁ, NECESITO—"

I stop in my tracks the moment I spot Wren seated in my childhood kitchen, a steaming cup in her hands.

"Hi," she says, voice almost muffled. Behind her, Callie is sitting on the floor, playing with Maybelle. "I came back from my run, and your mom was outside and invited me to stay for breakfast." The words come out of her mouth fast. I don't know why she's justifying herself. I don't mind that she's here. She doesn't look out of place.

However, I wasn't expecting our lawyer to be sitting in the kitchen when I came downstairs shirtless.

As if reading my mind, Ma turns from the stove where she's cooking that looks a lot like *mangú* and says, "**¡Aarón, ve a ponerte un poloche, por el amor de Dios!**"

Wren's mouth twists, like she's holding back her amusement. I don't think she understands Spanish, but with Ma's appalled expression, it's not hard to understand what she means.

Wren's eyes move away from me. I don't even know if she looked. I feel myself flushing from my neck up.

To no one in particular, I say, "Just give me one second." I disappear for a moment to the laundry room, then come back with a black T-shirt on.

"Good morning," I tell everyone as I walk to pour myself a cup of coffee.

When I look back at Wren, she says, "Again, I wasn't planning on coming in, but—"

"Hey, it's fine." I don't know why she's so bothered by it. Callie's laughing as she keeps making the tiny white dog sit, and Ma is cooking a breakfast I've been craving for weeks, so no one's going to complain about Wren being here.

After I sit in front of her in the kitchen nook, I take a sip of black coffee then say, "Are you planning on working today?"

She shakes her head, the short dark strands wilder than usual. "I don't usually work on Saturdays, no."

Her car is still at the garage—she told me yesterday that they said it should be ready by Thursday—so she can't go back home even if she's not working. The cabin is small, and there's literally nothing to do in there unless you've brought card games or VHSs to watch movies on the old TV.

"I'm going to be working on the farm all day," I tell her. We've just entered the busiest month of the year for us, and I know we'll get a lot of people coming in to cut their own tree. The self-service aspect of the farm is what makes most of its charm, according to clients. "But you can come with me."

Her jaw shifts.

"If you want, that is," I add. The last time I brought her to the farm to show her around, she seemed to have fun. It's always hard to tell with her, but I'm pretty sure I heard her laugh a time or two, so I'd say that counted as a win.

It takes a while for her to give me an answer. She does that often. As if she always needs to think carefully about what she's going to say. Maybe that's the lawyer in her that wants to make sure she never says the wrong thing.

In the end though, she gives me the answer I wanted.

"Sure, okay. Thanks."

I grin. I should be the one thanking her. Working on the land is one thing, but waiting around for people to show up and buy trees is pretty boring. I always love having company.

"Can I come too?" Callie asks from her spot on the floor.

I lift an eyebrow. "Tú nunca me quieres ayudar." *You never want to help me.*

With a lift of her chin, she says, "Bueno pues hoy si." *Well, today I want to.*

She then turns to Wren and says, "Maybe we can bring Molly too?"

That makes Wren light up, a true, bright smile on her lips. "I think she'd like that."

"Okay, now time to eat," Ma says as she brings a pan full of eggs and *salchichón*. I get up and help her bring the rest of the breakfast to the table.

"Where's Dad?" I ask.

"Still in the bedroom," Ma says. "Why don't you go tell him breakfast's ready?"

With a stiff bob of my neck, I nod.

"Do you need help?" Wren asks me, already halfway to her feet.

"No, I'm fine, thanks."

It's embarrassing enough that I'm avoiding him. I don't need her thinking I need help to go get my own father.

I turn and head to my parents' room, which we moved to the guest room on the first floor after his accident. When I'm not here, there's no way for Ma to help him up, and while he can walk with his walker, there's no way he could climb stairs. Hopefully, all the physical therapy he's in will allow him to one day, but we're not there yet.

As soon as I walk into the room, Dad's head jerks up from his spot in bed, then he tries to help himself up.

"It's okay, Dad, I got it," I say, rushing to his side.

His mouth opens, and he makes a sound, as if he's trying to

tell me something. A few muffled words come out, but none that make sense. My stomach twists. I look away as I help him get up, then drape his black dressing gown over his T-shirt and pajama pants, teeth clenched.

This.

This is why I can't wait for Wren to win our case. Not because I now need to take care of the farm, or because my dad isn't in the same physical shape as before. No, it's because my father was my best friend. The one person I could talk to about anything and who would never judge me. I love my mother, but when she doesn't agree with my choices, she'll never let me off the hook. Dad was the kind of person who would listen to all you had to say, then think about it and give you one or two sentences that clarified whatever situation you were in. He was a man of few words, but the words he did use were reflected on and always pertinent. And now he can't even tell me what he's thinking, no matter how much he wants to. And what kind of son would I be if I told him about my problems when I knew he couldn't help me with his advice, no matter how much he might want to? It would for sure make him feel even worse than if I said nothing, which is what I've decided to stick with.

Staying behind him, I make my way to the kitchen, where Wren says, "Good morning, Dennis." She's apparently less bothered than I am by the fact that he won't answer.

Hopefully, I'll eventually be able to learn from her.

"So," Ma says to Wren with a giddy expression once we've all sat down, "are you ready for your taste buds to be blown away?"

* * *

"So people just come here and pick the tree they want?" Wren asks me as we walk through the small portion of trees we keep for customer access. Fairy lights are strung above—a real pain to put up, trust me—zigzagging around the trail. "Baby Please Come Home" by Michael Bublé is playing in the hidden speakers while a light snow falls softly. That last part wasn't planned but definitely adds to the atmosphere.

"Pretty much, yeah," I say as I look at her. When we were about to go outside, I saw her grab her tiny pink coat, and I told her—in prettier words—that there was absolutely no way she'd survive the afternoon in negative-degree weather with that tiny thing. I handed her one of the old winter coats I wore when I was a teen that doesn't fit me anymore, yet even if Wren is a tall woman, she looks to be floating in fabric. I coupled it with old mittens, a hat, and a scarf. Nothing about the outfit matches, and she looked at me like I was crazy when she put it on, but her lips are perfectly pink, and I don't think any part of her is freezing, so I'd say it's good enough.

"People can always pick some of the trees we've already cut down, but usually when they come to Evermore, it's because they want to do it themselves."

"I can see that, yeah," she says while looking around. Her eyes are round, as if she's amazed by the whole ordeal. Seven or eight families work on finding the perfect tree to bring home—some large with five children, others with one or two kids who look old enough to be in college.

She points to one couple in their thirties who work on cutting a tree with a hand saw. "Is that hard? I thought you used chainsaws or something."

The smaller of the two women has the saw in hand while the other cheers her on. She's maybe halfway there.

"We do, but the clients use the safer tools."

She eyes the large saw before muttering, "Safer. Sure."

"It is. Practically foolproof."

Her dark brows climb on her forehead.

I smirk. "Wanna try?"

She takes a step back. "No." Her frown is as if I'd suggested she perform a tap dance in front of everyone.

"Come on," I say, walking toward one of the saws we left at the entrance of the farm. "I'll show you. It's not that hard."

"It's okay, I don't need to—"

"You think you can't do it?"

She stops in her tracks, then says, "Give me that saw."

I grin. Wren Lawson truly only needs to be dared to want to do something. Noted.

With someone who gives answers as scarcely as she does, you pick whatever you're given.

It's strange. I've always thought myself to be someone people felt comfortable with. When a friend has a problem, they often come to me to talk it through. Yet no matter how many times I see her, a mystery remains. And in the past weeks, I've thought more about the conversation we had on the day we met, and I haven't been able to stop thinking about it. She mentioned something about her genes being messed up, and I have no idea what that means. She's made one or two other strange comments that might be related to it, but she never went further than that. And, selfishly, I wish she would want to tell me.

But for now, I'll keep saving up the crumbs she gives me and hope to connect the dots one day.

Bending, I grab one of the saws we left next to the trees, then hand it to her. She takes it with her chin held high.

After shaking her shoulders, she tries different ways to place her hands so she has the best grip, neither of which is the one I would use, but I don't utter a word. She said she could do it.

When she has a handle she believes is good on the saw, she sends me a look that is so menacing it makes me want to laugh. "Which one do you want me to cut?"

"Whichever one you want."

Turning, she looks around her, then starts to walk around while examining all the trees one by one. I look over my shoulder and check to see where Callie is, finding her playing fetch with

Molly in front of the cabin. So much for helping me. At least there's no client waiting at the front to be led around the place. When I bring my attention back to Wren, she's standing in front of a tree, studying it. I guess that's the one.

"Do you want me to show you how to do it?"

"I'm fine," she answers with the most serious voice.

Don't laugh, Aaron.

"You don't even want a tip?"

She throws me a glare that tells me to shut up. I lift my hands in the air and stay silent.

Knees bent, she places her arms at an angle that I'd bet my balls isn't comfortable. The saw is barely notched into the dark bark of the tree as she examines everything one last time. When she looks confident in her angle, she starts sawing.

It doesn't go well, to say the least.

At first, the teeth are stuck in the bark, and she can't move the saw back and forth. Then, when she doesn't dig the teeth deep enough, the saw slides to the side and cuts nothing. With a small huff, she repositions herself. The saw glides in. She makes a few movements where the teeth dig in properly, and her lips curve just a little. She's doing it.

Her hair shifts on her shoulders as she uses all her strength to saw the tree. Her face is turning red, hat tilting on top of her head, but she doesn't stop. She's a girl on a mission.

It looks like she's doing good, yet something's off. I don't know if it's her position or the way she holds the saw or the strength she's using. She looks unsteady with each movement.

A second later, I learn what's wrong. Her balance.

With one harsh movement, she jerks the saw back, but she doesn't use the right amount of force, and with the way she's leaning back on her legs, everything goes to hell and she falls on her butt, the saw flying off somewhere behind her, her whole body spread like a snow angel on the ground.

I try, I really fucking try, to keep it together, but in the end, I fail.

I lose it.

"Stop it," she mutters through her teeth, not bothering to get up. Maybe she got the wind knocked out of her when she fell, but I'm laughing too hard to check on her.

"Was there someone back there you wanted to behead?" I say between two bouts of laughter.

She grunts.

"Be right back, I'll go grab my chain mail."

"I hate you," she says stoically, never moving from her star-shaped position.

That only makes me laugh harder.

"Please leave me here to die," she says. There's snow all over her head, and with the way she's positioned, there's probably some that's seeped into the collar of her—well, my—coat.

I sigh happily, then squat over her and extend my hand. "Come on."

She closes her eyes. "I said leave."

"Not a chance." When she still doesn't move, I say, "Come on, I'll show you how to do it the proper way."

As I thought it would, that gets her eyes to open. "I can do it by myself."

"Sure you can."

"Are you always this annoying?"

I answer with an oversized grin.

With a groan, she takes my extended hand and climbs to her feet. Once she's up, she dusts snow off her coat and pants. I work on the parts of her back she missed.

"All right, let's go," I say.

"I said I don't need your help."

I try really hard not to smile again. I have a feeling if I do, she'll for sure tell me to go to hell. "Stop being so stubborn, and let me show you."

She still gives me an unconvinced look.

"You've already shown me that you can do it," I add, pointing at the tree that's halfway sawed in two. "Point proven. Now let me teach you the proper way to do it."

She's still glaring. Only two people might dethrone her in the stubbornness competition: my mother and Callie.

"Fine, tell me," she ends up saying. She acts like she doesn't want to know what I have to say, but her eyes twinkle like she actually wants to learn how to do it right.

Maybe I'm finally starting to be able to read her.

"I'll show you instead." With a nudge of my chin, I say, "Grab the saw."

Like this morning, she looks at me for a moment before making the decision to listen to me. She turns around, grabs the saw, then looks over her shoulder.

"Good, now bend your knees."

She does.

"Okay now..." I don't know how to explain how she needs to position herself. There's something wrong with the way her knees are placed, but it'd be much easier to just show her how to position herself.

Fuck it.

I approach her with slow steps. The moment I near her arm, she tenses, but quickly relaxes against my touch.

"Just like this," I say softly before repositioning her body. My body is flush against hers, and I realize I look like a cheesy trope in a rom-com, but it truly is the easiest way to teach her how to do it properly.

"Okay?" she asks, her voice airy.

"Perfect. Now—" I put my arms over hers so I can position the saw at the perfect angle and height on the tree. Her breaths cloud in the cold air in front of her, coming in fast. She must be winded from the exercise from before. Cutting down a tree is harder than it looks. "Keep the saw at this angle, then use your thighs to create the force, not your arms. Like that."

We start cutting the tree, my frame circling hers. When I feel her body doing something wrong, I readjust it so she can only succeed. And it works. Once she's three-quarters of the way into the tree, I take a step back. She quickly glances over her shoulder, then returns her eyes to the task at hand. Not long after, the tree falls, the sound of her success a boom choked by the thick snow.

"See?" I say with a smirk. "Much easier like this."

"I guess, yeah," she says, lips pursed. "Thanks."

"You only had to ask."

She rolls her eyes. I internally high-five myself. Getting a reaction out of her truly is the best feeling. Like you've just aced something not many people have.

"Molly!" a small voice shouts behind me.

Wren and I both spin and start walking toward the sound. When we escape the area dense with trees, we spot Callie running after Molly who has a small, violet mitten in her jaw. Meanwhile, Callie has one naked hand.

"That little heathen," Wren mutters, lips pursed. I immediately snicker. There's so much more to this girl than the stern but polite attitude she constantly gives.

Before I know it, Wren joins Callie and is running after Molly. The girls are fast, but the dog is faster.

"You're not getting away with this, Molly Lawson!" Wren shouts, slightly breathless. "And you? What are you doing?" It takes me a second to realize she's speaking to me. "Come help us!"

What can I do but oblige?

"Let's take different corners," Wren the leader of operation shouts. We spread over the terrain, and when Molly heads my way to escape her mother, I try to catch her collar. I fail miserably.

"Come on, lumberjack!" she tells me. "You need to catch—" Her sentence is interrupted when Molly starts running her way. As soon as the dog is within reach, Wren jumps—yes, *jumps*—to land on Molly's back. However, the dog is too fast, so she lands face first in the snow.

God, this is really not her day.

I try hard not to laugh, but when I see the humored expression on her face as she gets back up, I let it out. To my right, Callie is giggling, a sound I haven't heard in so long. It makes me beam even more.

"Are you all right?" I ask Wren.

She gives me a death stare, this time clearly finding it funny. "Why don't you focus on your problems and I'll focus on mine?"

I snicker.

"Gotcha!" Callie says before using a similar strategy to Wren's, and failing just as bad.

Wren laughs. She doesn't ask my sister if she's hurt. I suspect she knows Callie wouldn't complain about it anyway. "Come on, Callie, let's get her!" Wren's cheeks are red, bitten by the cold, while her smile is as white and bright as the snow covering her hat.

Callie doesn't need to be told twice. She starts running after Molly, Wren joining her. Our lawyer must know they won't catch her that way. Still, they try, my sister finally given the chance to act like a little kid at home.

Yeah, I don't mind that Wren's here at all.

CHAPTER 11

Wren

THE AIR IS WARM AS I WALK INTO THE MEMORY CARE facility.

More than three weeks have passed since I've been here. I usually come visit every other Wednesday afternoon, but this week, I had a meeting with one of the doctors who works at the local hospital, and after that, Selina called me to talk about a new case the firm received that she would like me to take on with her in a few weeks. By the end of the conversation, the visiting hours were almost over, so I'd missed my chance.

Another reason why I don't like messing with my schedule.

"Wren, hi!" Jean, one of the nurses, calls from the medical care pod in the middle of the hallway. Her black braids have been styled in two buns, making the forty-year-old look closer to twenty-five.

"Hi, Jean, how are you?"

"Great, thanks. Melissa's had a great day today."

My expression remains the same. If I'm being honest, I'd rather she not tell me that every time I come here. It would make it less painful when my mom reacts the way she does to me if I thought she was like this with everyone.

"All right. I'll go see her now," I say.

She smiles, the corners of her eyes crinkling. "Have fun."

Sure.

I quickly find my way to room 42B. She's been in that one ever since she came to live here six years ago. It was my request, hoping she would become familiar to it enough to feel comfortable. So far, so good.

With a knuckle, I knock faintly on the door before walking in.

As expected, Mom is sitting in a chair facing her window. No music or television is playing in the room. It's only her and the silence. I'm not sure what she looks at when she gazes outside. The facility is located next to a forest, but nothing goes on out there except for the occasional squirrel walking by. It must get so boring.

And yet, every time I come in here, this is where I find her.

The faint sound of mumbling comes from her. Another thing I've gotten used to.

"Hi, Mom," I say softly, taking a seat next to her. I know better than to touch her. Wouldn't want to recreate last year's fiasco.

The mutter stops as her head turns my way in slow motion. The gray in her hair has become more apparent in the past three years, lining the black curls that used to shine in the sun. Her cheeks are hollow, the skin covering them wrinkled. Crazy, what eight years of not being able to take care of oneself will do.

It's rare that someone with eFAD survives this long. The nurses always tell me how lucky we are that she's gotten this far.

I'm pretty sure if they'd ask a thirty-year-old Melissa if that's what she considers luck, she would've hurled something at them. The mother I knew would never have been found outside without a full face of makeup, yet here she is, looking nothing like her old self.

It's not like I don't want to come care for her. I used to drive here every day after work.

No, it's the facility that has asked this of me. Understandably.

I brace myself for the moment her eyes meet mine. Every time I'm in this position, I feel like I'm sitting at a poker table, waiting for my opponent to reveal their cards.

Dull brown meets blue, and I know in an instant that today will be one of those days.

Still, I keep my chin up and say, "I'm sorry I couldn't come see you last week."

No reaction.

Actually, if there could be something less than none, this would be it. Like she's staring at a blank wall but she'd rather be looking anywhere else.

I notice her shirt is put on backward. It's something she keeps on doing, even when the nurses try to help her put it on properly. She'll just remove it and put it back on like this.

With a clearing of my throat, I say, "So, I heard you had a good day today. Did you play bingo with Frances or Cormac?"

Her eyelids lower down slowly, a sloth-like blink. Then, her gaze narrows. It reminds me of when she'd catch me still up after she came back from her evening shift at the restaurant when I was a kid.

Not a good sign.

Her lips part for the first time since I got here. My shield is on. Her bullets won't hurt me. I'm ready.

"What are you doing here?" The words come out raspy, nothing like the soft voice I heard her use when she had friends home and she let me drink bubbly apple juice with them. The cigarettes she smoked for years probably have something to do with it.

"What do you mean?" I say, trying to keep my voice steady. The last thing she needs is to feel threatened.

"Who are you and what are you doing in my house?"

My eyes close, only for a second. I need the respite.

God, I'm so naïve. Every time I think it won't be painful, and every time, it is. As if her words find the cracks around my breast plate and make their way right to my chest.

"It's me, Mom. Wren. Your daughter. I've come to visit you."

Creases form around her lips as she purses them. "I don't have a daughter."

Air whooshes out of my lungs slowly.

It's okay. It's got nothing to do with you.

"So, what have you been up to? Are you eating well?" I ask, forcing a smile. I've tried to confront her with the truth in the past. It did not end well.

She blinks again. "Are you stupid or what? I said who are you?"

"Mom, I—"

"Will you stop calling me that? I'm not your mom." She swats me with the back of her hand. "Now get out of my house."

"It's okay, it's okay," I say, hands lifted in front of me. "Let's just talk about—"

"I SAID GET OUT OF MY FUCKING HOUSE!"

My throat closes in on itself as I get up and start walking backward. Less than ten seconds later, a nurse comes into the room. She's new here. Maybe my age, with large glasses and a shawl covering her hair.

"Everything okay in here?"

"Yes, don't worry," I answer at the same time my mom says, "Mommy, thank God. This woman won't leave my house."

The nurse turns to me suspiciously.

"I'm Wren, her daughter," I say.

"Stop saying that, you liar! You want to kill me, is that it? I'll kill you first if you try. LEAVE!" She shoos me with her hands, like vermin infesting her place.

What she truly sees me as.

The nurse winces, then throws me a pleading look. I know it all too well.

"It's okay," I say. "I'll go."

I don't bother telling my mother goodbye. It would only anger her more.

"Leave me alone! Just leave me alone!" Her shouts resonate out of the room. "No, don't touch me! I want Daddy."

My heart beats wildly in my chest as I walk down the hallway leading to the front door of the facility. The air is too warm, too thick, constricting my trachea. Behind me, someone calls my name and says goodbye—probably Jean—but I can't stop to talk. My body is being compressed between four walls, no air left inside. Jean will forgive me for it. It's not like it's the first time.

And *this* is why I've had to come see her less often.

People with Alzheimer's disease usually recognize people from their family, at least in some way. They might not know their names, or realize what their relation is to that person, but they'll become calmer in their presence. Smile bigger. For my mother, it's the opposite. As if seeing me reminds her of her old life, and she'd rather forget all about it.

All the staff working with her at the Somerville memory care facility say she is a bright, lovely patient. That she is peaceful with most of the other residents. Mostly keeps to herself, but is polite and sometimes plays cards with some of them.

So imagine their surprise when they see how distressed she becomes when her own daughter comes to visit her.

You think you know pain until you are called into a meeting where people ask you to stop visiting your mother as often because seeing you makes her "unwell."

If I were a better person, I would stop coming here altogether. I'd let her live her life and be happy away from me. But I'm too selfish for that. What kind of daughter would I be if I all but abandoned my mother?

This one-visit-every-two-weeks arrangement is the compromise I've made with myself. Frequent enough that I can make sure she is well and receives good care, infrequent enough that the staff don't have to handle her crises every day.

The cold air hits my face as I open the front door, and for the first time this winter, I'm thankful for it. My feet stay in place as I take deep breaths, trying to let all that has happened in the past fifteen minutes disappear into the wind. It's okay. It doesn't matter.

At some point, my phone vibrates in my back pocket. I grab it to find my cousin Aqidah calling. The call is declined at the speed of light. No way can I deal with her today after what just happened. Putting the phone away, I close my eyes and continue trying to calm my heart rate.

The tips of my fingers are cold by the time I start walking back to Aaron's SUV. My car is still out of order, and I felt bad enough for having missed last week's meeting with my mother, so I asked him if I could borrow his car to go on an errand. Of course, he said yes. I don't think I've ever seen this man not be agreeable.

His smell surrounds me as I open the door and sit in the driver's seat. Not just from the car, but from the coat he's lent me that I'm still wearing. It's not the prettiest, but it's much warmer than mine, and it smells good. Really good. Like pine and a hint of cinnamon.

I put my hands on the steering wheel, but don't start the car yet. I think I need another minute.

Just then, my phone vibrates in my purse. With a wince, I pick it up, but exhale when I see it's not Aqidah again. Instead, it's one of the paralegals working at the firm under Selina.

Yes, work. Exactly what I need.

After a sharp inhale, I swallow down all the anguish that could fill my voice and accept the call.

CHAPTER 12

Aaron

I PUMP MY LEGS HARD AS MY SKATES SCREECH AGAINST THE ice.

The wind is freezing cold as it bites my face, but I don't care. I'm warm enough all over that it's only a relief.

I played hockey throughout middle school and high school. When the time came for me to go to college, I hung up my competitive skates, but I never stopped playing for fun. When it's just me, the ice, my stick, and a puck, I feel like I can let out everything I'm feeling inside. It's not exactly like drawing, which allows my mind to quiet. This isn't peace. It's a channeling of my frustrations and pains. Something that makes me feel alive. The small ice rink surrounded by large trees and a frozen pond in the Sonder Hill park is a perfect escape.

"Hey, dumbass, what are you doing?"

My eyes roll back. Today, I'm not exactly alone with my skates. The most annoying man I know is also here.

"Showing you how it's done," I shout back to Finn, skating fast next to him before shooting in his net. He tries to stop the puck from breaching his goalposts, but only ends up sliding facedown on the ice, missing his target.

He groans, getting back up.

"You've always been a shit goalie," I say with a smirk.

"Fuck off."

Nothing like riling Finn up to burn off extra steam.

Chuckling, I start skating backward when my phone pings in the pocket of my hoodie.

Wren: Callie asked if she could keep Maybelle with her for the night. Do you think your parents would mind?

"What's got you smiling like that?" Finn asks, making me realize my lips are turned upward. I force them back down and ignore him. I start to type an answer, but before I hit send, another message pops on my screen.

Wren: She really, really wants to. Think we can make it a secret between the three of us? Maybelle is well trained. No one will be the wiser.

Wren: :-)

A smiley face? Who would've thought. It's probably to make me lean her way; that girl is too smart to do anything without secondary intentions.

I was already going to tell her it was fine, but I erase what I'd already typed and make it seem like she convinced me. Maybe that will mean more smileys in the future.

Me: Sure. Sneak her in while Ma's cooking dinner. ;)

Wren: Will do. Thank you.

And there goes the friendly texting. Snickering, I put my phone back in my pocket.

"That your lawyer girlfriend?" Finn asks with a shit-eating grin.

I roll my eyes.

"So it *was* her."

I don't bother answering, instead skating away with the puck. If I try to refute it, he'll just get on my ass even more.

"You're fucking blushing," he shouts in a sing-songy voice.

I might kill him.

"Am not."

"Who knew you'd start crushing on your family's lawyer?"

My jaw tightens. I'm about to tell him to go to hell, but the words stick in my throat. Am I? Crushing? Jesus, that sounds like a word Callie would use when talking about her grade school boyfriends.

It's not like I've ever thought about that. Sure, Wren makes me laugh, and I'd have to be blind not to think she's one of the most beautiful women I've ever seen, but it ends there.

I don't share that thought with him. Instead I say, "No one's crushing on anyone. Now do you want to play or not?"

Finn doesn't take the bait.

"Hey, man, it's okay if you are. It's been a while since Amber."

He's not letting this go, is he?

"Have you even seen another girl since then?" he adds when I don't talk.

With a straight face, I say, "You know the answer to that." It's been more than six months since I've been with a girl. Before that, I'd been in a relationship for almost a year, so the last of my casual hookups goes a while back. Since Amber and I broke up, I haven't exactly been in the mindset to date, and meaningless sex is not something I'm interested in anymore. Without any kind of connection, it doesn't feel worth it to me. If what I want is something real, why would I waste time on something less?

"Then maybe hooking up with your lawyer is exactly what you need. You know, get you back in the game."

Goddammit. Why in the world did I ask him to come play with me today? I probably would've had a better chance of actually playing rather than having a heart-to-heart I never asked for if I'd brought a baboon with me.

"I'm not hooking up with my dad's lawyer, are you out of your mind?" Even if I were interested in some quick, hollow thing, I'd never do that with her. How awkward would that be? Isn't the rule of a fuck friend not to present them to your family?

Besides, if I *did* feel something for her, it wouldn't only be sexual attraction. She's someone I would want to get to know. Someone I'd want to explore, to discover what makes her cry or light up. Someone I'd know everything about.

Finn hums, skating toward me before sneakily stealing the puck from my stick. Damn, he's messing with my head. I skate toward him to get it back.

"So your little jealousy at the bar last time was nothing?" Finn says with another annoying smirk.

"I wasn't jealous," I answer, short of breath. Even in the cold, my skin feels warm under my thick hoodie. "You were just annoying."

"Of course." He passes me the puck, and I send it back to him, all the while skating backward. He might not fully believe what I'm saying, but at least he seems done questioning me about it.

A few minutes pass before his face lights up again, and there goes my hope of him being done. When's the last time he left me off the hook? It's not like I wouldn't do the same to him if our positions were reversed, but Jesus, he's getting on my nerves. I cringe, waiting for the blow to land.

"So if you don't want anything with her beside a professional relationship, it should be okay with you if I invite her to dinner?"

"Fuck no." The words are out of my mouth before I can think them through. And with the way his grin grows, he clearly knew what he was doing.

I brake abruptly then and glare at him. "You know what her work means to my family. *I* won't ruin that, and *you* won't ruin that. Got it?" I omit the fact that I definitely wouldn't want to see Wren with him for some reason I won't explore now.

He stops skating too, leaning his weight on his stick. "What about when she's done?"

My body freezes.

An image pops into my head, of Wren and Finn kissing at a family dinner during summer, Callie playing with Wren's dogs while I man the barbeque, alone. Something doesn't work there. I don't know why, but it feels wrong. Like if she were to be in our lives after the case is done, it would be because *I* asked her out on a date, not Finn.

Shit, maybe I do have a crush.

It doesn't mean anything, though. I'd never do anything about it, at least not now. Besides, it's not like Wren has ever acted like she'd be interested in me as anything more than an acquaintance. She's so closed off most of the time, she might hate me for all I know.

"That's none of your business," I end up answering. I'm not about to admit anything to him. If I give him an inch, he'll take a foot and start shouting from the rooftop that I'm in love with her.

"That's not what an uninterested person would say."

I roll my eyes with a groan. "Why don't we focus on your personal life instead, huh? Have you talked to that girl from Italy again? Have you gotten over her? Who are you fucking this week to keep your mind distracted? Or how about—"

"All right, all right," Finn says, surrendering with his hands in the air. "No need to get all defensive."

I really am getting defensive. I can be honest about that, at least. I'm not sure why he's riling me up so much today, but it's obvious. I can usually take all of his teasing easily. Today, it's like he's struck a chord I'd rather he'd left alone.

I give him a curt dip of the head.

"Seriously, though, I'm just messing with you man. I don't care if you want her or if you're in the mood to go pick a stranger at the bar and get laid. But truth is, you've looked happier this past week, and I can't help but think it's related to her staying in Sonder Hill. That's all."

I swallow, still unable to fully catch my breath. I don't bother thinking about what he's just said. I don't know if it's true, and I don't care if it is. It won't change anything.

In one swift move, I steal the puck from him and get back to the game.

CHAPTER 13

Wren

I KNOCK ON THE HEAVY, DETAILED WOODEN DOOR OF THE Scott-Perez house three times, then clasp my hands in front of me.

It still feels weird that I'm walking up to my clients' house for reasons other than work. I've never had the kind of relationship with any other clients that I do with the Scott-Perez family. It's not like I've voluntarily tried to insert myself into their lives. It kind of happened on its own. The majority of the time, I try to put some distance between us when I realize I'm getting attached to them as more than professional acquaintances, but it's hard. They're always so lovely.

The door opens, Martina's round face lighting up in a warm smile when she sees me. "Wren, hi!" She doesn't even look surprised that I'm standing on her porch a Sunday at 5:00 p.m. She's not wearing a stitch of makeup, her ears adorned with large black earrings.

"Hi, so sorry to bother you. I was looking for—"

"Aarón, alguien está aquí para ti," she shouts behind her before I've had the time to finish my train of thought. Turning back to me, she says, "He shouldn't be long." She even caps that with a wink.

Oh God. Is she getting the wrong idea?

I can't try to rectify things, though, because a second later, Aaron appears behind his mother. His hair is wet, dripping over his thick wool sweater. The maroon color makes his light-colored eyes shine even more than usual.

Lord, why did he have to be this handsome?

"Hey, what's up?" he says.

"Uh..." I trip over my words. That never happens. "I promise I'm not here to bother you, it's just that Maybelle doesn't have any food left, and she's super picky about her diet, and I don't want her to lose any more weight, and I still don't have my car, and..." Aaron's lips curve. I'm rambling. What is wrong with me? I clear my throat. "Would you mind letting me borrow yours again?"

He nods right away. "Yeah, of course, but there's no pet store open on a Sunday evening in town."

Crap. I didn't even think about that.

I shouldn't even be in this situation right now. I never run out of food for me or the girls. The thing is, I had planned on staying in the cabin for a few days at most. The garage wasn't supposed to take this long to repair my car. I would never have packed less food than what Maybelle or Molly needs. This is embarrassing.

I close an eye. "Does the grocery store have a nice selection of dog food?"

He chuckles. "Not sure about that, Wren."

No choice, then. "Okay, then I feel so bad asking you this, but do you think I could drive home with your car and bring it back later tonight?" It seems stupid to drive all this way, but the girls only eat a specific brand of food, and it *is* Sunday night. It'll probably be simpler to return home than to drive from store to store in the hope of finding on that's open and that carries their food.

Maybelle better never believe I wouldn't do anything for her.

"Yeah, sure." Quickly glancing down at his watch, he says, "Can you give me a minute?"

"Uh, yeah, sure."

He disappears down the hallway, and I stand on the front porch with his oversized coat around my shoulders. I could technically have put mine on, but I've gotten used to its smell, and I don't want to wear a coat that doesn't smell like Christmas cookies ever again.

Martina has gone back to the kitchen, at least if my ears serve me right. I can faintly hear her and Callie speaking in the background. At some point, a deeper voice joins them.

A moment later, Aaron comes back in front of the porch, but instead of handing me the keys he went to pick up, he starts putting on his boots and coat.

"What are you doing?" I ask.

He lifts an eyebrow as he puts his black hat on. "Getting ready?"

"Yes, I can see that, but for what?"

"To drive to Boston?" He looks at me like I'm the one who's said something ridiculous.

I shake my hands in front of me. "Oh, no, please, you don't have to. I'm perfectly fine on my own."

"It's okay, I needed to go drop some stuff at the office anyway."

Uh-huh. I believe him approximately one percent.

"Aaron," I state, arms crossed in front of me.

He stops moving and glares at me. "Wren."

I glare right back.

"Look, I'm not letting you drive two hours back and forth alone in the dark even if you give me the biggest stare-down in the world. Deal with it."

"But..." The excuses die down on my tongue. I don't want him to feel forced to come with me, but the thought of making the drive alone is not that enticing. "Won't they need you here?"

He shakes his head. "I talked to them. They'll be fine." He nudges his chin behind me. "Come on, let's go get the girls."

I lift an eyebrow.

"If we're going back, might as well stay the night in the city. We'll come back tomorrow whenever you're ready. Okay?"

I can't find anything else to respond, so I say, "Okay. But I'm driving."

He huffs. "Not a chance."

"Why?"

The grin he gives me is annoyingly cute. "My mamá raised me right."

That she did.

He dips his head again. "Come on. I don't want Maybelle to start gnawing on my hand if she gets too hungry."

I can't hold the snicker in. He's starting to get her.

* * *

"So where are we in the case?" Aaron asks as we near Boston. His eyes are on the road, which is thankfully clear of snow. We haven't talked much during the first hour of driving, mostly filling the space between us with soft music. It hasn't been uncomfortable, though. Silence is a norm for me. I'm not that much of a small talker, and I have a feeling he gets that.

"We're getting close," I answer, turning to him. "I got all the records from the hospital and had them reviewed by three medical experts. Unless something major happens, I should be serving them this week."

"And then we're going to trial?" He quickly glances my way.

"Well, that depends on what they answer and offer us." Most malpractice litigation gets resolved out of court with settlements. I mentioned that to him a time or three.

"We're going to trial," he says, as if he hasn't heard a word of what I just said.

I don't answer. We'll see when we get there, and there's no reason to talk about what's going to happen when nothing is certain now.

A moment passes where Aaron drives silently, one hand holding his head against the door, the other wrapped tightly around the steering wheel. Then he turns to me and says, "So the other experts confirmed it, then? That Dad could've avoided all that?"

I shift on the leather seat. "Well, Dennis did have an unusual presentation for a stroke, so that makes it a little tricky. They still confirmed that Dr. Groban acted carelessly and that he should've run more tests, but even if he had, they can't guarantee there would've been a different outcome. We can't predict what would've happened if things had been different, you know?"

His lips twitch, but he drops it.

It breaks my heart to see him like this. I know he'd do anything to get justice for his father, but that's the thing about working in this field. True justice is never met. You can't go back in time. The result of a trial or a settlement will never change the fact that the event happened. I would do anything to give him the chance to get his father back in the state he previously was, but no one can do that. Getting him legal justice is the only thing I can manage.

Ten minutes later, Aaron says, "Home sweet home," as we pass the *Entering Boston* sign. The tension in his shoulders has mildly gone down, as if getting away from Sonder Hill gives him some kind of relief. In a way, with all the responsibilities he has there, I'm sure it does.

Behind us, Molly and Maybelle start to bark, like they can feel we're close to home. I turn to them, then say, "Shh. We're almost there." Aaron has already driven us here just because he's a gentleman. No need to annoy him with high-pitched barking on top of it.

"Wanna remind me of how to get to your place?" he asks me, a small smile on his lips, which unties a small knot in my chest. Yeah, he's truly more himself when he looks happy.

I lead him through the city, and soon he's parking in my spot in the back of my building. And because his manners know no bounds, he of course gets out of the car to help me get my bags out.

As soon as I open the back door, Molly jumps down, then starts running toward the front door of the building.

"Molly!" I shout. How in the world did I raise such a hellish dog?

"I got it," Aaron answers, running toward her and grabbing her collar before she can do something crazy like run in front of a car.

I grab my bags from Aaron's trunk, filling my arms. Picking Maybelle up is a challenge of its own. When I reach the front door, a weight is removed from my load before I can say anything.

"Come on, I'll help you up," Aaron says, a hand around Molly's burgundy leather collar.

"Oh, no, you don't have to do that." It's becoming embarrassing how many times he gets me out of trouble.

"Yeah, I do." His brown gaze studies me. "Unless you'd rather I don't come up?"

"Don't be silly," I say before dipping my chin in the direction of the door. He opens it for me, my arms still too full to use, then follows me up the stairs to the third floor.

Just before opening the door to my apartment, I hesitate. No one I really know has ever come inside this place except me. My cousin Aqidah has asked me to come visit a few times, but I always suggested we meet up somewhere instead.

I don't know how I'll feel having someone else in my living space after being alone in it for so long. But we've just had a long drive, and I don't know if it's because I've become used to being surrounded by other people during the past week, but I don't particularly want to return to my typical loneliness tonight.

I open the door.

"Welcome to my humble abode," I say as Aaron releases Molly, who starts running in circles around the living room. After removing my shoes and placing them in their usual spot on the mat, I put my bags down, then go place Maybelle on her tiny bed.

When I return to the front door, I find Aaron looking around. Suddenly, I'm trying to consider the space from an outsider's view. It's extremely tidy. Not a single thing is out of place.

Being back here, with the lilac scent coming from the diffuser and the cold breeze coming from the window that doesn't close just right, brings me a sense of comfort. The cabin was fine—better than I'd expected, really—but I still had a moment of panic every time I opened my eyes in the morning. Home is better.

"It's very nice," Aaron says, standing in front of the door with his hands in his pockets. His gaze is wide while exploring the space, as if he wants to see all of it.

"Please, come in," I say before I can overthink it.

"You sure?"

"Of course. Let me just feed Maybelle, and then I'm all yours." I cringe. "Well, all *there*."

While Aaron removes his shoes and his coat, I go to the tote bag I had packed for the girls and open the front pocket to grab Maybelle's bowl.

It's not there.

No. It can't be.

I check again, but the pocket is empty. I close my eyes.

Breathe, Wren.

Not already. It's too soon. Way too soon.

"What's wrong?" Aaron asks, now crouching next to me. I don't question how he knows something's wrong. It's like a talent of his, to feel this kind of things. I've seen it often enough.

"Nothing." I inhale. "I just can't find May's bowl."

"Oh, the metal one?" He stands back up, then hurries toward the front door. "It fell earlier when I picked up the bag, so I put it right—" From one of the bags he was carrying, he pulls out something shiny. "—there. Sorry."

It's like he's taken three tons off my chest. False alarm.

"It's fine," I say as I walk to him and grab the bowl. "Just... Always in the front pocket of this bag, okay?" He looks a little confused, so I add a shaky smile for good measure.

"Got it."

"Thanks." Looking away, I go fill Maybelle's bowl, and while she can't see with her cataracts, her snout works fine. She gets to her food in less than a minute.

"You want something to drink?" I ask Aaron.

"What do you have?" His sly grin is still present, reassuring me. I'd rather he not see me as a crazy person, even though I might be. He seems to think of me as better than I am, and I'd rather keep it like that.

"Uh…" Yeah, I should've thought about that before offering. "Water, coffee, or tea."

He grins teasingly. "No alcohol?"

"I don't really drink."

He lifts an eyebrow. "I'm pretty sure the day we met, you were drinking at a bar alone."

Touché. "That was, um…an exception."

He hums. "I'll just have water, thanks."

I go fill two glasses in the kitchen, then come back and invite him to the living room. Since I only have one couch, we both sit on it, and Molly soon jumps up to lie between the two of us.

"So that night was an exception for you, huh?" he asks as I take a sip.

"And it wasn't for you?" I reply.

He snickers, though there's not much humor in it. "It was a fucked-up night for me."

I tuck my feet under my bottom. This conversation feels like walking a fine line. We may not be friends per se, but I've been wondering about that evening for so long. And now that it's been brought up, I can't make myself move on to another subject.

"What ended up happening after that night for you? Did you end up getting back with the girl?"

He shakes his head vigorously. "I told you I wouldn't go back to her. I want to be with someone who wants to be with me just as much as I want her."

I swallow. So he does remember a lot from that night.

"Was it hard?" I ask. "Keeping your word, I mean."

His shoulders give a lazy shrug. "It never felt *just right* with Amber. I'm not sure why. I don't even know why I proposed, to be honest." One of his hands move to pet Molly's furry back. "I tried to convince myself that everything was perfect, but once she said no, I realized that I was blinding myself with hope and it wasn't good enough."

I nod. It all sounds so mature. He's probably only a few years older than me, but he's already lived so much. Love and relationships and proposals and breakups. I can't begin to imagine what it all feels like. In some areas of my life, I'm a successful woman, but here, in my apartment, next to this man, I feel stupid. The girl who's never been with a man before—in all the ways that count. I've had my reasons, but it still makes me feel inadequate. Or maybe jealous would be a better word.

"Are you happier now than you were when you were with her?" I ask. I didn't even know I was wondering about that until the question leaves my mouth. For someone who hates talking about herself, I sure seem to love learning about others. Or maybe it's just him that piques my interest.

He takes a second to think before saying, "My life is much more complicated now than it was then, but in a way, I think I am, yeah."

"I'm glad."

"What about you?" he says as he leans an arm on the back of the couch. "You never did tell me exactly why you were there that night."

I don't speak.

"But there's one thing you mentioned that's been running around in my mind for a while."

Shit.

Please not that please not that please not that.

"You said something about your genes."

And there it is.

My nails dig into my palms as the sentence resonates in my mind like the boom of a gong.

What in the world made me share that with him? Sure, I never thought I'd see him again, but that only proves I should never talk about myself, even with drunk strangers.

Aaron's brows furrow when I don't answer.

"You can tell me anything, you know," he says.

I lick my lips. The thing is, I do know. I think I even knew that when we met. There must've been a reason that led me to give this little piece of myself to him. Maybe I saw the same thing in his eyes that I do right now. This spark of warmth. The one he shows his sister when he packs her lunch for school, or the one he gives his mother before kissing her cheek in the morning.

Aaron Scott-Perez makes me want to talk.

Actually, that's not quite right. He doesn't make me want to talk, but he makes me feel like he would understand anything I could tell him. And for someone who's been keeping things to herself for so long, it feels enticing to share with someone who will listen. Especially someone who you will never see again in a few weeks.

In a split second, I make a decision.

"There's something wrong with my brain," I say. "Or at least, there will be."

His frown deepens.

You can do this. Just get the words out.

I exhale sharply. "I carry the gene mutations for early familial Alzheimer's disease."

I don't remember the last time I've said this sentence out loud. It feels strange, to hear it somewhere other than in my own head.

Aaron starts blinking quickly. "What…what does that mean?"

"It means I will develop Alzheimer's at some point, and at an age younger than most patients. My grandfather had it, then my mother, and then my uncle. I'm next."

His eyes are still round. "I didn't know Alzheimer's was inherited."

"It usually isn't. But we have a specific type of the disease that is passed from generation to generation and that affects younger people." As if feeling my emotions, Molly places her heavy head on my thighs. I give her a scratch, the feel of her wiry hair grounding me. "That night at the bar, I'd just gotten the results of my genetic test. I always suspected that I'd have the disease, but the test confirmed I truly only have a few years left with my mind."

Aaron doesn't speak for a while, frozen in space.

Oh boy. I probably shouldn't have said anything.

After a moment, he moves again, then says, "I'm so sorry, Wren." His voice is so raw, it sends a shiver down my spine.

I purse my lips and shrug. I'm not going to tell him it's okay, because it's not, but it is what it is.

"And is there… Is there a possibility that you have the gene but won't develop the disease?"

I puff my cheeks. "Not really, no. There are studies that show the gene doesn't have a perfectly complete penetrance, which means that some people might have the gene but not necessarily the disease, or maybe they could develop the disease, but not as severely." I give Molly another head scratch. "But the vast majority of people do develop it. My family all did."

Surely, I will too. The sentence hangs in the air between us, even though it was left unsaid.

His jaw shifts back and forth. I've rarely seen him looking so distraught, maybe except for the time we couldn't find Callie. I don't like it.

"And what does 'early' mean here? What's to be expected?"

This is the answer I hate the most. The one I try to avoid

thinking about as much as possible, even though it's always in the back of my mind.

I clear my throat. "Technically, it's anything before sixty-five years old, but some cases can be in the thirties, forties, or fifties." The youngest case ever recorded was a twenty-three-year-old man. I've thought about this man more times than I can count.

Aaron drags a hand down his face. "Fuck."

"Yeah."

"And… And if you *do* get it, how long until…"

"People can survive years with AD. The lifespan is usually shorter with eFAD, though." I swallow. "My mom's a unique case, in that sense."

He frowns. "I thought your mom had passed."

"I know. I'm sorry for not saying anything." Not meeting his eyes, I say, "I didn't correct you before because in a way, I did lose my mother." The most important way that counts, really. Her body is still there, sure, but *my mom* isn't.

"I can't…" He gets to his feet, then crosses his arms behind his head.

He looks too affected by this. As if I just told him someone in his family would develop AD.

Is it because of the legal case?

"Don't worry, though," I reassure him. "It's not like I won't have the time to complete my contract. I wouldn't have accepted it if I didn't think I could."

He spins to me. "I don't give a fuck about that right now." His head shakes quickly. "I just can't believe that someone like you…" He doesn't complete his sentence.

"I've made my peace with it." Accepted that I wouldn't be here for long, and took all the precautions that come with that. Still do.

"But you shouldn't have had to." His eyes bore into mine. "I'm so fucking sorry, Wren. I can't imagine what that's like."

My mouth twitches to the side. "Thanks."

Finally, he comes to sit back down and says, "Thank you for sharing that with me."

I nod. It feels weird to have the fact out in the open. Kind of like getting naked, but knowing at the same time that the person will hold a cover to your body whenever you need it.

"And you probably have other people to talk to," he adds, which almost makes me want to laugh, "but if you need an extra set of ears, I'm here, okay?" His fingers land on my wrist, warm and newly calloused. Goose bumps cover my skin. "I'm always here."

"Thank you."

He gives me a smile that is nowhere near his typical Aaron smiles, but the fact that he's able to grin for me right now makes me realize walking away from him after his father's case is done will be a lot harder than I'd once imagined.

CHAPTER 14

Aaron

I HEAR HER VOICE DOWNSTAIRS.

Because I started my day on the farm early this morning, I allowed myself some time to work on the game design this afternoon. However, I hadn't expected the sound of her voice would mess with my focus this much.

It's been a week since Wren and I discussed her diagnosis—or at least the diagnosis she will likely one day receive. The morning after her revelation, I drove her back to Sonder Hill mostly in silence. The discussion we'd had the night before hung heavy between us, and while I wished I could say something, my mind was too overwhelmed to think of the right thing to say.

She didn't seem bothered by the silence. In fact, she didn't seem bothered by anything. Her expression was neutral when I picked her up, and it stayed that way the whole ride. As if she hadn't dropped a bomb on me the day before. As if she wasn't troubled by it at all. I guess she's had a lot of time to wrap her head around it, but still. If I was in her shoes, I don't think I could ever accept a thing like that. I would spend my life thinking of all the things I would eventually miss and would be constantly angry. She's clearly a better person than me.

When we arrived at my parents' house that day, she got a phone call almost as soon as we stepped out of my SUV—her car was finally ready. She then left with a quick goodbye and has worked in Boston ever since. Today's the first time she's back. She met with the hospital's lawyers for the first time this morning. I'm letting my parents discuss things with her first—both because I know I tend to monopolize the conversations when I'm there, and I want them to have the chance to ask all they want to ask, and because I want to delay seeing her again as long as I can.

"¿Aarón?" Ma calls from downstairs. I asked her earlier to let me know when they were done.

All right, time to do this.

After releasing a short breath, I get out of my so-called office and walk down the stairs.

And there she is.

My jaw tightens as I look at her. Her glossy, dark hair. The small pearl studs on her ears. The pressed blouse she's wearing. The calm look in her almond-shaped eyes.

I was right to be scared of seeing her again. Because right now, the only thing I can think about as I look at her is how unfair it is that something so bright will eventually dim.

Her gaze flits up to me. "Hey."

"Hi," I answer, forcing my lips upward. The last thing she needs is to know how deeply her confession affected me. She's the one living with this. If she can be strong enough to move forward despite it, then I can only do the same, or at least act as if I'm not devastated for her and for all the people who will one day not be able to be in her presence.

"Are you all done?" I ask.

"Yes," she answers as she packs her satchel with her computer and papers.

I peek at my parents. Dad's eyes are a little droopy, as if the meeting they just had drained him of his energy. His skin is paler than usual, or maybe it's just the lighting. I would be worried if I didn't see Ma, who looks calm and happy, next to him. That must mean they received good news, or at least didn't receive bad news.

"You mind talking for a second?" I ask Wren.

"Sure." She turns to my parents, then says, "I'll update you once I receive their official response."

"Thank you, hon," Ma says. I don't know when she switched from "Ms. Lawson" to "Wren" to "hon," but based on the small rise of Wren's lips, I'd say our lawyer doesn't mind.

I lead Wren to the living room, where a fire is burning in the stone alcove.

"So," we both say at the same time once we're out of my parents' hearing range.

With a chuckle, I say, "You go ahead."

She bobs her head up and down. "I just wanted to start by saying I'm sorry if I made you uncomfortable last week. I don't know why I told you about—"

"Hey," I interrupt. "No need to apologize for anything." That's exactly why I tried to not let my emotions show in front of her. Clearly, I failed. "I'm happy you told me."

She curls her lips behind her teeth.

"This changes nothing," I add, because really, it doesn't.

"All right," she concedes, not appearing to believe me. Clearing her throat, she switches the subject. "So the discussion this morning went well. I laid down all the facts that support your claims and expressed what your family's intentions are."

"And what did they say?"

She takes a seat on the arm rest of the leather couch closest to the fireplace. "Well, they couldn't say much at this point. They need to talk to their client and will get back to us once they've decided whether they want to make a settlement offer, which is what will likely happen."

I scoff. Of course they'd rather make a deal for some amount of money that's probably nothing to them and just sweep this ordeal under the rug. As if it's not a human life they fucked with.

"You know," she says, "this—"

"Dennis? DENNIS! ¡AYÚDAME! ¡AARÓN!"

In an instant, I'm on my feet, running to the dining room. Wren's feet slap the floor behind me. This is the second time my mother has called me in the span of five minutes, except the two calls were as opposite as can be. When she wanted me to come downstairs and meet with Wren, her call was warm, loving. This one is full of fear and urgency.

The moment I step into the dining room, I understand why.

Dad is sprawled on the hardwood floor, convulsing. The muscles of his whole body seem to be contracted. Ma is kneeling next to him, her mouth open wide as if she's wailing inside her head.

And I'm frozen in place.

No. This cannot be happening again.

"¿Que está pasando con el? ¡Ayuda! ¡Que alguien me ayude!" *What is happening to him? Help! Somebody help!*

My mother's pain-stricken words make me move. I kneel next to her, but I'm not of any use. I look at my father but can't come up with a single useful thought. I can't do anything for him. I'll have to sit next to my mother and look at my father have another stroke and possibly die in front of me, and I won't be able to do anything about it.

"What's going on?" a small voice says behind me.

I turn to find Callie staring at us with eyes wide like saucers, filling with tears when she looks down and says, "Dad?"

Oh God. I'd forgotten that Callie was home. Fuck. Fuck, fuck, fuck. She'll see our dad die too. And still, I can't do anything about it.

"Look away, Callie," I plead, but of course she doesn't. She just stands there, crying more and more until her sobs match my mother's.

"I called 911," Wren says as she enters the room.

I never noticed she'd left. I also never thought to call 911. What the fuck is wrong with me?

"The ambulance should be here in five minutes." Wren analyzes the scene, the only one who's logical here. When she spots Callie, she automatically rushes to her side. "Here, sweetie, let's go wait for the ambulance somewhere else." She leads a devastated Callie away from the dining room while I stay with my mother. I've never been more grateful for someone.

After what feels like an eternity, Dad stops convulsing. I didn't even think to time the seizure. That's something we're supposed to do, right? I didn't think of anything, as a matter of fact. I kneeled there like an idiot, not even finding the right words to comfort my little sister.

Even though he's not seizing anymore, Dad still hasn't opened his eyes. Now that I've regained some of my wits, I think of taking his pulse, which I thankfully find. It's weak, but it's there. I don't know what just happened to him, but he's not dead. I'll hold on to that until I can't.

A few minutes later, we hear sirens, followed by two paramedics entering the house. Wren probably led them in. They don't ask me any questions, so I assume Wren also answered what they wanted to know.

Quickly, they lift my father on a gurney and lead him outside toward the ambulance, a thin metallic cover spread over his body. We all follow him, and when I go to climb into the ambulance with Ma, I'm stopped by one of the paramedics.

"Only one of you can go with him," the middle-aged man says with an empathetic smile.

Shit.

I nod even though it's killing me to know I won't be there with him and Ma. What if something happens in the ambulance?

The man closes the back door of the ambulance, then walks to the front, where he climbs in.

"I'll follow them with my car, then," I say to no one in particular.

"But… Aaron…" Callie's weepy voice makes me turn to her.

Wren's arm is wrapped tightly around her shoulders, but she looks inconsolable. It doesn't matter how old she acts most of the time. Right now, she looks like a little kid. A kid who has been exposed to way too much already at such a young age. "What will happen to…to…"

I close the distance between us and hug her to my chest. Wren subtly peels away, watching us with concern.

"It's okay. Everything's going to be fine," I say, although I don't even know whether I believe the words or not.

She only cries harder.

Fuck. I need to comfort her, but I need to be there for my mom too, and I can't do both. Callie can't be at the hospital. It would only be more traumatizing for her to wait for news in the cold waiting room.

I'm torn in two. Again and again and again, the story repeats itself.

"I'll go."

I turn to Wren, who has a determined air to her.

"But…" I start.

"You need to stay with her," she whispers behind Callie. "She needs you."

I know she's right. Still, it doesn't make me want to stay away from my parents any less.

"I'll make sure Martina is okay," Wren says as if reading my thoughts, "and I'll give you updates whenever we get them."

Callie's fingers grasp the back of my shirt even tighter.

"Okay," I tell Wren.

She throws me a look that means more than words.

"Thank you," I add. I don't know what I would do without her. Again.

With a dip of the head, she turns and runs toward her car.

CHAPTER 15

Wren

MOST PEOPLE HATE THE SMELL OF HOSPITALS.

I don't. It makes me feel safe. Taken care of. I'd rather smell antiseptic than nothing at all.

Martina is sitting next to me, eyes closed. Her hand is shaking in mine, which is why I'm not letting it go. I know what it's like to wait for news, not knowing whether it'll be good or bad. A few months before my mother went to live at the memory care facility, she was hit by a car while I was at work and she'd wandered out of the house. The driver had slowed down enough that her injuries were superficial, but the minutes I spent alone in the waiting room, wondering if she'd be okay, were some of the worst I'd ever lived. No one should go through that alone, and especially not someone as good as Martina.

My phone vibrates against my thigh, like it has been doing on and off for the past hour.

> **Aaron Scott-Perez: Are you sure he's not being treated by the same doctor as last time?**

> **Me: Yes. I just asked again. He's being seen by a certain Dr. N'Diaye.**

It was the first thing I made sure of when I got to the hospital. Martina hadn't thought to ask about who would be treating her husband, which makes sense considering she's not exactly in her right state of mind right now, but this is part of my job. Making sure my client is not being assessed by the doctor we are currently suing. There's only one hospital close to Sonder Hill, so we had no choice but to come to the place where he was treated the last time, but at least the doctor he's with now seems qualified and aware of his condition. That's all we could hope for.

Aaron Scott-Perez: Thank you.

Martina's gaze flits to the screen. "If something happens..." she starts.

I squeeze her hand tighter.

She inhales shallowly. "If something happens, I will ask you to call Aarón. I don't think I could..." Her accent is thicker today. As if the stress is pulling it out.

"Don't worry," I say. "I'll do whatever you need from me." I don't tell her I won't need to deliver bad news because I don't know that. Empty words of encouragement are meaningless, and I know how painful and angering they can be.

She nods repeatedly, lips tight. "He trusts you, you know."

I don't say anything because, frankly, I'm not sure whether this is a good thing or not. It's kind of ironic, how I trust this man more than most people, yet I don't know whether I like that he might think the same thing of me. Can you trust someone you don't care about?

We return to our silent waiting, the faraway beeping of machines and the faint sound of a news broadcast filling the room. Martina's eyes are closed while her lips are moving softly, as if she's praying.

"Mrs. Perez?" a Black lady in a white coat says as she walks into the waiting room.

Martina and I both get up. I don't let go of her hand.

"I'm Dr. N'Diaye," the lady says, a warm smile on her lips. "You can sit." She grabs a chair and drags it in front of the seats we were using. We reluctantly sit. Is it bad? If she wants us to sit, is it because we need to brace for bad news?

I straighten my back. I'm here for Martina. She needs someone who will be her rock if she feels like crumbling.

Martina's mouth opens, but no sound comes out. As if she's afraid of asking something she doesn't want the answer to.

"Is he okay?" I ask. A simple question that will hold all the meaning we truly need.

"Yes, he's okay."

All the tension leaves my body—and Martina's—with these two words. I'm not the praying type, but right now the only thing I can think of is, *thank God.*

"Did he have another stroke?" I ask. Aaron's mother is still holding onto my hand, but her shaking has already started to subside.

"We don't think so. Mr. Scott actually had a really high fever when he got here, and according to his labs, he seemed dehydrated, which is likely the cause of his seizure. We'll still do a CT scan to make sure, but with rehydration and fever medicine, he should be much better."

"A fever?" Martina asks, eyes in a daze. "But he didn't even let me know."

Dr. N'Diaye gives her a sad smile. "We're still trying to find the cause of his fever. Was anyone sick at home recently?"

Martina takes a moment to think. I haven't been with them since I got my car back, so I can't answer for her.

"My daughter had a cold a few days ago. Didn't think much of it," she says.

"So this is possibly just a virus," Dr. N'Diaye says. "We'll keep him here to run more tests, but this is very reassuring. If you want to see him, I can take you to his room."

Martina blinks fast.

"Thank you," I tell the doctor. Turning to Martina, I say, "If you're okay here, I think I'll go back to your place to update Aaron."

She acquiesces. When I get up, she follows me, and before

I have time to say anything else, she steps forward and wraps her arms tightly around me.

"Thank you, Wren. No sé qué hubiera hecho sin ti."

I'm not exactly sure what she just said, but it sounds like she's happy. I hug her back. "It's no problem. Truly."

After I leave her with Dr. N'Diaye, I walk outside to my car. Just before leaving, I grab my phone and text Aaron.

Me: He's okay. I'm driving to you now.

* * *

When I park in front of the house, Aaron is already outside. I wonder if he's been waiting there since I sent him my text. As soon as my headlights turn off, he starts jogging toward me.

"Hey," I say as he opens my car door and I get out.

"Hi. What happened?" His eyebrows are drawn together, portraying everything he's feeling so clearly. The anguish. The fear.

"He's okay," I tell him again, just to make sure he truly understood this.

He nods, but his face doesn't relax. Instead, he looks at me as if he'll find answers there. No question leaves his mouth, but I know he wants me to tell him everything. So I do. I go through what the doctor told us, neglecting no detail. Aaron wouldn't like it if I did.

"And how's my mother?" he asks once I'm done. Most of the stress has left his face, the same way it did for me when I got the news, but he's still not fully himself.

"She's good. She'll stay with him for now."

He nods again, this time with more resolution. Like he can now truly be at ease.

When he looks back at me, his eyes are warmer. "You must be cold. Let's get you inside." As if he's not the one who's been waiting for me in front of the door without a coat on.

"Sure," I say, then follow him inside. After hanging my coat, I walk to the living room, where he disappeared. There on the rug in front of the blazing fire, lies Callie, her black curls tousled across her face.

Aaron is quietly watching her, arms crossed. When I get closer to him, he turns to me and whispers, "She didn't want to go to sleep in her bed until she knew Dad was okay."

My heart splits in two.

"At least now you have good news to tell her," I say.

"Yeah. I'll carry her up soon." Still, he makes no move to lift her. As if he doesn't want to disturb her sleep. I can understand. She looks so peaceful.

"Thank you for today," he tells me, the fire cracking in the background. His eyes look darker in the dimness, only reflecting the flames behind me. Was he always this close?

I blink. "It's nothing."

"No, it's not. Callie was so scared. *I* was so scared. If you hadn't taken control and offered to drive to my mom, I don't know what we would've done."

"I'm just glad I was able to help."

His gaze stays on mine for a long moment before drifting back to his sister. "It's been really hard for her. Her entire life has been flipped around in a few months."

"Yeah, I know what you mean." Illness often forces you to grow far too fast.

"I wish she could be just a kid for one day." He drags a hand down his face. "And now her birthday is coming up on Saturday, but I don't think Ma has had the time to organize something, and I have no clue what a soon-to-be-eleven-year-old could want for a party."

My gaze flits back to the small figure lying on the carpet, curled into herself.

"I mean..." I wring my fingers together. Why am I nervous? This is fine. "I could help you."

He automatically shakes his head. "No. You've done more than enough. This isn't on you."

"Aaron, I don't mind. I *want* to help." They deserve it. Plus, it's not like I have better things to do at home. I could always rearrange my typical Saturday schedule. Now that I've done it a few times, it's much less frightening to change things up.

He continues examining me like he's looking for a lie.

"Besides," I say, "if I do nothing, Callie will probably have a lumberjack-themed birthday party, and literally no one would want that." I keep a straight face and only crack up when Aaron bursts out laughing. On the floor, Callie shifts at the sound, but thankfully doesn't wake.

"You're right, I'd probably mess this up."

"You can't have *all* the talents," I say with a shrug.

He grins. "Are you absolutely sure, though? I don't want us to be your burden."

"I am very sure."

He has no idea just how unburdened I've felt ever since I got to know them.

I look down at my watch, wincing when I spot the time. "Okay, well, I guess I'll get going now."

"What?" he says, head snapping up. "No way, it's too late."

"It's fine, I'll—"

"Wren, please," he interrupts. "Let us at least do that for you."

I shift my lips to one side. It *is* almost 3:00 a.m.

"I guess I could stay in the cabin until tomorrow." I've slept in it so many times; what's one more? My neighbor's fed the dogs already. At this point, it won't make that much of a difference to them if I show up at 5:00 a.m. or a little later in the day.

"Thank you," Aaron says, eyes tired but a smile still present on his lips. He starts walking toward the front door, his hand barely grazing the small of my back. "I'll just—" His steps stop abruptly. "Shit, I forgot, but a family's rented the cabin for the week."

I wave him off. "It's fine, Aaron, really. I'm not even that tired." A white lie never hurt anyone.

"Stop it," he says, his tone serious. "You're staying here. Just… take my bed."

Heat creeps up my face instantly. I can imagine myself being wrapped in his soft sheets, the smell of him all around me. I would probably get addicted to it. A way to get close to him without being close to *him*. It wouldn't matter that he wouldn't be there. It would be just as intimate.

"No," I say, "the couch will do just fine."

"Wren," he pleads.

"Final offer." No way am I burying myself even deeper into him.

He hesitates for a moment, then says, "You sure?"

I lift a side of my lips. "I'm sure."

"All right. But know I don't like this."

Chuckling softly so as not to wake Callie, I say, "Oh, I know. I've been told your mamá raised you right."

"That she did." With one last quick smile, he disappears down the hall, coming back a minute later with a bundle of sheets and pillows.

"Thank you," I say as I grab them from his arms. "Goodnight, Aaron."

His hand lingers a second longer next to mine before he pulls away. "Sleep tight." With one last look, he turns to pick Callie up, then carefully heads up the stairs.

With the knowledge that he'll be sleeping right above me, I doubt that'll happen.

CHAPTER 16

Aaron

SHE'S A GENIUS.

I haven't seen my little sister this happy in a long time.

Callie and five of her friends are lying on their backs on makeshift chaises lounges, cucumber slices over their eyes and exfoliating masks on their faces. Soft music with rainwater and birds singing plays in the background. The lights are dim.

"I have never been so relaxed in my life," Stephanie says. Or is that Chrissy? With the towels over their hair, it's hard to tell.

"Me neither," Callie answers, looking giddy.

I walk away from the doorway and turn to Wren. "You've done some magic," I tell her. It's true. Ever since she texted me the day after my father's episode, I knew this would be an incredible birthday party. Wren has thought of everything. If she hadn't been there to create the whole schedule and tell me what to go buy, I never would've been able to give Callie something like this. All credit goes to the girl standing in front of me, a simple black dress covering her lithe body. "Your kids are going to have the coolest birthday parties ever."

Wren's eyes become two wide orbs before she says, "I won't have kids."

"Oh. Sorry."

"It's fine." Leaning down to pick up a cucumber slice that fell on the floor, she says, "I'd just never want to pass down my genes."

My throat feels tight.

"But do you want kids? Because I'm sure there are options."

She shakes her head as she gets back up. "No. I wouldn't want to put anyone through what I lived with my mother."

"Right." She hasn't explained much of what it was like to take care of someone with Alzheimer's, but I can assume it's been far from easy. Her reasoning makes sense, as much as it breaks my heart that the decision was made for her the second she was born.

"What about you?" she asks. "You want kids."

"I don't know yet," I answer honestly. "My life is busy as it is, and I wouldn't want to have a kid only to half-ass the job."

"Why am I not surprised by your answer," she says teasingly.

I smirk, then point back at the room the girls are lounging in. "All that to say, I'm very glad you have those organization skills. I never could've planned all this by myself."

"It wasn't that hard," she answers in a lighter voice, apparently relieved at my switch in subject. "Just had to think of what my ideal birthday party as an eleven-year-old would've been."

I lean back against the hallway wall. "And what was your eleventh birthday party like?"

She looks up. "I don't remember exactly."

Four words. Enough to make me feel like I'm choking.

My face must change because she lifts her hands in front of her and says, "Not like that. I just meant that my birthdays have never been something that memorable."

Oh, thank God. I nod, forcing my lips into a smile. "Oh, yeah, okay."

"Don't get weird on me now," she says.

"I won't," I say, hoping I'll be able to keep that promise.

I don't know how she lives like this. It must be so hard, forgetting something and not knowing whether this is simple human forgetfulness or the beginning of her disease. I don't even remember what I ate for breakfast yesterday, but I don't have the fear that this might be due to something else—at least not yet.

It must be why Wren has one of the most impressive capacities for memorization I've ever seen. Ask her anything; she'll have the answer. Just this morning after she arrived from Boston and hung out with me while I had breakfast, she completed the *New York Times* crossword puzzle in seven minutes—yes, she timed herself. It's as if she reads encyclopedias before bed and absorbs all the information she reads. I'd rarely seen anything so impressive.

And to think that this might eventually be gone…

"What are you thinking about?" she asks, brows slightly cocked.

"Nothing." I clear my throat. "So you never did anything special for your birthdays?"

Her eyes narrow, but I don't think she picks up on my change of subject. At least if she does, she doesn't say.

"No. I remember going to the library after school with my mom at some point, but I think I was the one who'd asked to do that."

"Why am I not surprised?" I can't imagine a Wren that wants to make a big fuss about her birthday.

She goes to peek in Callie's bedroom once more, then comes back. "I'm giving them ten more minutes, and then I'll tell them to get ready to eat." Gaze tipping down to her watch, she says, "Pizza should be here soon."

"Sounds good."

She stands in the hallway, her back straight. Poised and in control, like always.

I let my head bob to the left. "So if the gingerbread-house making and the at-home spa was your dream party at eleven, why didn't you ask for it?"

Leaning back against the wall, she says, "My mother was busy. She worked two full-time jobs, so time at the library sounded easier for her." She shrugs like it's no big deal.

"I can see why you and Callie get along." Two of the most selfless girls I know.

Wren looks back at my sister's room. "She's a good kid."

"The best," I say.

That earns me a smile.

And what a beautiful smile it is.

* * *

"Okay girls, what do you want to listen to?" I ask, scrolling through my phone for a good playlist.

The six of them are seated at the dining table, a feast of pizza, french fries, and chicken wings spread over the balloon-covered tablecloth. I'd bought cone-shaped birthday hats for all of them, but when I pulled them out of the plastic bag, Wren very *un*subtly smothered a grin and told me the girls might be a little too old for those.

I don't know. In my head, Callie will always be the tiny monster who would run around the house wearing pants as a headpiece.

Now that I look at them, though, I'm happy Wren was there to tell me not to get the party hats out. Callie would probably have worn it just to be nice, but I'm sure it would've been embarrassing for her. Preteens can be ruthless.

"Why don't we let the birthday girl choose her music?" Wren suggests, plucking my phone from my hands and handing it to my sister. When she comes back to me, she whispers, "You know, just to make sure you don't make them listen to old people music."

I scoff. "My music tastes are great, thank you very much."

With a lift of her brows, she says, "I've been on long drives with you a couple of times. It's too late to convince me."

I throw my head back with a chuckle. "You really are something, aren't you?"

She doesn't answer, instead going to help one of the girls who can't open a can of soda.

"There," Callie says as she hands me my phone back, a Latino singer I've never heard before filling the room. Once everyone's settled, Wren and I both grab a slice of pizza and eat it in the kitchen, giving the girls a sense of independence.

Right before we're done with our food, the front door opens, and in comes my mother.

"¡Mamá!" Callie shouts, getting on her feet. After she looks around her, she hides a little of her excitement by sitting back down, but there's no mistaking the happiness in her expression.

Ma goes to her and hugs her tight while saying, "Oh, mi corazón. No podía faltar a tu cumpleaños." *Oh, my heart. I couldn't miss your birthday.*

My father is still in the hospital, although he should be able to get out tomorrow, according to his doctor. After all the tests they ran, they concluded that his seizure really was due to the fever, and he hasn't had another since. It was good news, but it still pissed me off. For some reason, he didn't let us know how bad he was feeling. I don't know if it's because he physically couldn't tell us or because he didn't want us to worry, but either way, I'll need to have a talk with my parents to figure out a way for this not to happen ever again.

But that's a problem for another day.

Callie squeezes our mother for a long time before pulling away. "You want to see how Aaron and Wren set up the living room for my pajama party? Everyone loves it."

Ma bobs her head multiple times, then follows my sister to the room where we set mattresses covered in fluffy blankets on the floor, giving the illusion of one giant bed. Another one of Wren's genius ideas. I almost broke my back bringing some of these mattresses into the room, but it was worth it. Before leaving, Ma looks at Wren and I and gives us a look that shows me just how grateful she is.

"Thank you again," I tell Wren once we're alone.

She rolls her eyes, then picks up both of our plates and brings them to the sink. "Stop thanking me and start washing instead."

I shake my head. How a person can be so calm yet so commanding, I will never know.

I start washing the dishes, Wren drying beside me. The girls eventually bring their plates back to the kitchen before making their way to the living room with Callie and my mother. In the background, I hear high-pitched shrieks, followed by the opening credits of a movie Callie watches every single year.

The music my sister selected still plays from the speaker I linked to my phone. I still don't know who the singer is, but he's pretty good.

"Are you dancing?"

I turn to Wren, who's watching me with a raised brow while drying a plate.

"So what if I am?" I say.

Her eyes narrow, although a twinkle of amusement fills them. "You dance?"

I laugh. "I'm Dominican, *cariño*. Of course, I dance."

She hums, then returns to her drying. My hips never stop moving. I wasn't lying: when there's music, I can never *not* dance. It's automatic.

"What about you?" I ask with a smirk.

"What about me?"

"You dance?"

She shakes her head vigorously. "Nope. Can't dance to save my life."

"Come on, now," I say while drying my hands on a rag. "Everyone can dance. It's natural."

"No, it's not."

It might be the two beers I just drank, or the fullness in my chest from seeing my sister so happy, or just that damn black dress, but something pushes me to extend a hand and say, "I'll show you."

Her eyes triple in size, and before I can remove my hand, she whips it with her dish rag. "I'm not dancing."

"Why not?" I smirk. "Scared?"

"I'm not *scared*."

Hips moving left and right, I move closer to her, hand still extended. "Then you have no reason not to let me teach you."

She rolls her eyes, but when she sees I'm not letting this go, she puts her hand in mine. Her skin is warm, even a little clammy. I take her other hand and start walking backward, dragging her slowly with me.

"There you go," I say, moving to the beat. Meanwhile, she barely shifts. Her body is so stiff, it looks like she's made of ice. Her burning skin is the only thing telling me she's really here with me. "Get out of your head, Wren. Just feel the music."

"Easy to say," she says, but after she lets out a long breath, she closes her eyes and starts relaxing. Her upper body starts moving with the music, still rigid but dancing at last.

"See? You're a natural."

"Stop teasing, or I'll stomp on your toes."

I laugh, then move one of her hands to my shoulder, my own going to her hip. I've rarely been this close to her, and now that I am, I can smell her subtle perfume. Something floral. It's so good it almost makes me weak. I'm pretty sure it'll be imprinted in my nose even once she's gone.

Finn's voice resonates in my head, telling me I've got it bad. I push him away. This is nothing. Just two friends dancing.

Her eyes are still closed, but she's truly starting to get it. Slowly, her hips start swishing to the rhythm, a mirror image to mine.

I lean forward, her soft hair brushing my cheek, before murmuring in her ear, "Good." Then, I push her body and keep hold of her hand so I can spin her around once, twice. I catch her hips at the end of her last turn, this time her back to my front. Wren's breathing is loud and shallow. Her smell is everywhere.

Jesus Christ, this was a bad idea.

And it only gets worse when she starts moving her hips, now grinding her ass against my groin.

Fuck. Fuck, fuck, fuck.

Think of something else, Aaron. Something that doesn't involve a dream-inducing body with plump lips and a witty humor.

Neither of us talks, but something is exchanged through the dancing. I couldn't say what it is, except that Wren's slender fingers wrap around my wrists and hold me as I grind against her. I can feel myself getting hard despite all my best efforts, but I can't for the life of me pull myself back. She's a drug. I can't get enough.

Wren stretches her neck back so her head leans against my shoulders. My forehead slowly drifts to hers. She exhales shakily.

Then, in a second, she's off me, spinning so we're now face-to-face. Her eyes are no longer closed; in fact, they're wide open. Her chest rises and dips fast, probably not so unlike mine.

She swallows, then looks away. "I, uh… I'll go check on the girls."

I don't trust myself to speak, so I just nod. Without a second look, she's gone, leaving me alone in the kitchen, breathless.

Fuck. Finn was right.

CHAPTER 17

Wren

"I'M NERVOUS."

Aaron turns to Martina and lays a hand on her shoulder. "You don't have to be nervous. It's going to be fine." Lifting his dark eyes at me, he adds with a smirk, "Besides, Wren's here with us."

I force myself to breathe in, then busy myself looking for a pen in my bag even though I already put one in my front pocket.

It's been three days since Callie's birthday party—and Aaron and my little dance session. To say I haven't been able to stop thinking about it would be an understatement. Whoever pictured sirens as females never danced with Aaron Scott-Perez. When I went to bed that night after the party, the feeling of his hands on my hips and his hardness on my lower back was all I could imagine, over and over again. Even my vibrator hasn't been able to quench my thirst. Which made me realize that maybe my feelings toward him aren't entirely neutral after all.

Which in turn made me realize I need to be even more careful with him.

I haven't gone back to the farm since, but since Dennis got released from the hospital two days ago, Dr. Groban's legal team asked to reschedule the meeting we missed due to Dennis's illness. Today, we're finally going to receive their response to our lawsuit.

"Hey, you doing okay?"

I only realize Aaron spoke to me when I lift my head and find him right *there.*

"Mm-hmm."

He frowns. "Sure?"

I nod, and thank goodness, the door to the waiting room of the lawyer's office opens at this exact moment. One of the two men I met two weeks ago—Mr. Ragsdale—comes out and says, "Hi, everyone. Are we ready to begin?" He must be in his early forties, with a clearly expensive gray suit and short brown hair.

I look to my clients, who stand up, not a hint of a smile on their faces. It almost feels weird to see Martina so expressionless. Without a word, Martina helps Dennis get up from his chair and enter the room.

This office is nothing like what I'm used to. While Silver & Prescott's offices are sleek and modern, this one is full of heavy wooden furniture and darkly painted walls. The room Mr. Ragsdale leads us into contains a long conference table surrounded by eight large chairs, reminding me of a boardroom in an ancient university.

Dennis sits in the chair closest to the door, with Aaron and Martina by his side. I enter last, closing the door behind me. The second lawyer working on the defense's side, Mr. Beischel, is an older man with pale hair and paler eyes. He's already seated in a chair on the side opposite to us, documents spread in front of him on the heavy oak wood table. I take a seat at the head of the table while his colleague joins his side.

"Thank you for meeting with us today," the older lawyer says, with a smile I'm not sure is sincere, to the Scott-Perez family.

If looks could kill, Aaron's returning glare would've shot this man dead. Thank goodness Dr. Groban isn't here. The way he's reacting to the lawyers alone makes me think it would've ended in a brawl.

"We're happy you came to a decision," I say, placing my pen and a notebook on the table.

Mr. Ragsdale stretches his lips tightly. "Right." Turning to Dennis, he says, "We'd like to start by offering our sincerest apologies for what has happened. Our client would like to apologize in person as well, if you so wish."

"I think we'll pass, thanks," Aaron says, jaw clenched.

Oh boy.

The younger attorney hides a wince, but thankfully doesn't bring the subject up again. Instead, with the tips of his fingers, he slides a pile of papers toward me. His colleague does the same to Martina, Dennis, and Aaron. I automatically start turning pages to find the official offer.

All right. This isn't too bad.

"We have worked very hard with our client to find a deal that we think could be advantageous for everyone involved. We're offering a settlement of $500,000 to compensate for your inconveniences, as well as—"

"I beg your pardon?" Aaron says, voice cold as snow.

The older, less smiling lawyer says, "My colleague said we're offering—"

"You said you're offering to pay us off to shut up."

Crap.

"Aarón, please," Martina starts. "Let them speak."

He turns to her, flabbergasted. "You can't be serious." Shaking his head, he flips back to the lawyers and says, "You can take your offer and fuck off."

Mr. Ragsdale's eyes become wide as saucers as he says, "Mr. Scott-Perez, please—"

"We'll see you in court," Aaron interrupts.

The sound of my chair scraping the floor makes everyone turn my way. "Aaron? Can we talk? Outside?"

He stares at me in silence for a second.

Please say yes. Don't mess this up.

I try to let him read me. To tell him without speaking that I understand what he's going through, but that this is definitely not the way to go.

Something softens a hint in his gaze. He doesn't answer, but he does get up. I exhale in relief.

"Sorry, everyone," I tell the defense team. "Can we take five?"

"Sure," the older lawyer says while throwing a side look at his partner.

With a quick step, I lead Aaron outside, closing the office door behind me. Then, I cross my arms and whisper-hiss, "What the hell are you doing?"

"What do you mean?" he says sternly.

"Don't play coy with me. What was that in there? You want to ruin this deal?"

"What deal?" he answers, anger building in his voice. "The one where they're offering us something that is pennies to them instead of giving us actual justice? You know this isn't what we want, Wren."

"I *am* getting you justice. This is a good deal. I wouldn't have accepted to come here today if I thought they would offer us something unfair. And I'll negotiate it so that—"

He steps back. "So you knew they were going to try to settle?"

"I expected it, yes."

"And you still brought us here? When you know we want a real trial?"

I pinch my lips. It's not his fault. I would be acting just like him if I were in his situation. I did everything I could to get the best care possible for my mother years ago, even when the state gave us barely enough services for her to live with a remaining sense of dignity. I still need to go to war for her sometimes, and I do, gladly.

Keeping my voice calm and soft, I say, "I know you want a trial, but you don't realize that a trial could go both ways. Your father had a strange presentation for a stroke. I told you that could play against us because it makes it more understandable that it wasn't caught early enough."

"Understandable?" he explodes.

I lift a hand. "Please let me finish."

His mouth closes.

"It's hard to prove that any good doctor would've acted differently in his situation, and since it's so rare to present like this, there's no way to prove that Dennis wouldn't have developed aphasia even if his stroke had been detected right away."

Aaron's lips twist to the side as his eyes alternate between both of mine. "And you think my parents will agree with that?"

"They already did."

Shaking his head, his gaze gets lost. "It's not enough. They ruined my dad's life. They forced Callie to grow up with a mother who's busy being a nurse and a dad who can't play with her like he used to. They made me lose a job I love to keep my family's legacy alive. They made my mother age ten years in four months." He looks back at me. "They think five hundred grand is enough to compensate for *that*? Because it's not. It's fucking not."

His face holds so much sadness in this moment, I don't know how my heart doesn't physically break.

"Aaron," I say, walking slowly toward him. "I could negotiate this deal for years. I could bring this to court. I could get you more." When I'm close enough, I take his hand in mine. I don't think about my feelings outside of this. He needs the comfort. "But all the money or the court wins in the world won't bring your dad back to the way he was." I shake my head. "It won't. Nothing will."

Aaron's Adam's apple bobs, and as he stays still, his eyes fill with water.

"But it's all we have left," he says, voice cracking over the last word.

Without thinking, I break the space between us and wrap him in my arms. His chest is shaking against me, and I soon realize he's started crying. It's the kind of sobbing that doesn't let out a single sound, the anguish too heavy for words or cries. Grinding my teeth together, I squeeze him tighter, no space left between our bodies. His smell of fresh pine and cinnamon fills my nose as I rub a hand up and down his back. His fingers clutch at the back of my shirt, like he's scared I'll let go. I won't.

He's fought this for so long. For months on end, he convinced himself that winning a court case would make this okay somehow. I think he just realized that the only way for their lives to ever be okay again is for them to start accepting what happened.

"Let me negotiate this deal," I finally say softly as I continue holding him. "Let me get you the most money I can from this man, and once the settlement is accepted, the medical board of Vermont will automatically start an investigation. It might not be what you expected, but you'll get justice, Aaron. I swear you will."

He sniffles in the crook of my neck, then pulls back. Unashamed of his wet cheeks, he says, "Are you telling me this as our lawyer or as my friend?"

The answer comes out automatically, surprising me.

"Both." It's too late to pretend I don't care about him when I so clearly do. And for the time we have left in each other's company, I can admit it out loud.

Dark hair tousled, brown eyes glinting, he gives me all of his trust with a single nod.

It's one of the most beautiful gifts I've ever been given.

CHAPTER 18

Aaron

"LAST SIGNATURE."

Wren points to a line for my mother, who signs her name as my father's Power of Attorney given that he cannot write, and there. It's done. I watch them with tense shoulders.

In the end, Wren got us a great deal. Even I have been able to realize that, after a few days of reflection and lots of phone calls with her. Besides, she was right. I needed a wake-up call that nothing about this would ever be okay and that pursuing this trial thing forever would not necessarily be a good thing for my father. It was a hard realization, but I needed it.

"That's it?" Ma asks as she lets go of Dad's hand, his name written on the line in shaky handwriting.

"That's it," Wren says, collecting the papers. "We're officially done."

Ma's face breaks out into a large smile before she hugs Dad tightly. "Se acabó, mi amor." *It's over, my love.*

Dad leans his head on hers, a peaceful look on his face.

And this is what my acceptance of the situation was for. This sense of peace.

Throat tight, I turn to Wren, who's gazing at my parents with eyes crinkled in contentedness. This is all her. I don't know how we could ever thank her enough. She singlehandedly put this look on my parents' faces.

As if feeling me, she looks up. And as soon as she catches me watching, her smile dims.

I don't know what's going on with us. Not that there is an *us*, but ever since Callie's birthday party, she's been distant. Even though she confirmed that she sees me as a friend when we were at the lawyers' office, she's been a little cold toward me. I don't know if it's something I said or did, but I can't shake off the fact that she seems to want to put space between us.

I don't know how to feel about that. Especially since this feeling of knots in my stomach is still very much present—more than present—when she's next to me.

Done with her embrace with my dad, Ma climbs to her feet and jumps toward Wren, wrapping her in a tight hug. "Thank you so much," she says, her voice sounding emotional. "You've given us so much."

Slowly, Wren raises her arms so she can hug her back. "It's been a true pleasure."

When their embrace is done, Wren exchanges a look and small salute with my father, then turns to grab her stuff.

This is it. The project is over. She's officially not working on our case anymore.

Jesus, why am I feeling nauseous?

Once she has her bag in hand, she waves one last time at my parents. She then turns to me, but just as she opens her mouth, I say, "I'll walk with you to your car."

I don't know if it's because she doesn't want to part ways just yet either or because I didn't phrase it as a question, but she doesn't argue me on it.

Once we've put our coats and boots on, I open the front door and lead her out.

Head low, she stays silent as we start walking, the only sound the crunch of snow under our boots. All the precipitation of the past week has transformed the farm into a true winter paradise, which has increased our sales a lot. I guess people are more interested in going to cut their own tree when the landscape looks straight out of a movie. Or maybe it's just that Christmas is next week and people visited later than usual this year.

I can't wait for the season to be over and to be able to take a small breather.

Even though it's only 5:30 p.m., the sun has already set, night occupying the space. The Christmas lights I hung on the roof illuminate our path, the moon barely a sliver of light.

"So..." I start, although I don't know what to say next. This strangely feels like a hard goodbye even though we haven't spent that much time together.

Besides, it doesn't have to be goodbye.

A few days ago, I came to the conclusion that with these feelings I couldn't tamp down, maybe it would be worth it to ask Wren whether she'd like us to see each other once she was done working on my father's case. Maybe what I'm feeling for her is only a representation of my gratefulness (highly doubt it), but it would still be worth it to see whether there could be something more.

But with the distance she's kept between us, especially today, I don't think I'll risk it. She's not even looking at me, for Christ's sake.

"I'm happy it all turned out well," she finally says. "I know the medical board's investigation will begin soon too, so that's more good news."

"Right."

To our right, the commercial zone of trees still hosts a few customers. Even though it's dark, fairy lights keep the farm workable during the evening, and people seem to love to come at that hour. I can understand why. This makes for an extremely romantic setup. If I were dating, I'd for sure bring someone here at night. The cold temperature that makes you want to cuddle, the lights that create a cozy atmosphere, the soft Christmas music playing in the background. It's all perfect.

Sadly, the only person I would want to take on a date right

now is the one who's walking to my left and possibly disappearing on me in the next few minutes.

I don't know why I said I'd walk her to her car when I can't find any appropriate words to say. I feel like an idiot.

After another minute of silence, Wren says, "Looks like the rats have new roommates now."

I look up to find a family of three, all dressed in plaid shirts and flap-eared hats, walking into the cabin Wren used to sleep in.

I grin. "There were never any rats, and you know it." The traps never caught anything, and I've checked them every day since.

Finally—fucking finally—she turns to me and deadpans, "There. Were. Rats."

"Sure, cariño. Keep telling yourself that."

She huffs, but the tension is slightly less heavy than before, so I'll count it as a win.

Hands in her pockets, she looks around the land as she keeps walking. "Your family really has a beautiful place."

"Yeah, they do. *We* do." If I'm to officially take over, I need to start treating this place as my own sooner rather than later.

We reach her car, which is parked close to those of the customers, and just as I open the passenger door for her to drop her stuff in, I remember something.

"Be right back," I say before running to the side of the commercial zone. When I walk back, I have a small but beautiful tree in my arms.

After putting her bag inside the car, Wren turns around, and as soon as she spots me, her eyes widen.

"Is that for me?"

I shrug, as if I didn't spend thirty minutes roaming the lanes to find the perfect tree for her apartment. "I thought it could be a nice thank you gift."

She looks it over, even going so far as touching the green of the soft needles. "It's beautiful."

We're only a few days away from December 25th, but I still risked it. "I hope you hadn't already put one up?"

She shakes her head. "I don't really celebrate Christmas."

"What?" I say, eyebrows narrowed. How can she not celebrate the best holiday there is?

"Not much fun in celebrating alone," she answers casually, like she hasn't said one of the saddest sentence I've ever heard. Here, Christmas is spent singing and dancing and cooking and baking and hugging. Maybe this year will be a little different, but I know even with the illness that carved its place into our home, it can't not be a beautiful day.

The fact that she doesn't have that, and probably hasn't had that for a while, breaks my heart into a thousand pieces.

"What about friends, though?" I ask. Christmas doesn't have to be about blood family. Surely, there are people who'd love to celebrate with her.

She snickers, though there's no humor in it. "I don't have a lot of people around me."

"Why?" The question comes out automatically. It doesn't make sense.

Kicking a rock on the ground, she says, "It wouldn't be fair to them."

A crease forms between my brows.

"I'm like...a wildfire," she says. "Right now, my fire is contained, but when I eventually start forgetting, I'll torch everyone around me, and I'd prefer avoiding that." With a lift of her shoulders, she adds, "*I've* been burned, and it's not something I'd wish on anyone."

What...

How can she see herself that way? Like no one could benefit from having her in their life. I've never heard something so untrue.

When she sees I'm about to tell her something, she stops me

in my tracks and says, "I'm really thankful for this, though." She pets the tree as if it's one of her animals. "I promise I'll decorate it."

I lick my lips, tipping my head toward it. "If ever you need help with that, let me know."

She looks down again. "Well, I better get going if I want to get the girls out before a mess happens."

"Sure," I say, my voice sounding strange. Popping her trunk open, I put the tree in, then close the door.

Right before walking over to the driver's side, she gives me a hint of a smile and says, "Bye, Aaron."

I open my mouth, but before I can find what it is I want to say to her, she's inside the car. The wave she gives me is so quick I almost miss it. And in an instant, she's driving away, never looking back.

Fuck.

I spend a few minutes looking the way she left, taking the time to calm down. When I get back inside, Ma might ask me questions, and I need to look okay.

Because in reality, I don't have reasons not to be okay. This was always supposed to happen. Wren never signed up to stay in our lives forever.

Maybe she'll contact me later. Or maybe I'll grow some balls and contact her at some point.

With one last look toward the road, I walk back to the house, then hang my coat on the rack. As expected, the second I'm inside, Ma pops her head in the foyer and says, "¿Cómo estás?"

"Bien," I answer, clearing of my throat.

She doesn't say anything in response, which means even more than words. Ma never stays silent. She has the biggest mouth I know.

"It's fine, Ma. She was a friend, that's it."

Again, she stays silent.

Fuck that. Without looking at her, I walk up the stairs. I don't need to get her third degree tonight. Instead, I go to my office. Maybe I'll be able to do some work tonight. Turn this shitty evening into something productive.

But of course, that was wishful thinking. As soon as I open my software and look at the landscape I haven't worked on enough in the past weeks, the only thing I can think of is the fact that I'll need to quit this job I love soon.

Just as I let my forehead fall to the desk, a knock comes from my office's door.

"Yes?" Please not Ma. I can't with her psychoanalysis right now.

Instead, Callie walks inside, a shirt I'm ninety-nine percent sure I saw on Wren at some point on her back. It wouldn't surprise me that Callie asked her if she could have it. She's a sneaky little creature, and Wren is someone who'd give the shirt off her back if someone asked. Literally.

"I saw Wren leave," Callie says.

"Yeah, she had to go home. She's done here."

"So when will we see her and the dogs again?" my little sister asks like it's evident they'll come back to us at some point.

"I don't know, Callie. I don't know."

CHAPTER 19

Wren

THE DEEP RED OF MY NAIL POLISH GLINTS IN THE WHITE tree lights as I spin an ornament hanging from a branch.

I'm pathetic.

Truly, extraordinarily pathetic.

Ever since I got back from the Evermore farm ten days ago, I've been unable to stop looking at my tiny tree. It fits perfectly next to my couch between the two windows showing me a starlit Boston. As if it'd been tailored to my place.

I wasn't lying to Aaron; I'd never put a Christmas tree up in here before. With my mother, when she was still herself, we would decorate for the holidays, but ever since I've been alone, I haven't seen the point.

But the moment I came upstairs with my small tree, I put it on a makeshift stand, and the next morning, I went to buy ornaments and tinsel garlands to make sure I did it justice. As if having it in my apartment would let me keep a small part of the farm with me.

As I said, pathetic.

But the worst part was what came *after* that.

After driving away from Evermore, this painful lump had taken residence in my stomach. I wouldn't see them again. I wouldn't see *him* again. I'd kept my distance, just like I'd planned. Every time he'd had the opportunity to approach me, I took a step aside. It was the best thing I could do for him.

That didn't mean I didn't feel like crap leaving that place.

After I'd come back and decorated the tree, I stared at it for a long while. It looked so pretty in here. Made me feel so special. I even drank a glass of wine while staring at it.

And I don't know if it was the wine or the nasty feeling that wouldn't let me go, but something pushed me to snap a photo of the tree and send it to Aaron with a smiley face emoji.

See? I'm a mess.

He texted me back less than thirty seconds later telling me it was beautiful. Something sparked in my chest at the sight of his name on my phone, but as much as I wanted to, I forced myself not to text him anything else. This was supposed to be a clean break, and my text had only been a small lapse in judgment.

And now here I am, days later and still very much hung up on this stupid tree from this stupid farm that this stupid man gave me.

At least I did what I was supposed to do. Aaron is free of me. I'll survive this silly... What even is this? An infatuation? It feels stupid, but I guess it is what I'm feeling.

It's probably due to the physical contact we shared over the weeks. I'm not used to being so physically close to young, extremely attractive men, and I guess my inexperienced brain clung to it. It's only a case of sexual frustration that's making me so obsessed with him.

It'll go away eventually. I can only hope.

Behind me, someone whines. I spin to find May's head leaned on the armrest, eyes sad.

"What's up?" I ask my dog. "You miss him too?"

Surely not. She hasn't seen him enough for that. She's probably just hungry for dinner, and I'm projecting my thoughts onto her.

"Come on, let's eat," I tell her as I lift her off the couch and carry her to the kitchen. As if she heard the words, Molly also comes running from my bedroom, her large tongue hanging out of her mouth.

"Jesus, all right," I say with a chuckle as she starts wagging her tail so hard, the one picture of my mother I have in here almost falls off the small buffet.

After putting food in their respective bowls—and watching them eat like one little and one big hyena—I open the fridge and pick up the single portion of turkey and stuffing I bought from the grocery store. I'm the worst cook I know, so no way was I attempting to make a Christmas dinner, especially only for myself.

I put the plate in the microwave, and once I've taken it out, I sit at the table, where one set of utensils welcomes me. There's also the thriller I picked up from the library two days ago. Sinister to read this on Christmas night? Perhaps, but can't be worse than continuing to mope. Next to my chair, Molly and Maybelle are still gulping their food down. Maybe I'll give them a piece of my meal as a special treat.

"Merry Christmas, girls," I tell them before picking up my fork. But just before I can start digging in, something weird happens.

Someone knocks on my front door.

What the hell? Who bothers people on December 25th? If it's carolers, it might just bring me to tears. I always thought I liked being alone, but after the day I've spent, this loneliness is bone-chilling.

My mother's residence organized a special dinner for the residents and their families tonight, and I've been told how much she enjoys attending it each year. I didn't want to ruin it for her, so I went to see her this morning instead. I probably shouldn't have, but I couldn't imagine not going to see my own mother on Christmas Day.

In the end, I only stayed ten minutes. Mom obviously didn't recognize me. She called me a thief, then started hysterically crying while begging me not to hurt her. Someone came and asked me to leave, but I was already halfway out the door, nausea churning in my gut. She'd rarely reacted this strongly—and negatively—to me.

It was one of the worst days of my life.

So tonight, I really, *really* have no patience left in me.

I get up, ready to tell whoever it is to leave me alone, but words die on my tongue as soon as I open the door.

Impossible.

Aaron is standing on my landing, dressed in dark jeans and a clean white shirt, a dark wool coat on top. Snowflakes dust his dark hair, which is combed to the side.

He's a dream.

I mean, I must be dreaming.

"What..." I start.

He smiles, which makes him even dreamier. "Merry Christmas, Wren."

"But... How... What are you doing here?" I end up saying, mouth hanging open like a fish out of water.

"Figured you hadn't changed your plans, and no one should spend Christmas alone." He looks down, then extends his hand, a red container in it. "Oh, and Ma made way too much *puerco asado*, so I thought I'd bring you some."

I keep staring at him like I've lost my mind, taking his extended container numbly.

He drove here. On Christmas night. Because he knew I would be alone.

Not much gets to me in life. Without wanting to throw myself a pity party, I've gone through a lot. It's gotten hard to phase me.

But this? This brings tears to my eyes.

After another long moment of my silence, Aaron says, "So... can I come in?"

Still in a daze, I step back so he can walk inside. He removes his coat and hangs it on the rack that only holds my winter coat, giving me time to finally find my words.

"I can't believe you're here."

"Good surprise, I hope?"

To hell with my distance, at least for tonight. I nod eagerly. "Good surprise."

He smiles again, as bright as a thousand diamonds.

Paws pitter-patter behind us, and a second later, Molly's face is brushing against Aaron's pants, her tail again wagging like crazy.

"Molly, stop it," I chastise.

"It's okay," Aaron says as he pets her. Leaning closer to her ear, he then whispers, "I've missed you too."

Aaron Scott-Perez alone? Very handsome.

Aaron Scott-Perez on my landing on Christmas night with a Tupperware full of food he knows I couldn't cook for myself? Sexy as hell.

But Aaron Scott-Perez talking to my dog while petting her? I'm melting. Literally. I'm so hot, I think I'll need to reapply deodorant in a few minutes.

"I hope you didn't miss Christmas dinner with your family, though," I say, guilt starting to claw through me as I realize it's only 7:30 p.m.

"Nah, don't worry. We ate early because Dad doesn't go to bed late anymore."

"Oh, okay, good."

He looks around the place, his gaze sticking to the tree. "It looks good in here."

"I love it," I say honestly. I don't know how I'll ever be able to spend a Christmas without a natural tree emanating a strong scent of pine that fills the room. It's not a simple decoration; it transforms the place in its entirety.

Looking back at me, Aaron simply smiles, as if the fact of being here, in this apartment, makes him happy.

It certainly makes *me* happy to have him here.

"Thank you," I say in a low voice. I don't think I need to explain what I'm thanking him for. He knew I'd feel lonely, probably before I even realized it. He's truly something else.

He grins, then says, "Oh, and before I forget." With a fast pace, he walks to the coatrack and pulls a large white envelope from inside the pocket of his coat. On it is written my name in a beautiful calligraphy, four simple but bold letters. And at the top of it is a tiny red ribbon made of tinsel.

He brought me a gift.

He drove here and brought me a gift, and meanwhile I am here, empty-handed and feeling so inadequate I could die.

"Aaron, you didn't need to—"

Handing the envelope to me, he says, "Don't worry, it's nothing."

I lift my brows. I don't think this man could ever give a meaningless gift even if he tried. Somehow, I know that about him. He's the type of person who would handpick the perfect item for every single person around him, taking hours to do it if he had to.

And I guess he considers me one of these people now.

"I swear," he says with a laugh.

Heartbeat accelerating, I slowly open the envelope, the sound of paper tearing clashing against the silence in the room, then slide my hand inside the envelope.

It feels like a piece of paper.

"Come on, you're making me nervous now," he says.

I look up to find his amused eyes on me. Quickly, I pull the sheet out of the envelope.

My world blurs, heart beating in slow motion.

On the thick cream paper is the most realistic drawing I have ever seen, a scene with my two dogs playing in the snow, a horde of coniferous trees in the background. Maybelle looks like a tiny ball of cotton, her frizz perfectly depicted, her dark eyes popping against the light background. And Molly. Oh, Molly. Her colors are so vibrant, each strand of hair looking realer than life. As if I'm truly witnessing my girls romping through snowdrifts.

"Aaron," I start, voice wobbly.

He clears his throat. "You like it?"

I don't have words. There's no way I could find the right thing to say. It's too beautiful, and more importantly, it means more to me than any other piece of art ever could've, which Aaron must've known somehow. He's just ruined all the future presents I might one day receive with a single one of his. So, instead of talking, I take a step forward and wrap my arms around his torso, so tight I'm probably crushing his lungs.

After a moment of stiffness, he relaxes against me and puts his arms over my shoulders, squeezing my head against his chest. He smells so good, like snow and cold air and *him*, his warmth enveloping me, and for a second, I find myself thinking I never want to step away. I could stay like this forever. His muscles are hard under me, flexing as he pulls me even closer against him.

I swallow.

"Merry Christmas," he whispers over my hair.

"Merry Christmas, Aaron," I say, keeping him against me just a second longer. I need one more.

There have been a lot of occasions when I've wished I could have a normal brain and get a normal future. When I've had to refuse coffee dates with Selina or any of my colleagues. When I made the decision to never have children. When I lost the will to travel, knowing it might make me heartbroken to create memories only to lose them.

But this moment probably tops them all. Knowing that I'll never have this man for myself.

God, this infatuation is definitely not going away anytime soon.

But as long as it stays one-sided, everything should be okay. Protecting Aaron is the only thing that matters.

Finally forcing myself to take a step back, I bring my attention to the drawing again. It's even more impressive on the second look. The more I study it, the more I wonder how he made something that looks like a real-life photograph with simple strokes of his hands. There's more to it than skill. There's passion, and a gift too.

"Aaron," I say, "you can't give this up."

"What do you mean?"

I look up. "Your art. You're too talented to stop."

Scratching his head, he says, "I'll keep it as a hobby. Don't worry."

That's not what I meant, and he knows it. He needs to keep his job. No one with this kind of genius should step away like that. Plus, he loves it. It's written all over him.

But tonight isn't about having hard discussions. Aaron is here, after driving two hours on Christmas night, to celebrate with me.

So that's what we'll do.

"Come on," I say, cocking my head toward the dining table. "Let me try that *puerco* something."

Aaron laughs, the sound warmer than anything I've ever experienced.

* * *

A warm nuzzle touching my hand jerks me awake.

As I scan my surroundings, it takes me a second to remember where I am.

In my apartment, on my couch, Molly and Maybelle at my side. I must've fallen asleep after…

My head snaps toward Aaron, whose small, tired eyes are on me from his side of the couch. His hair is mussed, and a crease of pillow lines his golden cheek.

"Were you watching me sleep?" I say, skin warming up.

"Couldn't pass on the opportunity."

My deadly stare makes him chuckle, the low sound vibrating through my entire body.

"Kidding," he says. "I just woke up too."

I blink a few times as I look down at my watch. It's almost four in the morning. We must've fallen asleep at some point during the night.

After I ate all the food Aaron brought me earlier—it was so good I couldn't stop—we sat at the kitchen table and talked for hours. It wasn't festive per se, but it was enough to make me happier than...well, come to think of it, pretty much happier than I'd ever been. I wasn't alone. For this moment in time, I was part of something bigger than my own tiny life. Rarely had I felt something so refreshing.

It was around midnight when Aaron got up from his chair. I followed him to the door, not ready for him to leave just yet but also unable to keep him any longer. However, just as he reached for his coat, he spun around and said, "How about a Christmas movie?"

I exhaled in relief, then nodded as eagerly as a little kid.

We started watching *How the Grinch Stole Christmas,* and I guess I drifted off at some point, too cozy between my knitted throw blanket, my dogs sleeping at my feet, and Aaron's body heat next to me. He sat far enough that it was appropriate, but close enough that I felt pure comfort. I'd rarely felt this good, but coupled with the stress of the day, I passed out after the opening scene.

With a big stretch of his arms, Aaron gets up from the couch, careful not to untuck me from my covers. "Well, guess it's time for me to get going."

I follow him to my feet. "You're not going back to Sonder Hill at this hour, are you?"

"Nah, I'll crash at my place," he says while walking to grab his coat.

I swallow, rooted to the side of my couch. Poor him. It's so late. He's still here because of me. I'm sure he somehow felt my need for him to stay a little longer earlier, and now he has to drive home in the middle of the night.

As I watch him put his boots on, it's on the tip of my tongue to tell him to forget it and just stay. It's not even a big deal. He could stay on the couch, or I could give him my bed. Friends do this all the time. We *just* spent hours sleeping side by side, and everything was fine.

Still, even I can feel some lines were blurred.

So in the end, once he straightens himself, all dressed up to face the cold outside, I stay where I'm standing and say, "Thank you again for tonight. You have no idea..." My voice dies in my throat, emotion clogging it.

He smiles softly, which leaves my chest feeling ablaze. "It truly was my pleasure."

And for some strange reason, I believe him.

CHAPTER 20

Aaron

I CAN HEAR HER BEFORE I EVEN SEE HER.

I haven't wrapped my head around the fact that she's here. Ma told me she'd invited her to celebrate New Year's Eve with us—after learning that she'd been alone for Christmas, my mother was out of her mind—but I still couldn't believe that she'd said yes. That Wren, who's closed off most of the time, had agreed to come celebrate with us tonight, for something completely unrelated to her work, even if she knew we had guests.

Yet, here she is. I could recognize her voice anywhere. I've just realized that. It's strange, how accustomed I've become to her in such a short period of time, but when I woke up in her apartment on Christmas night, I remembered where I was before even opening my eyes, simply by recognizing the scent of her perfume around me.

I just came out of the shower, so before going down to greet her and start partying, I head to my room with a towel wrapped around my hips and change into black slacks and a burgundy sweater. I may or may not spend a few extra minutes to make sure my curly hair doesn't look like total shit.

Once I reach the main floor, it sounds like chaos, in the best possible way. Laughter is coming from everywhere. I halt for a second, wondering whether I've jumped into another dimension while I was in the shower. The house hasn't sounded this alive in months.

And when I enter the living room, I immediately understand why.

I don't know how it was possible for them to find a way to embarrass me in less than five minutes, but this proves I should never underestimate my family. Because in the time it took for me to change, my sister, my mother, and my cousin Will have jumped on the opportunity to go pick up my old photo album and start showing it to Wren. Or maybe that was their plan all along, and the album was already in the living room, ready to be studied.

Fuck me.

"And this is the day Aarón lost his first tooth," Ma says as she points at a picture. The album is open on Wren's thighs, who's studying it like it's a work of art. "He was so scared, he started crying so much he peed his pants."

Wren throws her head back, her laughter brighter than the sun. It almost makes this intense embarrassment worth it. Beside her, Violet, Will's wife, is laughing with them, discovering the pictures at the same time. I've seen her a couple of times since she and Will reconnected a few years ago and made things official, but I guess she never saw photos of me as a snotty kid before.

Hiding my smile, I say, "I see my traitor family has showed their true side."

They all lift their heads in my direction, but I only stare at Wren. It's as if her gaze is magnetic. I have no choice but to maintain it.

Two weeks ago, I would've said that was pathetic of me. She was avoiding me at all costs, for one reason or another. I'd made up my mind that I wouldn't try to get closer to her. I was convinced she wouldn't contact me again. But the moment I saw her name on my phone, with the sweet image of her Christmas tree decorated in a simple but glittery fashion, I knew I was done for. It was the smallest of signs, but it was all I needed to start hoping again. I never would've gone to her on Christmas night if I'd thought she didn't want me there, but the fact that she'd texted me first told me maybe, just maybe, she missed me too.

And I'm so glad I went.

After the evening we spent together, which fast became one of my favorite to date, she didn't text me. I didn't text her either. The ball was in her court if ever she wanted to see me again. After a week of radio silence, I thought that was it.

But here she is, sitting in front of my dad, between my mother, sister, and cousin-in-law, a smile on her lips as she's going through my baby pictures.

"Oh, come on, Aarón. We're just showing Wren and Violet here a bit of our history," my sneaky mother says.

"More like showing them all the times I was humbled."

To my surprise, Wren is the one who answers. "Just shut it and let me go through these." She's trying to keep a straight face, but I can see her lips twitching.

I fake an annoyed huff. "Sure, whatever."

Triumphant, she returns to her browsing, with Ma and Callie commenting. Meanwhile, Dad looks at them, not speaking with them like he usually would on New Year's Eve, but still looking happy to be here with all of us.

"Hey, man," Will says to my right as he comes out of the bathroom.

"Hey," I greet him before hugging him and tapping his back twice. It's so good to see him. We don't travel to each other's places as often as we'd like, but I know whatever happens in my life, I can always text him and he'll answer as fast as he can. "I'm so glad you could make it."

"Me too," he says, pulling away. "Violet felt bad about making us miss New Year's with Sam and my mom for her exposition in Boston tomorrow, but being able to come here and see you makes it better."

I couldn't imagine not spending this time with my family, but I guess for Will, Violet *is* his family.

"Maybe next year we can all spend the holidays in New York,"

I say, already thinking about how to arrange a trip like that for Dad. "I miss everyone."

"Please do. Mom would be ecstatic," Will says. "She's got this new man who's kind of a tool, but he makes her happy, so who cares, right?"

I chuckle. He's a good one.

To our left, someone shrieks as they move through the photo album. I must take that thing away from them at some point tonight and burn it.

"So, new girl, huh?" Will whispers.

I shake my head, no matter how much sometimes I wish I could nod. "Nah. She's a…friend."

"Sure thing," he says, grinning. "As if I've never seen that kind of face before."

My brows furrow. I don't remember ever feeling that way when looking at Amber, but maybe I did look like this and I just didn't notice.

But that's not what he meant.

"Every time someone takes a pic of me looking at Violet, I have that same stupid expression," he says, eyes on his wife, and I can't deny it. He does look lovesick, even more so than when I first saw them together at eight years old, when I'd gone to spend a few days at the beach house that their families owned in Southern Maine.

"I don't look at her like that," I say, voice filled with less conviction than I'd hoped.

"Oh, buddy," Will says as he turns to me and shakes his head. Then he claps my back again, as if in consolation. For what, I don't know.

"Mamá," Callie says in a loud voice, bringing my attention back to the girls, "isn't that the time Aaron got sick everywhere after Halloween?" She's pointing at a picture of me dressed up as a zombie, maybe fifteen or sixteen years old.

"Uh-huh." Ma side-eyes me. "Someone had just discovered the wonders of alcohol and had no control over himself."

Will laughs sharply as I grab the glass of water I left in the living room earlier and take a big gulp, hiding my face. Yeah, that wasn't my brightest hour. Ma had torn me a new one.

Still looking down, Wren mutters, "I guess he didn't learn his lesson."

Water spills out of my mouth in a jet spontaneously. Jesus. I wasn't expecting that.

In a second, Callie's laughter fills the room, loud and clear and so intense, it becomes contagious. This kid still laughs at the stupidest things. Including when her big brother makes a mess.

Wren grins, not hidden one bit this time.

"Your brother's really classy, huh?" she asks Callie, but her eyes are on me. Fighting a laugh, I give her an annoyed look. Meanwhile, Callie only laughs harder, which makes Ma and Violet join too.

It's like one's amusement only strengthens the others'. At some point, I'd bet everything I have that they don't even know what they're laughing about anymore, which in itself makes them unable to stop. I can't help but join in, seeing all of them folded in two and brushing off tears.

And then, the most surprising thing happens: a sound I haven't heard in so long joins the mix.

Dad is laughing.

I turn to him, my face becoming serious all of a sudden, although no one notices.

My father has never been very expressive. He would rarely laugh, and only do it when he thought it was really worth it. But since his accident, I hadn't heard him laugh. Not once. I'd noticed faint smiles here and there, but that was it.

And now here he is, laughing at my family and Wren having the time of their lives.

It both breaks my heart and mends it back together. He's still there. He'll never be like he used to, but my father is still in there, able to joke around with us. Maybe he just needed a push.

My gaze moves to Wren, whose laughter has slowly calmed down. As if feeling me, she looks up, her straight white teeth lighting something up inside me.

I'd call hearing my father laughing a holiday miracle, but somehow, I know it's a Wren miracle. There's something about her that I can't explain, but which acts as a glue in my family. Holding us up, and eventually bringing all of us back to our true selves.

She's pure magic.

* * *

I've rarely been this full.

We ate and ate and ate, for hours on end. Ma cooked *pollo asado, pastelón de plátano maduro, ensalada rusa, pastelitos,* and *pasteles en hoja*. It was a real feast, and not only was I happy to eat it, but I loved seeing Wren experience it all for the first time. Plus, Ma sprinkled Dominican traditions throughout the night, like putting her old broom out the door to throw it away tomorrow and hanging twelve grapes outside the house. In the Dominican Republic, she would've spent the night—the party going strong until dawn—with her big family, but in the States, she only has us. She doesn't seem too sad about it, at least. Plus, she has three extra guests this year, which I can see makes her even happier.

Everyone is dancing. It's ten to midnight, and for the past hour, we've been playing Latin music and moving our bodies to it. Everyone save for Callie has their glass of *ponche,* which has been refilled multiple times throughout the night. Callie is currently holding Wren by the hand, twirling her around, which seems silly given their heights. However, Wren looks so much more comfortable dancing today. I don't know if it's that she knows us better or that she's had alcohol or that I'm not the one pressed close to her like last time, but she seems to be having a lot of fun.

I am too.

Next to them, Violet has her back stuck to Will's front, both moving their hips to the music. His head full of black curls is bent over her shoulder, and when he whispers something into her ear, she bursts out in giggles, a blush covering her cheeks. They don't notice me watching. I have a feeling when they're together, they don't see anyone else. I was present when they got married on the beach next to the house they currently live in, and I'd rarely seen two happier people.

To my right, Dad is leaning over his new cane and swaying with Ma, who's hugging him tight. They're not dancing to the music at all, but neither of them seems to care. They're lost in their own world.

Even after all these years, they look like they couldn't love each other more.

That's what I want. Someone there for me through the highs and the lows. Someone who wants to grow old with me. Someone who won't give up on me, just like Ma never gave up on Dad and Will never gave up on Violet.

I don't know why my eyes roam in the Wren's direction, but they do. However, she's not where she was dancing a second ago. Spinning on my heels, I look around the room, but she's nowhere to be seen. Callie doesn't seem to care, eyes closed and moving her hips to the voice of the singer she recently made me discover.

It's almost midnight. We'll soon be turning off the music to count down and celebrate the new year. Where is she?

Leaving my family to their small party, I move through the house, looking for glossy brown hair and a sparkly black dress. I look down at my watch. 11:58. The kitchen is empty, as are the living room and foyer. The bathroom doors are open, and no one is standing in the stairs.

In the end, I find her seated on the floor in a hallway upstairs, her chin resting on her knees, back curved. As soon as she sees me, she gets to her feet.

"What are you doing here?" I ask her.

One of her hands rubs the opposite arm. "I, uh…" She clears her throat. "New Year's is always a weird moment for me. You know, time passing and stuff."

Her words feel like a punch to the solar plexus. That had never even crossed my mind.

"I understand," I say, looking back toward the stairs. "Do you want me to leave you alone?"

She shrugs. "I don't want to keep you away from your family."

That, in Wren's words, means *please don't go*.

Instead of telling her I'm not going anywhere, I say, "Would anything make this easier for you?"

Her lips twist to the side. "I mean, I guess not being alone is something new."

"You like it?" I take a step forward.

My watch glows in the dimness of the hallway. 11:59.

Her throat bobs. She stays silent as she nods slowly.

"Good," I say in a low voice.

The air is thick around us. Downstairs, the music stops, and I hear Will asking Ma in a loud, tipsy tone if she has any party horns, but surprisingly, no one calls me to come join them. As if they know that whatever I'm doing, it's important to me.

And it really is.

Wren's perfume envelops me just like on Christmas night in her apartment as she takes a micro-step closer. Lilacs, and something citrusy. It's addictive. The second I inhale it, I know I want more.

But really, I just want more of her.

Her breathing is getting faster. I can see it from the way her chest rises and falls, the sparkles on her dress making her look like a shooting star.

As I shift forward, her face only a foot away from me, something catches my eye above us. I'd missed it before.

Mistletoe.

A side of my lips curls up. Callie placed mistletoe all across the house when she decorated with Ma a few weeks ago. I'm not sure why. Maybe precisely for this reason.

And it's in that moment I realize I *will* make a move. There's no way I won't. She's here, so fucking beautiful I lose my words when I look at her, her smell and voice and laugh all I can think about. I don't know when I started craving her this much, but now, it's right there in the middle of my brain.

Will was right. She's what I want.

Downstairs, everyone starts calling the countdown, starting from twelve.

Twelve seconds away from starting a new year. From beginning again.

Eleven.

Ten.

While my eyes move from the mistletoe to the woman standing in front of me, hers climb to the branch hanging above us. I wait for her to step back in shock.

Nine.

She doesn't move.

Eight.

I need to make sure I'm not imagining this. Slowly, I lift a hand and tuck a strand of hair behind her ear.

Seven.

She leans against my hand, her skin soft and warm.

Six.

Her eyelids flutter. I'm barely touching her, but her pulse is erratic against my fingers.

Five.

With my thumb, I caress her cheek.

Four.

Is this okay, Wren? Am I making a fool of myself?

Three.

Her eyes open.

Two.

She stares straight at me, but never moves away. There's fire blazing in her gaze.

Fuck the mistletoe. I want to kiss her because she's her.

One.

Below us comes the sound of my loved ones celebrating *Cañonazo*. Neither one of us moves.

In a voice almost too low for me to hear, Wren says, "Happy New Year, Aaron."

I answer by swallowing the last of the space between us and kissing her.

Wren gasps as my lips meet hers, but she soon returns my kiss. Breasts pressed against my chest, she brings a hand against my back, making me hotter than ever before. Her bottom lip is in between both of mine. I bite it softly, and she moans.

Jesus fucking Christ, she feels like heaven.

Taking a step forward, I push her against the wall so I can get more of her. My tongue enters her mouth, and hers immediately connects with it, making my cock twitch in my pants.

Jesus Christ.

My other hand climbs up so I can hold her head firmly, fingers tangling in her hair. With a sound so sexy I could die, Wren presses even closer, taking control of the kiss for a moment. I let her, so fucking glad that she wants this as much as I want her.

Her nails dig into the skin of my back through my shirt as she licks my lips, then plunges her tongue back inside my mouth. She tastes like *ponche* and chocolate and something unique to her. If I thought her smell was addictive, it was because I hadn't tasted her yet.

She breathes fast against me as she presses herself to my groin, and the moment she feels my hardness, she gasps. In response, I grind once against her.

The moan she lets out in answer just about ends me.

Our kiss is relentless, maybe from fear of this moment ending. Because what will it mean then? I don't even want to think about it. The only thing I want on my mind right now is her delicious lips and body fitting perfectly against mine.

Pulling back, I whisper against her lips, "Make me burn, Wren." Then, I bring her mouth back to mine. Tilting her head back, I gain even better access, kissing her deeper, stronger. From there, I lose control, my lips moving from her lips to her neck, leaving a path of wet kisses down the column of her throat.

And that's when the bubble bursts.

In a moment, we go from being tangled into each other to Wren having taken a step away, then another. Her breathing is erratic, hair all over the place, as if she's just been thoroughly kissed. Because she has.

I don't move, only watching her while trying to catch my own breath, which seems impossible right now.

"I'm… This can't be happening. I'm sorry," she says, not quite meeting my gaze.

Before I can ask her what she means, she's gone from the hallway, leaving me panting and empty.

CHAPTER 21

Wren

THE LAST FIFTEEN MINUTES HAVE BEEN FILLED WITH ENDless pacing around the cabin.

I must have done something to piss off someone in another life. Why else would the Universe want to punish me like this?

Throwing Aaron in my path was a cruel thing to do. Giving me something I want more than I can wrap my mind around, but making it forbidden to me. I feel like Eve, looking at the apple, knowing it can only bring bad things but still deciding to have a taste.

It's not like I haven't kissed anyone before. I might have stayed away from men from the moment my mom got sick, but I'd kissed guys in high school before that.

Except that what we just shared wasn't just a kiss. It was *the* kiss. The one that makes you feel like the earth has stopped spinning. The one that makes you wonder how you ever thought kissing someone other than them was nice. The one that could make anyone do something stupid. Case in point: I let it go on for way longer than it actually should have. I kept telling myself, *just another second.*

And now here I am, completely obsessed, knowing full well it can't happen again. Or at least *shouldn't* happen again.

For some people, maybe one kiss would've been enough to fill the well of need, but for me, it's the opposite. I've tasted him, and now I want more. There's this lump in my stomach, this heaviness between my legs, and it's nothing short of uncomfortable, to say the least.

I've rarely felt the need to have sex with someone. Sure, at times I thought it would be nice to share this experience with someone other than myself, but I always thought abstinence would be what's best for everyone. No sex, no feelings. But somehow, Aaron's touch has lit something in me. Something foreign. A desire stronger than anything I've ever felt before. I can't stop replaying the moment in my head. The feel of his lips on mine, of his hands on my body, of his hardness against my belly, is too strong to ignore.

Just as I walk toward the small bathroom in the corner of the cabin, three heavy knocks come from the front door.

Crap.

Of course, it was foolish of me to think we could just sweep this under the rug and act like the kiss didn't happen. And apparently, this needed to be addressed right this moment, regardless of the fact that it's past midnight.

With a sharp exhale, I head for the door. I dug my own grave. Time to own it.

The first thing I see when I open the door is the size of Aaron's pupils, strangely. They're wide, the amber of his irises only a faint circle.

"Hi—"

"What was that?" he interrupts, standing stiffly on the front porch. He doesn't push to come inside, but the seriousness of his voice does all the heavy lifting.

"I..." The words don't come, maybe because they're nonexistent. I can't explain why I kissed him. It was instinctual, and it was also a mistake.

"You can't just *do* that," he says.

My eyes close. "I know, I'm sorry. I promise it won't happen again."

"What won't?" His brows are drawn in confusion.

"The kiss."

"What?" This time, he does take a step forward, and I don't stop him from walking in. We need to address this at some point, so I guess now is as good a moment as any.

"I'm not talking about the kiss, Wren."

It's my turn to be confused.

"You can't just kiss me and leave like it means nothing," he says, taking another step my way. His scent reaches me, and I stop breathing.

He doesn't care that we kissed. He cares that I left.

"Aaron, I—"

My sentence is interrupted by his hand reaching for my cheek, his touch so tender all of a sudden, I feel my heart fall to the floor.

"Don't do this," he says, his soft breath touching my lips. "Don't shut me out." I exhale shakily as he whispers, "Not when I know you want this too."

I swallow, eyelids fluttering. Of course I want this. Who wouldn't, in my position? This man makes me feel things I never thought were possible. He makes me feel beautiful. He gives me warmth. He lights me up.

The delicate press of his lips against my temple makes my legs weak, and all at once, the beautiful promises I made to myself a minute ago to stay away from him fly out the window. Is this even avoidable at this point? My body is in a frenzy. It wants and wants and wants, consequences be damned. I was strong enough to break away from this once, but I don't think I could do it again.

I'm not alone in this. Aaron's heart is beating fast under my hand—one I hadn't even realized I'd placed there.

"What's going on inside that beautiful head?" he whispers.

"A lot," I sigh.

I want him. With the way his body reacted to mine, I daresay he wants me too.

"Don't overthink this, Wren." His nose brushes mine.

"Easy to say."

"Easy to do," he replies, tilting my head up. "I know you're feeling this too. Just let yourself go for once."

Could I simply let go and forget about possible feelings developing? I never did in the past, but is it so crazy to think we could get physical without having emotions involved? Plenty of people do it. It can't be impossible.

God, I can't believe I'm even considering this.

"Just tell me what you're thinking," he pleads on a sigh.

I blink, his gaze on mine centering me in the here and now. "I'm thinking this is the only thing I could offer you."

"Huh?"

"Casual. No falling for each other." My head bobs up and down as I convince myself. "That's my ground rule." I gulp again, feeling my resolve melting under his stare. "Take it or leave it."

A beat passes before he so much as moves. That's not what he was expecting, but it's what I can give him.

"All right," he says.

"All right?"

"Yes, cariño. We're doing this."

That damn nickname. I have no idea what it means, and it drives me crazy. I won't look it up, though. I like wondering about it. Imagining it means something nice.

Before I can respond to his agreement, he grabs my backside and pulls me to him so my body slams into his. I gasp.

Through the window, I spot a flurry of snowflakes falling, a storm brewing. As if we're being warned about this. *Too late.*

Slowly, he leans forward. My lips part as the tension in my body reaches its breaking point.

"Now," he murmurs above my mouth, "can I kiss you?"

The second I nod, he dives in, and I know this was the right decision. The taste of him is exactly what I imagine the minute after jumping off the plane to be like, just before the parachute opens. Pure ecstasy.

Immediately, I climb on my tiptoes and pull at his hair, kissing him harder.

His tongue slowly enters my mouth, and I know I'll never get enough of this. He fits perfectly against me. Our kiss is just as electric as the first, like two tidal waves meeting and forming something even bigger.

I can't breathe. It's so much better than anything I've ever experienced.

And still, I can't help but dive back inside my head. With the way he's kissing and touching me, reducing me to a pile of goo on the ground, he must've done this a thousand times before. Meanwhile, my last kiss goes back to high school and my only sexual experiences have been with myself. This is going to be a disaster. An embarrassing disaster.

Pulling his mouth away, Aaron opens his eyes, frowning. "You're tensing up."

My lips twitch.

His right index finger traces my bottom lip, causing goose bumps to erupt all over my body. "Relax. It's just me."

He's right. He's just him. Aaron. The man who danced with me even when I must've looked like an awkward worm, and who played in the snow with me and my dogs, and who let me look through childhood pictures of him with his mother and sister because he knew it made me smile.

He's the best of them all.

Instead of answering, I put my hands on his chest and kiss *him* first this time. Our tongues tangle, slowly at first, then gaining fire as I wrap my arms around his neck. Aaron's hands climb back to my head, holding me tight as he deepens the kiss, making my stomach fill with a swarm of butterflies.

In one swift movement, Aaron grips the back of my thighs

before lifting me up, as if I'm weightless. Then, he starts walking, never breaking away from our kiss. I don't even know if he's seeing where he's going, but to be honest, at this moment, I couldn't care less. It's so unlike me, to go in blind, both figuratively and literally, but he makes me feel like nothing could be more important than this, right now. His teeth nipping at my bottom lip. His large hands gripping my butt. The sounds he makes when I tug lightly at the roots of his dark hair.

I'm not sure how, but eventually, Aaron drops me on my back on the bed. He's standing in front of it, not moving, simply looking. His gaze is dark, roaming. I'm still dressed, but from the way he's gazing at me, you would think I was completely naked. A large bulge is teasing at the seam of his jeans, making me blink. I feel wetness gathering between my legs, and I squirm on the bed, trying to ease some of the tension. I don't think I've ever wanted anything as much as I want this. Enough to make me forget about all the possible consequences.

Gaze never wavering, Aaron prowls forward before he starts to unzip my dress, going so slow I almost die. Once he's done, I shrug it off, lying down only in my matching black lace lingerie set.

Being this bare in front of someone, I should be embarrassed, but somehow, I'm not.

"Goddamn," he mutters before covering the outline of my bra with kisses. I throw my head back, enjoying every single touch from him. I could never regret this. I know this now. How could I think something that feels this good was a mistake? Dying without having experienced Aaron's lips on my body would've been a sin.

The way he looks at me gives me a confidence I didn't know I had in me. So much that I don't hesitate when I start tugging at the hem of his sweater. He leans forward to help me pull it off him, and then I start kissing down from his pecs to his taut stomach. This man couldn't be hotter if he tried. I knew this before, but this just confirms it.

"Fuck, Wren," he says when my mouth reaches his navel. His words just prime me even more, encouraging me to press wet kisses and lick the line of skin above his pants. A groan booms from his chest.

"Is this okay?" I ask as I continue kissing his chest and belly. I feel like what I'm doing is good, but maybe this isn't quite what he wants from me. And if I want this deal to be worthwhile for him too, then I need to know whether he likes what I'm doing or not.

The moment the words leave my mouth, his gaze burns deeper. Without a word, Aaron grips my hand and leads it to his erection, which seems even harder than it was before.

"Does that answer your question?" he whispers in my ear before he gives my earlobe a soft bite.

"Uh-huh."

Aaron's hands never stop trailing my body, as if he wants to imprint the feel of me in his mind. I can understand the feeling.

"How can you be so perfect?" His nose trails my neck before he starts kissing me between my breasts, then lower. When he reaches my panty line, however, he doesn't stop. His lips press on top of the black lace, where I can feel my pulse increase. Instead of being bent on top of my body, he drops to his knees, then pulls at my legs so I'm hanging on the edge of the bed, his head between my knees as he looks at me like a predator would his prey.

And when he moves forward and gives one slow stroke of his tongue over my panties, so warm and wet, I almost pass out on the spot. I must say something of the sort out loud because he chuckles slowly before repeating the motion. Then he hooks both of his index fingers in my panties and says, "Can I?"

I nod eagerly, but when he doesn't get up and instead starts pressing kisses on top of my center, I lift myself on my elbows and say, "You don't have to do that."

He only flicks his eyes my way with a raised eyebrow.

Cheeks warm, I say, "I thought we'd agreed on something

more...mutually pleasing." My voice climbs at the end, as if I'm asking a question.

"Oh, trust me, this is pleasing me all right." Then, before I have the time to argue, he presses his tongue against my middle, and I know there's no way I can tell him to stop.

His movements are slow at first. As if he's tasting. Teasing.

It's a torture of its own.

I don't think I could ever feel something better than the way Aaron licks me thoroughly as his hands hold my thighs in a tight grip. His stubble scratches my skin, bringing me into sensory overload. I don't ever want to come down.

My breathing comes in pants, and when the flicks of his tongue start to accelerate, I reflexively take a hold on his hair as my back bows.

He hums.

Wetness drips down my thighs as he continues lapping against me, his rhythm now steady. It's so good it's almost painful. Too much. Without realizing it, I start writhing, but he soon presses a large hand on my belly, keeping me in place as the pleasure he gives me only multiplies.

"You're unreal," he whispers, something almost like awe in his voice, before returning to work.

No, *this* is unreal. The wet sounds he makes as he eats me, the way my legs are starting to shake, the grip I know will leave a bruise on my skin.

And when he adds a finger inside me, hitting the perfect spot right away, it brings me to a whole other place.

"Aaron, I..." My thoughts are too scrambled for me to even be able to talk properly. There's nothing on my mind other than this moment. The feel of his finger as it goes in and out of me while his tongue continues working wonders on my middle.

"You gonna come for me, cariño?"

I can only reply a high "uh-huh" before the orgasm hits me

harder than a tsunami. I pulse around Aaron's finger, my hands pulling at his hair as I moan his name, over and over again. It's so good it makes me forget everything else for a moment. I don't know who I am, or who we are as a pair. I just know I want this forever. Aaron never pulls away, continuing to kiss me even as I come down. Once I get too sensitive, though, I need to pull back.

He grins as I do, his lips gleaming. "Sorry. Couldn't stop."

I can only let out a breathless chuckle. I can't believe this just happened. I had my first orgasm with someone else. And it was better than even in my wildest dreams. It's like Aaron didn't need words to know what to do, like it was instinctual for him. As if he'd always known me.

"This was...I..." My thoughts are scrambled. Aaron has just wreaked havoc in my mind.

"I know," he says, as if what I just said made sense to him. Maybe his brain is as messed up as mine right now.

With the stealth of a panther, Aaron gets back up, kissing back up my body until his lips land on mine. Our tongues tangle slowly as one of his hand moves to my breast, which he cups over my bra.

I want it off.

Wriggling on the bed, I unclasp it with one hand as I continue kissing him. The moment it's off, Aaron fingers start playing with my nipples, making me even wetter. I want him. All of him.

While his mouth moves down to suck on one nipple, I start to undo his belt, all the while humming at the sensation. When I finally get the belt off, I unbutton his pants and pull them down his knees. He helps me by taking them off completely, leaving him clad in only his boxer briefs, his erection obvious.

"You want this?" he says, an air of confidence in his voice.

I nod, my hands getting clammy no matter how much I'm trying to will my mind to relax. It's okay if I'm not the best he's ever had. This is Aaron—he won't mind. Plus, it can't be that hard, now, can it? And I'll learn. I'll make it good for him the next time. If he wants a next time.

Sitting up, I tug his black briefs down, freeing his length. Licking my lips, I try to keep my face neutral and not freak out at the size of him.

I must do a bad job at it because, with a smirk, Aaron says, "Don't worry, it'll be fine."

He turns to grab a condom from his wallet, then puts it on his length. When he's done, I pull back so he has space to climb onto the bed.

The sight of him on all fours as he looks at me like I'm the most beautiful thing he's ever seen is…something.

"I think you might be the death of me," he says as he spreads my thighs open, two of his fingers dipping inside me. I moan, then grab his shoulders so he can get closer.

"You sure you want this?" he says once he's settled between my legs.

"Very sure," I say.

His gaze holds mine, and for a moment, it's like we're the only two people in this world, and the earth rotates for us. Then he kisses me, all the while positioning himself with his hand.

And then he's inside me.

My eyes squeeze tighter as he pushes himself further in. I continue kissing him, hoping he won't see my reaction. I try to hold it in, but it's impossible. The sheer size of him feels like he's tearing me in half. I was expecting discomfort, but not a sharp pain like this.

"Whoa, whoa, whoa," he says, suddenly stopping. I don't know if he's all the way in, but I don't see how I could take more than this. "What's wrong?" He pulls back, not completely but enough to make me release a breath of relief.

I shake my head. "Nothing, I'm fine. Go on."

"You're not fine." He lifts a hand and caresses my cheek with his thumb, the touch so tender it almost makes me whimper. Why does he have to be so attentive?

I force a smile to my lips. "I'm telling you, I'm okay."

"Now that smile just proved you're lying." Another brush of his thumb. "You want to try another position?"

"No, let's just keep going," I say, pulling at his back, but he doesn't budge.

"Did you have pain in the past? With, uh, other men?" He continues searching my eyes like he'll find his answer there.

"Uh..." Shit. This is not how it was supposed to go.

"You can tell me," he adds, his voice so warm and calm, it makes me feel terrible for omitting the truth.

"I... I mean..."

A notch forms between his eyebrows. "You *have* had sex with other men before. Right?"

I close my eyes, teeth clenched. How did I ever think this would go unnoticed?

Barely more than a whisper, I say, "I told you I've always avoided getting close to people."

He blinks twice, as if he needs to absorb the words. Then, he says, "Are you kidding me?" Pulling out of me completely, he rests on his knees and adds, "Why didn't you tell me?"

"Because this changes nothing."

"This changes everything!" he snaps, sitting on the side of the bed with his head in between his hands. "We can't do this."

"Why?" I try to mask the hurt in my voice, but I don't think it works.

"Because your first time shouldn't be with someone you only see as a friend. It should be..." He rubs a hand over his forehead as he mutters, "Fuck, how did I not see this? I'm so sorry, Wren."

"I'm the one who didn't tell you." How could he even think to blame himself?

He doesn't answer, so I shift until I'm on my knees next to

him. Then, I place my chin on his shoulder and say, "I want it to be you, Aaron. Please."

He turns to me, face gentle. His lips are pinched as he studies me, so long that I start feeling self-conscious. Maybe I'm making him feel like he needs to do this.

"If you don't want to…"

"If I don't want to?" He laughs then, his smile still successful in taking my breath away. "Wren, on what planet do you live?"

I'm the one who has nothing to say now.

Aaron turns to me and presses a soft kiss on my lips. "Are you a hundred percent sure?"

"Yes," I say without a single moment of doubt.

His jaw shifts before he says, "All right." Leaning down, he licks my middle again, making me even wetter. When I squirm, he comes back up. "We'll try to make it as easy as possible, okay? And I need you to tell me to stop if you're in pain. Those are *my* conditions. Do you promise?"

I grin, an honest one this time. "I promise."

"Good." Slowly, he shifts on his back and says, "Let's try with you on top. This way you'll be able to control the depth."

His length is back to being big and hard, ready for me. I didn't expect to do it like this, but maybe he's right and it'll feel better like that. Nodding, I move forward and straddle him.

Eyes on me, he takes one of my hands in his, interlacing our fingers together before he gives me an encouraging squeeze.

Slowly, so slowly, I sink down on his length.

I'm about halfway down when I wince, the discomfort still there. Aaron's free hand automatically lands on my hip, pulling me up so I don't take him deeper.

I was right about this. It was always going to be with him or no one else.

With his fingers digging into my skin, I sink back down, able to take a little more this time before coming back up. I repeat the movement again and again, the discomfort easing the more I move on him.

"You're doing so good," Aaron says, gaze never wavering. In response, I take more of him. He's almost all the way inside now, and by the way he's clenching his jaw, I'd say he's liking it as much as I am. Yes, there is still some pain, but I'm also starting to see how this could feel really, *really* good once I'm more used to it.

I ride him up and down again, until finally, I take him all the way in. My body stills, giving myself a moment to adjust to the stretch of him.

"Fuck," Aaron groans, his eyelids squeezing shut. "¿Cómo podría resistirme a ti?"

"English, please."

He snickers. "Just saying this feels amazing."

A surge of pride fills my chest. This isn't just for me. He likes it too.

I return to moving on top of him, his hand still guiding me. The discomfort is moving to the back of my mind, leaving only pleasure.

"I won't be able to hold off for long," he says through gritted teeth as he lets go of my hand to cup one of my breasts, thumb flicking the bud.

His words give me even more confidence, so much that I start riding him faster, trying to take hints from the sounds he makes or the expressions he gives me to know what he prefers.

Eventually, his fingers tighten on my skin, and he closes his eyes as he orgasms, soft groans leaving his mouth. I continue moving until I feel him soften inside. Then, I slowly climb off and lay next to him, languid.

"Jesus, Wren," Aaron croaks, eyes still closed.

I laugh as I put a hand on his chest. Somehow, that simple movement feels almost too intimate, which is crazy considering what we just did.

"Thank you," I whisper.

He turns to me, face so serious it scares me for an instant. "I'm the one who should thank you." There isn't a trace of a smile on his lips.

I bite my lip.

This is much more than just physical pleasure. Preventing my feelings from growing will be near impossible, being this close to him, feeling him like this.

But now that I've tasted this, I know I could never back down, not even if I wanted to.

CHAPTER 22

Aaron

"HEY, WHAT'S UP WITH YOU?"

I lift my head to find Finn standing in front of me, his fists on his hips. A black wool hat covers his buzz cut, the rest of his face bitten red by the cold.

"Huh?"

With a dip of his head, he says, "You've been looking at that trap for the past five minutes."

"Oh." He's right. I haven't even installed it properly.

Since Christmas season has come and gone, I've spent most of my time inside, working on accounting bullshit. For a week, I've only been looking at numbers after numbers. I've never been a fan of this type of work, so yesterday, I went on a walk, hoping it would clear my mind, and in some part of the woods, I found some of our trees had had their bark ruined with scratches and holes, despite the plastic protectors we put on last October. Exactly what it might look like if we had a squirrel problem. It might not seem like a big deal, but when people pay a nice amount for our products, we like to give them trees that look perfect.

So, I called Finn and asked him if he'd come help me set up some traps today. He could've done it alone—it's his job to be on the field during winter season—but I couldn't stand staying inside with more sets of numbers for another day, so I joined him.

I return to my trap installation, trying to keep my mind focused for once. However, the snow crunching beside me tells me Finn hasn't moved.

"So?" he repeats once I'm done and am back on my feet.

Wiping the snow off my knees, I say, "So what?"

"So, what's up with you, dumbass?"

"Nothing," I answer as I grab another trap and walk away to install it somewhere else. I need to work on a better poker face. Finn will never let me off the hook if he can always tell when I'm conflicted.

"Oh, don't feed me that bullshit." He follows behind me.

I sigh.

When I don't answer, he says, "It's about her, isn't it?"

Eyes closing, I stop in my tracks.

Yes, this is about her. When has anything *not* been about her? It's like I can't remember a time when she didn't occupy my every thought. When I woke up in the morning and my first thought wasn't, *I hope I see Wren today.*

But now, it's even more difficult than before. Because now I got to feel her.

I got to kiss her, to inhale her moans and swallow her cries. And fuck me, I can't take my mind away from it. Her taste is imprinted in my head.

It's been three days since we had sex, and I haven't heard from her yet. I haven't texted her either. She needs to know that if she wants something more, she'll need to be the one to make a move. I wouldn't want her to feel pressured to see me again, especially after what I did.

God, I still can't believe Saturday happened. That she gave me this part of herself, and that I actually accepted it. She deserved so much better for a first time. She deserved for the guy she was with to actually know it was her first time, *goddammit.* But how was I supposed to know? With a girl so fearless, so beautiful, so sharp as Wren, it never even occurred to me that she might not have done this before, especially once she suggested we start casually fucking.

And yet, it had happened. She'd kept silent as I entered her, even though she was in pain. If I'd known, I would've been so much gentler.

God, I'd rarely hated myself that much.

I was serious when I pulled away and said we shouldn't do this. It was a moment that should've been shared with someone she loved. That's the way things should be for everyone, man or woman. But then she said she wanted it to be me. *Me*. I might be a bastard, because when she said those words, I knew there was no way I wasn't going to give her everything she wanted. Not when I wanted her more than I'd ever wanted anyone, and certainly not when she said my name with so much trust.

She has me wrapped around her finger, and I don't even think she realizes it.

Why else would I have agreed to enter a casual relationship when being her *friend* is the last thing I want? After Amber, I'd sworn to myself I'd only get attached to someone who wanted the real deal with me, but that was before I met Wren. She's a tough one to crack, and I realized something when she offered something casual: it might be the key to her heart. If we started sleeping together, then maybe I could get her to start caring for me, and then she'd realize the two of us together makes sense. She might see that her genetic heritage doesn't change anything for me. So, I agreed to it, even though I want more. So much more.

But I'm not about to tell all that to Finn. Instead, I say, "Whatever."

A burst of laughter resonates behind me as I continue walking. "Really? You're actually not going to say anything?"

"Yup."

"You're no fun," my best friend says.

"Tough luck," I say, blowing him a kiss over my shoulder.

His eyes narrow before a smirk slowly curls his lips.

Ah, shit.

"If I can't get any information from you, then I'll need to go ask someone else. So you better tell me everything before I go ask someone what's up with the two of you."

I stop walking.

With a rub of his chin, he says, "I could call Will. Surely he knows something."

My jaw clenches. I knew I should never have introduced those two.

His eyes widen in amusement. "Or I could walk a few steps and go ask your mom."

"You wouldn't."

"Wanna bet?"

I really need to find new friends.

"Fine," I admit. "We may have slept together once."

He gasps like a schoolgirl before getting up and slapping his hands together. "Ha! I knew it!" With a quick stride, he joins me before punching my shoulder.

"Ow!"

"And you weren't going to tell me? I'm hurt."

I roll my eyes.

"So?" He waggles his eyebrows. "How was it?"

"It was good." I turn and get back to my trap installing so he doesn't try to wring any more out of me. Good doesn't even cover how it was. I don't think a word could do justice to what it felt like to be with her in that way, even if I had to leave afterward when all I wanted to do was stay in bed with her.

And there's no way I'm telling Finn about it being Wren's first time. That's something that's purely between her and I. For some reason, I got lucky enough for her to decide to share this moment with me, so there's no way I'm ruining it by telling Finn.

"Just good? That's it?"

I throw a snowball at him. "Stop fishing for details. You're not getting any."

"Wow. She got you all secretive and shit. This is serious." He grins.

"Far from it," I mutter as I finish setting up my trap and move to another.

"What does that mean?"

"Since when are you so nosy?"

"Humor me."

I feel like rolling my eyes again, but I don't. This, I could actually use someone to talk about with.

Grunting as I pull the trap in the right position, I say, "She suggested that we enter a friends-with-benefits kind of arrangement." At least that's what I think she meant.

"Whoa. Wasn't expecting that."

Me neither, Finn. Me neither.

"But didn't you say you were against a casual fuck after Amber?"

"I didn't have much choice in the matter." If I did, I'd never have suggested something like that. "It's what she offered, so I took it."

"And you're gonna be able to keep things casual?" Finn isn't working one bit, now only watching me, arms crossed.

I clear my throat. "She said that her only condition for us to do this thing was that we keep feelings out of it."

"Oh, man, you're so fucked."

I lift an eyebrow at him.

"You're not as subtle as you like to think you are," he gives as an answer to my unspoken question. That's the second time someone's told me something like that, and I don't like it.

Not answering, I return my attention to my job.

A few moments pass where Finn finishes installing another trap. Then he comes back to me and says, "Seriously, though. You think you'll be okay?"

My jaw twitches. "I hope I'll be." This is as honest as I can get.

I can't speak the entire truth out loud. That I'm starting to see this might've been a mistake. If this continues, and I realize my gamble was wrong and she'll never develop feelings for me, then I'll be at an impasse. Because there's no way I'll get over her. Not if I get to spend more times like the one we shared in the cabin. Even if we don't repeat the experience, I don't think I could ever forget about the night we shared.

Look at me. Three days without a text, and I'm already getting lost in thoughts of her every chance I get.

Finn probably sees something in my face that tells him I can't speak about this anymore because he changes subjects.

"How's your dad?"

For once, I'm happy to talk about him.

"He's okay. Ma's with him at physical therapy right now." Testing the solidity of the trap, I add, "He's improving a lot." It's clearly made him happy to regain some motion. Sometimes, he's able to make a few steps without his walker.

"That's great."

With this final trap put in place, I turn to Finn and say, "All done?"

"Think so, yeah."

We start back toward the house and the garage in front of which Finn parked. The farm is at its quietest after Christmas, but when we exit the forest, I spot two people on the land. Squinting, I see it's Dad walking around the driveway, Ma by his side.

"He looks good," Finn says.

"Yeah." I grin as I watch him. It's been a wild ride, but we've passed through the worst of it. "I caught him laughing on New Year's."

"Really?" Finn says before wrapping an arm around my shoulders. "I'm happy to hear that, man."

I don't mention to him that I know part of it is because Wren was there and changed the dynamic of our time at home, but it's all I can think of.

"If he's that improved, you think he might decide to come back to work after all?" Finn asks.

"Nah. And even if he physically could, I wouldn't want him to handle that kind of stress."

His lips purse. "I wish you'd—"

Finn's words are interrupted by my phone ringing. I pick it up, finding Wren's name on my phone. She's Facetiming me.

"Wait a second, Finn."

My pulse skyrockets as I take the call, but just as Wren's face pulls onto the screen, I feel my phone slipping out of my hands.

"Hello, there," Finn says, smiling wickedly at Wren.

"Finn," I hiss, trying to steal back the phone, but he takes a step back.

"Oh, huh..." Wren starts. I can picture the little notch between her brows as she tries to figure out stuff. "I'm sorry, I thought I'd called Aaron."

"You did," Finn says, flicking the camera my way for a second before returning it his way.

This is useless. I give up trying to get my phone back, instead glaring at Finn with my hands on my hips. He better not say something stupid.

"Oh," Wren repeats. After clearing her throat, she says, "Well, you two must be busy, so—"

"Not at all," Finn says, sending a shit-eating grin my way. I answer with a middle finger up. "I was just telling our dear Aaron how crazy it is to give up his life to take on his family's work. We've been working for an hour, and I don't think he's smiled once."

Okay, that's enough.

Taking him by surprise, I push his shoulder so he drops the phone in the snow. We throw ourselves on it like two hyenas, but in the end, I come up winning.

"Hey," I say, slightly breathless. "Sorry about that."

God, it feels good to see her. To know she called.

"No, that actually sounded important," she says, eyebrows furrowed just like I'd imagined. "I'll leave you to it and call you later, okay?"

"No, it's—"

The call ends before I get to say anything else.

My heels dig in the ground as I spin slowly toward Finn.

"I will kill you."

He doesn't even have the decency to appear remorseful. "She seemed to be agreeing with me."

I blink.

"You have three seconds to run," I deadpan.

Grinning, he obliges.

I count to two until I start running, but just as I take my first step, my phone pings.

The air is particularly cold and dry today. Enough to enter my lungs and make me feel like I'm inhaling pure ice. I felt bad for having asked Finn to come work outside today—before he betrayed me, that is.

And yet, the moment I hear the notification on my phone, I remove my gloves to grab it again, frozen fingers be damned.

Wren: Sorry about that. I shouldn't have called before texting.

Me: No, don't worry about it!

Me: Was there anything you wanted to talk about?

A pause.

Wren: Nothing important. Just wanted to know if you wanted to come to my place tomorrow night after work?

Another text comes in.

Wren: :)

Not important, my ass.

The pinch of the wind on my skin doesn't even bother me. Not when it's to answer that kind of text.

Yep. Truly fucked.

CHAPTER 23

Wren

Wow.

I went wrong somewhere in my life. Because why in the world did I decide to deprive myself of this feeling?

Aaron is lying next to me in my bed, chuckling as he catches his breath. "That good?"

"Huh?" I'm in a daze. I've rarely felt this blissful.

"You're smiling at the ceiling. I'm guessing that means I did something right."

Shifting to my side so I face him, I say, "You know you did."

The smile he gives me is larger than the sun.

Reflexively, I lean forward and brush my lips against his. I usually try to keep kisses to a minimum when we're not actively having sex, just to make sure we don't act like we're in a relationship, but he looks so good now. So familiar. I can't help it.

When I move away, Aaron doesn't let me. Instead, he puts his arms around my back and spins me so I'm on top of him. I can feel his hardening length under me.

He's unstoppable.

It's been three weeks since we started sleeping together, and to say it hasn't been incredible would be a lie. I never thought I could like it this much, yet now, I feel addicted to him. Maybe it would've been like this with anyone else, though I doubt it. There's something about Aaron that makes me feel so at ease to try new things and to express myself.

I'm drowning in him.

But I also try to refrain myself from texting him all the time. If it was only up to me, I'd see him every day, but this could lead to expectations that would then lead us somewhere I don't want to go, so sometimes I just have to wait until he texts me first.

I usually don't have to wait long.

Slowly pulling away from my lips, Aaron whispers, "I can't get enough." His hands are cupping my butt, calloused fingers against soft skin.

"Likewise." He's shown me ways to pleasure I didn't even know existed.

Suddenly, the bed dips under a new weight at our feet. Spinning off Aaron, I sit up to find Molly now nestled on my bedspread against Aaron's legs.

Gasping, I tell her, "You know you're not allowed to get on the bed." I turn to Aaron. "Did you let her up while I was in the shower?"

He gives me a guilty smile. "Maybe?"

I let myself fall back against pillows. "It's too late, then. She'll never take no for an answer anymore."

"Stubborn like her mother?"

"It's always run in the family," I answer truthfully. My mom has the same trait. My grandpa too. Aqidah's probably the worst of us.

Aaron shifts so his head is propped on his hand. "Is your mom similar to you?"

My gaze shifts to the fan on the ceiling. "In some ways, yes."

"I wish I could meet her."

My head shakes left and right automatically. "That would be a very bad idea." For more reasons than I could count. It would be way too much. Not at all keeping a safe distance between us. Plus, I can only imagine how traumatized he'd be if she reacted to him the way she does to me. Maybe he'd be lucky and she'd like him more than her daughter, but I wouldn't risk it.

"Tell me about her then?" He says it like a question. Like he'd really like to know, but is still giving me the choice. It's something he does often. Giving me the final say on how things will happen, even if he already has something in mind.

I puff my cheeks before letting the air out. Talking about my mom to someone other than her caregivers is always a bittersweet thing. But it's been a long time since I have, and I don't want to feel like the memory of the *real* her is slipping away. It'll happen eventually, but I want to hold it off as long as possible.

"She is...hard to approach. Always has been." Her diagnosis has only made things worse.

Aaron cocks an eyebrow.

"Don't get me wrong, I love her, and she was pretty much my whole life for a long, long time, but she was so...unhappy, sometimes."

Fingers land on my arm, stroking it up and down. I don't even think Aaron realizes he's doing it.

"What do you mean?" he asks.

I scratch my head with my free arm. "Even before she got AD, she was so bitter about life. She had all these things happen to her, and she never recovered. She never wanted kids, and all of a sudden, she had me by herself. She never ended up getting the degree she wanted. She worked at a place she hated for most of her life to pay the bills. And then her dad developed dementia, and she had to take care of him." The simple contact of Aaron's fingers on my arm tethers me to the moment. Allowing me to face these facts for what they are: facts.

I pull my lips to the side. "She tried her best with me. We weren't that close, but I knew she loved me. And even then, it was clear there was always this part of her that was resentful of this life. I think the happiest I ever saw her was actually when she started forgetting who she was."

That's such a sad statement to make, embarrassing, even, but I still let it out.

"And do you feel the same way as her?" Aaron asks, focused on me and only me. There's no judgment in his voice. It's an honest question he has.

I take a moment to think about this before I answer. It's not a simple yes or no question. It's one that appears simple, yet is anything but.

Finally, I shake my head. "No, I don't think I do. I'm not resentful of my life. It is what it is, and I made good with what I was handed, I think."

Aaron stays silent for such a long time, I feel like he's having some kind of blackout moment. But just as I'm about to ask him if he's all right, he leans forward and kisses me. And again, I can't resist kissing him back.

His tongue enters my mouth, slowly and purposefully, as he gently cups my head to bring me closer. I put a hand on his pecs, then slide it down, my nails barely scratching his skin. He groans.

He might now know ways to make me go out of my mind, but I've also found a thing or two that works for him.

Just as my hand reaches his navel under the covers and he groans again, a tongue that doesn't feel nearly as good licks my chin, making me pull away. Molly isn't only jumping on the bed now, apparently. She also does her best to keep me from getting what I want.

"Molly, down!" I say as I point toward the floor, unable to stop myself from laughing. She's so cute, with her tail wagging like she just wants to cuddle too. I pet her head before ordering her down again.

"Perro maldito," Aaron grunts as he runs a hand through his hair.

"What did you say?" I say with a poke of his chest.

He smirks. "Nothing."

I follow the track of his eyes, which land on my naked breasts. It's so strange, that I'm not uncomfortable one bit from being this exposed in front of him. Maybe it's that I know he wouldn't judge me, no matter what he was seeing. Or maybe it's the fact that every look is filled with reverence.

"I wish I could understand you when you speak Spanish."

His gaze lifts back to mine, twinkling. "Do you, now?"

My chin dips. "I never know whether you're speaking behind my back when you talk with your family. Can you imagine the stress?"

Velvety laughter fills the room. "Don't worry, cariño. We've never spoken bad of you." With a lift of his hand, he adds, "Scout's honor."

"Still. I always want to know what's going on."

"Trust me, I know that."

I swat him with the back of my hand, which makes him laugh.

When he's recovered his cool, he says, "I could teach you, if you wanted."

"You would?"

"Sure."

I clap my hands once. "Okay, where do we start?"

"Now?"

I nod eagerly.

"Okay, then, how about the basics?" he says.

I frown. "That's boring. It's going to take too long." Grabbing a pillow and putting it in front of my chest so I can lean my chin on it, I say, "Just tell me something and then tell me what it means." I've never been patient with languages. As much as I can read for hours at the office without batting an eye, I don't like having to start something from scratch. I want to know it all right away.

I wait for him to give me a sentence, but like earlier, he only observes me for a while. When I start feeling scrutinized, I touch my hair to make sure I don't have crazy bedhead. "What?" I say, chuckling.

He shakes his head, then says, "Nunca me habia sentido asi por alguien."

I repeat the words, which makes the corners of his lips tilt up. I probably destroyed the entire sentence with my pronunciation, but he doesn't tease me about it, so I take it as a win.

"What does it mean?" I say.

"Just…" His throat bobs. "We should watch a movie or something."

"Oh. That's what you said?"

He nods. I don't know why, but something in his face has changed. As if he doesn't feel like teaching me Spanish right now.

"What kind of movie are we talking about?" I ask.

"Whatever you want."

"You're giving me free rein? Really?"

He nods again, his traits soft in the moonlight coming from the window next to my bed.

I hesitate for a second, but then kill the doubts inside my head. We already watched a movie together on Christmas night, and it was more than fine. Totally platonic. It's not something exclusive to romantic relationships. As long as we don't cuddle, it's fine.

Teasing his leg with my big toe under the covers, I say, "You like horror movies?"

"Hate them," he answers.

"Really? Why?"

"Being so tense I can't move is not my thing. Especially when the movies involve evil dolls."

Hand on my heart, I say, "But those are the best kind."

"Then we can watch that."

"You sure? You won't wake up my neighbors with your screams?"

He smirks. "Will you still love me if I do?"

I freeze. He freezes.

"I mean… You know what I mean," he says, stuttering.

I force a smile. "Don't worry about it." A simple slip of the tongue. It happens. With a clear of my throat, I say, "How about a compromise and we skip the evil doll for a mass murderer?"

Seemingly as happy about the change of subject as I am, Aaron says, "Sounds like a plan."

CHAPTER 24

Aaron

"WREN?" I CALL AS I ENTER THE KITCHEN OF MY parents' place.

"In here!"

The sound comes from my mother's large pantry, so I follow it and find Wren on her tippy toes, arms stretched up to grab something on a high shelf.

"You okay in there?" I ask, leaning against the wall.

"Fine. Just trying to reach the rice cooker."

Ma decided to organize a dinner party tonight to celebrate Dad's birthday, and without asking me, she invited Wren. I don't think she's aware of what's going on between her and I because knowing my mother, she would've asked me about it already if she suspected something. Wren agreed to come and offered to help cook dinner.

"Hm," I answer, smirking.

With a spin, she squints at me. "Of course, don't offer your help. I don't look like I'm struggling at all."

A smirk climbs up my lips. "Oh, cariño, you just had to ask."

She scoffs, but I still catch the hint of a smile on her lips.

Pushing off the door, I walk to her, then mold the front of my body to her back. Her breath catches in her throat, so loud I can hear it.

Teasing my nose on the side of her throat, I whisper, "Aren't you going to say please?"

With a shaky exhale, she mumbles, "P-please."

With one arm caging her against the shelves, I put a hand on her belly, letting it slowly drift down. "Please what?" The last word comes out on her skin as I kiss her neck, then her shoulder. Her head bobs to the left to give me easier access. I don't even think she realizes she does it, but every time I step closer to her, she adjusts her body so it's easier for me to touch it.

It drives me fucking crazy.

"Please, help me…pick up the rice cooker," she finishes, her voice airy.

"With pleasure." I lift the hand leaned against the shelf to grab what she came here to get, but keep my other hand on her, fingers dipping slowly into her jeans. She gasps. The sound alone makes me hard as a rock.

"Is that all you want?" I ask as two of my digits graze her lips, already wet. I clench my jaw as I start rubbing her slowly. In response, she pushes her ass against my cock, making me groan.

"Maybe I want something else," she whispers, writhing against my fingers. So perfect.

And that's when we hear, "Aarón? Wren?"

Fuck me.

My mother's voice isn't coming from far away, but from the sound of it, she's not in the kitchen yet.

Wren shifts to move away, but I don't remove my hands from her pants. Why not thrill her, just a little.

"Hush," I whisper in her ear as I dip a finger into her wet pussy. She gasps, and I shush her again.

"Aaron…"

"Where are you guys?" Ma repeats, louder this time. Closer.

Wren tells me that we need to go, even though her body tells me otherwise. But I'm afraid this can't go on for much longer, unless I want my mother to find me fingering our ex-lawyer in our pantry.

Finally, I remove my finger from inside Wren. She sighs—in

relief or disappointment, I don't know. I suck on my finger to get all the taste of her I can get, then whisper, "This isn't over."

She turns around, facing me now, and the look in her eyes tells me exactly what I hoped she was thinking: *I hope not.*

* * *

"This tastes amazing," Wren says as she takes a bite of *albóndigas guisadas*. After we got out of the closet with the rice cooker and a bag of rice, Wren helped Ma cook the meal, but I guess she didn't try to steal a bite while cooking. Of course she didn't. She's way too in control of herself for that.

"Thank you," Ma says as Dad hums beside her, eating eagerly. His mood has been great in the past few weeks. I don't know whether the legal case being closed helped him or whether it's his physical rehabilitation making him feel better, but the progress is undeniable. He still can't pronounce more than the few words he's gotten a handle on with his speech language pathologist, but I need to focus on the positives, so that's what I'm doing.

"You'll be able to make it too, now," Ma tells Wren.

"Hopefully I'll remember everything."

"Well, if not, you can just call me." Ma looks my way. "Or Aarón. He's been watching me cook this since he was a kid."

Was this supposed to mean something?

Wren nods before digging in again. While her mouth is still full, she stops chewing all of a sudden, grabbing her phone from her pocket. When she looks at the screen, she swallows forcefully, then declines the call.

"You can take it, if you want," I whisper.

"No, it's fine."

"Come on, it's okay," I insist. She should feel as comfortable here as if she were home. At least that's what I want for her.

She eyes me for a moment before getting up. "I'm so sorry,

I'll be right back," she tells the rest of the family. We all tell her it's fine before she disappears down the hall.

"Who is it?" Callie asks beside me, her mouth full.

"How would I know?" I answer.

It's the truth. While we might have been sleeping together for the past month, that's all it's been. At least technically. Sure, she has opened up from time to time, but there's still so much about her she keeps hidden.

We eat in silence until Wren comes back a few minutes later and sits down at the table.

"Sorry again," she says before grabbing her fork.

"Do you have a boyfriend?" my sneaky sister asks without a warning.

"Callie!" Ma bellows. I should say something too, but my thoughts freeze for a moment. Or more like catch fire. The thought of her with another man makes me feel like I'm swallowing pure lava.

"It's fine," Wren says. I'm not sure whether I imagine it, but I think her eyes flit my way before she returns her attention to Callie. "No, I don't have a boyfriend. That was just my cousin."

Huh. I thought she didn't have any family left apart from her mom. Why didn't she spend the holidays with her?

Callie tilts her head. "What's her name?"

I snicker. My sister is such a gossip. Not with everyone, though. She only gets curious about the lives of people she likes.

"Aqidah."

Callie's brows furrow before Wren adds, "Her mom's Pakistani."

Didn't know that either. It's like outside of her place or mine or the farm, I don't know who she is.

I also have no idea if I ever will.

"Is she your age?" I ask softly.

"A little older." Wren picks up her glass of water and takes a huge gulp.

Clearly she doesn't particularly want to talk about it, but the curious side of me takes over. "Did she have anything important to tell you?" Wren cocks her head, so I add, "I mean, I've never heard you take a call from her before." My voice is low enough that others can't hear.

"She, um, wanted to invite me to her and her husband's ten-year anniversary party."

"So she's really old, then," Callie says, not a bit ashamed of her eavesdropping.

Ma laughs. "That's not insulting at all."

"When is it?" I ask Wren.

"In two weeks." She shakes her head. "But I'm not going."

"Why not?" Ma asks. Another one who loves getting invested in other people's business.

Wren shrugs. "Oh, you know, we're just not that close." She looks at me again, and I see right away there's more to the story than what she's letting on. Under her breath, she whispers, "We have different views on...things."

By the seriousness in her expression, I assume this has something to do with their shared heredity.

"It might be fun," Ma says, unaware of what Wren just said. "If you don't want to go alone, Aaron could go with you." She side-eyes me.

Okay, she's definitely figured something out. I don't know why she hasn't brought it up with me, but it probably won't be long now.

"No, no, don't worry about it," Wren says before taking another bite. Ma shrugs and does the same.

When everyone's attention has drifted to Callie's crush from school—which makes Dad's eyes bulge out of his sockets—I lean toward Wren and whisper, "If you want to go, I really could go with you, you know."

She frowns. "You're already coming with me tomorrow. That's enough."

Right. Tomorrow. For her yearly appointment with her neurologist.

Last week, when she mentioned it, she tried to sound casual, but it was clear she was dreading it. Her voice even became shaky when I asked her what kind of appointment it was. So, I offered to drive her there. Obviously, she would fight me on this, so I told her I was just worried about her driving if ever it didn't go well. If I'd told her I only wanted to be there for her, she would have freaked out. She normally would've freaked out only with the offer to drive her somewhere, but she didn't, which gave me an even bigger indication that she needed me there with her.

"So?" I say, nudging her thigh with my knee under the table. "I don't mind."

"You don't have to."

"I know. But I want to. Big difference." To be frank, I don't care one bit about her cousin, but I never pass on an opportunity to spend time with Wren, especially if it's for something that's important to her.

Lips pinched, she watches me for a second before muttering, "We'll see."

I guess that was as good as I was going to get.

* * *

"Thank you for dinner, it was absolutely amazing," Wren tells my mother before turning to my father. "And happy birthday again, Dennis."

He opens his mouth as if to thank her, but the only word that comes out is, "Huh..."

She smiles at him and nods. Some things don't need words to be conveyed.

With a wave, Dad leaves toward their bedroom, Ma in tow.

Wren's supposed to be sleeping in the cabin tonight because it's too late for her to drive back to the city. The dogs are currently waiting there. Obviously, I'll join them later, once everyone is asleep. Can't say I'm a fan of sneaking out like a teenager, but I don't have much of a choice.

When they're finally out of earshot, I grab Wren's hips and say, "Guess that leaves just the two of us."

She lifts her brows. "Whatever will we do with ourselves?"

"Got a few ideas." I kiss her softly. Tenderly. "How about a hot tub?"

"Hot tub? Since when do you have a hot tub?"

"Since forever. You just were never invited."

She gasps, then pushes my chest. I laugh.

"Sorry to tell you, though, but I don't have a bathing suit." Her beautiful lips form a pout.

"Who said you had to wear one?"

"Aaron!" she whisper-hisses while looking left and right, as if someone could suddenly hear her. "Your family's here."

"So what? They're in bed. And even if they get up, their windows point toward the front of the house, not the back."

She doesn't seem convinced.

"Come on, cariño. Live a little."

After a moment of hesitation, she says, "Fine."

I smile grandly, then kiss her. Hard. When I pull back, I grab her hand and say, "Okay, come on."

We pass by the laundry room, where I grab two towels, then lead her out the back door.

"What about shoes?" she asks.

"No time. Just run." Then, I follow my own command, her feet padding behind me. She shrieks at the cold, but I don't stop, no matter how much the soles of my feet are burning from the snow.

When we reach the tub, I jump from one foot to the other,

getting undressed as fast as I can. Wren watches me for a second before imitating me, as if she's too cold to back down now.

Even though I'm naked much before her, I wait for her to be ready before getting inside.

The sigh we release as we dip into the hot water is one of pure bliss.

"God, that feels good," Wren says with her eyes closed, her feet nudging my thighs.

"See? Taking risks can pay off sometimes." I try not to sound like my words have a second meaning.

"Tell that to the third-degree burns on the bottom of my feet."

"Now you're just being dramatic."

"Am not."

I slide closer to her, my skin now burning for a completely different reason. "Guess I'll just need to make it worth it now." Under the bubbles of the jets, I let my hand wander between her thighs.

She inhales sharply. "What are you doing?"

"If I remember correctly, I said that what we started earlier today wasn't over."

"And you want to—" Gasp. "—do this here?"

"Why not?" I kneel in front of her, my thumb slowly stroking her clit as my other hand plays with her breasts.

"I…" She never finishes her sentence as her eyes roll back and her lips part. I love seeing her like this. Abandoning herself.

"Shh." I continue rubbing her with a rhythm I've come to learn drives her wild. "Stop thinking. It's just you and me." My cock is hard as ever as I look at her chest coming out of the water, dripping wet as she pants.

"Aaron," she sighs.

"I'm here," I say, kissing her neck, her chin, her ear. "I'm right here." Lower, I add, "Always." Then, I push one finger inside her, and right away, I can feel she's close.

Pumping slowly in and out, I lick her nipples, pebbled under the cold air. Our faces should be cold, exposed to the January air, but blood is rushing everywhere in my body. Wren's cheeks are pink, the little puffs of air she let out condensing on top of her lips.

"I'll never get enough of this," I say before claiming her lips and kissing her deep and strong. My tongue tangles with hers while her fingers pull at my hair.

I keep pumping inside her and circling her clit, and it only takes a minute before she pulls even harder on my hair, moaning and gasping into my mouth as she clamps around my fingers, a feeling I could never get enough of.

When she finally comes down from her orgasm, I pull my fingers out and tuck some hair that fell from her tight bun behind her ear.

"Good?"

"Good," she answers, still not completely back to her right state of mind. Her eyes are reflecting the twinkling lights from the trees behind us, but also seem to be shining from within.

"Now," she says as she shifts so she's straddling me, "your turn."

"Uh uh."

"What?"

I rub her hips with the pads of my thumbs. "Tonight was just about you."

"Why?" She cocks her head. "That's not fair."

"Yes, it is." I gave a peck on her lips. "When are you going to realize that making you happy makes *me* happy?"

I'm afraid that she's going to think I'm too much, but instead, she blinks and grins softly. "You're too good for me."

"Wren," I say as a gush of wind drags snow around us, shining in the moonlight. "Nothing could be too good for you."

CHAPTER 25

Wren

"YOU OKAY?"

The leather of the chair I'm sitting on squeaks as I turn toward Aaron. "Huh?" I might've been lost in thoughts for a moment.

"I asked if you were okay," he says.

"Oh. Yeah, fine."

While he doesn't push it, he clearly doesn't believe me. And he has every reason not to.

Coming to my yearly neurology follow-up always makes me want to throw up. For 364 days of the year, I can pretend that everything is right, or at least that nothing has changed. I can convince myself that all my exercise and my good diet and my organization and my brain-stimulating job and my crossword puzzles have been efficient, and dementia is a faraway threat. Cinderella always knew she'd have to go back home, but as long as the clock didn't strike midnight, she could still enjoy her time at the ball.

It doesn't help that I went to see my mother this morning and she somehow seemed worse than usual. The image of her trying to eat soup with her fingers sears my brain, over and over.

I notice that my leg is jumping up and down as we wait for my name to be called. Aaron notices it, settling a hand on my thigh as a comfortable weight.

"What can I do to help?" he asks.

Oh, Aaron. You've already done too much.

For the first time since we started...*this,* I woke up this morning and found him sleeping next to me, his chest rising and falling softly. His dark lashes fluttered for a moment, but he didn't open his eyes. And I just laid there, admiring him.

I didn't like how it felt to wake up next to him. Not one bit. Because the flickering I felt in my chest meant I'd gone wrong somewhere. I hadn't respected the one rule I'd given him: I'd developed feelings. Sure, I already liked him when we got together for the first time, but this was nothing like now. And as I watched him sleep, it only became clearer that I'd get my heart broken once this eventually ended. I was so afraid for him, I forgot to build my own shield.

But that's okay. As long as he keeps seeing me as just a good friend, it won't destroy him when I'll forget about him. When I won't be able to say what his name is, or where I know him from. Or possibly even when he'll approach me and I'll shout in fear, not recognizing the seeming stranger wanting to hug me. If he doesn't love me, then it'll be easy for him to leave me and move on when it happens.

It's not like I don't think I deserve love, from him or others. I do. But I also know that I don't want to be responsible for making him feel any kind of pain. Deserving isn't part of the equation here. Keeping feelings at bay is a simple, well-thought-out decision.

"Nothing, I—"

"Wren Lawson, room three," a voice calls on the overhead intercom, making my heart rate speed up.

Getting up on wobbly legs, I turn to Aaron and say, "Wish me luck."

"I'll wait here." He takes my hand in his and gives it a quick squeeze. "It's going to be fine."

I don't know how to answer, so I don't. My stiff legs lead me to the room I've been called to, where Dr. Steinberg is sitting at his desk when I walk in. He wears his signature bowtie, his bald head reflecting the overhead light. He must be around sixty, but I couldn't say for sure. I've known him for years, and I feel like he's never changed through time.

"Ms. Lawson, come on in!" he says with a pleased expression, not showing that he's at the end of a long day of seeing patients.

"I already told you, please, Wren is fine," I say, trying to reciprocate his calm and happy expression as best I can.

"All right, then, Wren." With his eyes on his computer, he scrolls through my file, probably reading what he had noted in the evaluations of the past years. "Are you ready for some questions?"

I nod, and we get started.

These exams are always more or less the same. Dr. Steinberg asks me questions about general culture—who's the current President, in what museum resides the Mona Lisa, what's America's Independence Day. He asks me if I've gotten lost recently, or if I've been struggling at work or during my daily tasks. I'm then told to draw a clock, to name some animals, to retain seven numbers and to tell them back to him after a minute, in different orders. I have to do basic math calculations and other tests I think might be new, and finally, after a quick physical exam, he asks me questions about personal things I told him in the past—what's my mother's date of birth, where did I grow up, when did I graduate college.

"And that's it," Dr. Steinberg says after what must've been thirty minutes of testing my brain. He smiles, but that smile could mean anything. Doctors are taught to keep a reassuring face no matter the circumstances.

In reality, I think I know that I'm okay. I was able to answer his questions, or at least I think I was. Do people who lose their minds realize that they're not answering properly? I never thought to ask my mom or my uncle or my grandpa. And now two of them are gone, and one can't answer any question I ask her, and no one can tell me whether I would know if I'd drastically failed my test.

With a swallow, I force out, "So?"

"So everything looks great."

I let out a huge breath, just like I do every time he tells me that sentence. Because one day, he won't.

"Thank you, Doctor," I say as I get up from my chair.

He frowns before folding his hands over his belly and leaning back. "You know, Wren, there's a lot of uncertainty regarding Alzheimer's. I wish you wouldn't trouble yourself so much at your age about this."

I don't answer.

"Chances are, you have many, many years in front of you, if it ever does occur."

"Right. Thank you," I say before waving and leaving his office. The moment I walk into the waiting room, Aaron is on his feet, my purse and coat in his hands.

"So? How did it go?" he asks. The room is empty—a perk of having the last appointment of the day—so no one's here to listen to our conversation.

"Good." My hands are shaking. I ball them into fists. "I guess I passed another year."

"That's good news, though." His eyes dip to my hands, then to my wobbly legs. "Why aren't you happy?"

"I am. Really." I hug my middle, trying to control my breathing. *It's done, Wren.* "It's just...coming here never gets easier."

This might sound crazy, being more shaken after than before the appointment, but Aaron's nod only makes me feel understood.

And when he puts an arm around my shoulders and kisses the top of my head before saying, "Well, now it's done, so we can get out of here and go home," I feel the most intense urge to wrap my body tightly against his and ask him to never let go.

I don't want this to end.

Biting my lip hard enough to draw blood, I squeeze my eyes shut and breathe him in. He's so warm. So comforting.

In this moment, I realize if there was one thing I could wish for, it would be to live in a world where time stands still. Where

Aaron and I could keep living without growing old, our bodies stuck in this place in time. This way, nothing would stop me from begging him to stay with me. I wouldn't ever get sick. He'd never have to say goodbye. We could just *be*, together.

It's a childish dream, I know. But the way he's looking at me right now, I—

Ringing.

With a wince, Aaron pulls away from me and grabs his phone out of his wool jacket.

"Hello?"

I faintly hear the sound of a feminine voice speaking fast.

"Wait, wait, wait, Callie, slow down. Tell me what happened."

While my heart was beating fast minutes ago, it's jackhammering against my chest now. It could be anything. Dennis having another stroke. Callie getting hurt. Martina falling down the stairs.

But when Aaron turns to me with sympathetic eyes, I realize I forgot one important option.

The girls. Callie was with the girls today. She had a day off and had all but begged me to leave them in Sonder Hill for the night. I'd gladly accepted.

Aaron doesn't need to tell me something happened to one of them. I can read him like an open book. Plus, I've seen this look a thousand times before. The bad-news look. It's one I welcome like an old friend. And with the step back I've just taken, he must know I know what's coming.

"What vet are you at?" he says softly.

The voice answers something, then Aaron says, "Okay. Stay with Mom. We'll be there as soon as we can."

* * *

The veterinarian hospital closest to Sonder Hill is not particularly big. In fact, it's quite small. So the moment we step inside, we spot

Callie and Martina huddled together in the brightly lit, sterile waiting room.

Aaron's footsteps hurry toward them as I keep a slow pace, doing everything I can to control my breathing. While driving out of Boston, Aaron explained to me what happened, or at least what little he had heard of the situation. Even with that information, I feel like I'm currently walking into the unknown and need to be ready for anything, which explains my holding back from going to question them right away. If I do, I probably won't be able to stop talking and panicking.

Although Aaron does enough panicking for the both of us.

"How did this happen?" he utters midway into the room, making heads turn toward him, including his mother's and little sister's. Callie's cheeks are drenched in tears, her face turned into a deep scowl.

Instead of speaking to him, though, Callie gets up and runs in my direction. "I'm so sorry, Wren. I turned around for one minute to grab something in my closet, and next thing I knew, Maybelle was falling down the stairs." The last words come out as wails. "I'm sorry. I'm so, so sorry."

"Hey, sweetheart," I say, crouching a little so we're eye to eye. "It wasn't your fault. May is old and can't see, and it's something that was likely to happen at some point." I don't allow the lump in my throat to grow or to clog my voice. This little girl who's gone through so much needs my comfort. This is what I need to focus on.

From the corner of my eye, I see Aaron briefly talking to Martina before he rushes to the front desk, maybe to ask questions. I should've thought of doing that before. My mind is a complete blur.

"But I was supposed to watch over h-h-her," she cries again, her brown eyes drowning in tears.

"It wouldn't have changed anything if it had been someone else. She is fast, and she could've fallen from somewhere with me too." I use the word *is*, but it very well might be *was*. Maybelle is old, and she's small and frail. There's a chance that—

No. I won't even think about it. Not until I'm alone at home and can truly break down.

"I went after her when I heard her shriek, and I tried to see if she was hurt anywhere, but there was blood and—"

"Come here, sweetheart," I say before pulling her into my arms, closing my eyes long enough for me to regain some self-control. "I'm not angry at you. It wasn't your fault, and I need you to understand that."

Callie doesn't answer, only sobbing into my arms. I rub a hand over her back when a hand lands on my own back. I gaze up, and Aaron's there. I don't know how long he's been standing there, listening to us. I should probably find a way to get a bus back home. I don't think I'll be able to drive in this current state of mind.

When Callie pulls back from my hug and wipes her eyes with the sleeve of her sweater, Aaron's fingers drag down my back once again as he murmurs, "Got some updates. Mind if we step outside to talk?"

Right. Callie doesn't need to hear whatever bad news he's about to give me. She's been through enough today.

With a last squeeze of her shoulders, I follow Aaron outside. The air is frigid, but I feel even colder. Like there's ice freezing my veins.

"So, they're currently operating on Maybelle."

I keep my face neutral despite the fact that it feels like he's just punched me in the stomach. *Operating.* Meaning it's bad.

"Do they know the severity of the injuries?" I ask, breathing slowly. My voice is stable. Strong. Someone should give me a trophy for this.

"The receptionist wasn't sure. She said the surgery is supposed to last around an hour and a half, so we still have some time to wait."

"Okay," I say, then wrap my coat tighter around me.

With a step in my direction, Aaron asks, "Are you okay?"

I acquiesce, but I don't meet his gaze, hoping he'll get the message and leave. I can't have him here, asking me how I'm doing. That can only lead me to break down, and that has to wait. I'm already attached enough. I can't have him here for me all the time. It'll give us both the wrong idea.

And yet the moment he places his hand on my cheeks, I feel an immense amount of comfort.

No matter how much I shouldn't.

Tears threaten to spill from my eyes the longer I stay within Aaron's orbit, so I take a step back. I can't leave yet, not as long as I don't know what's going on with Maybelle, but I need to step away.

Breathe in. Out. In. Out.

"I'm really sorry, Wren," Aaron says, giving me space while not walking away.

Oh goodness. He can't do this to me. Not right now.

Voice nearly breaking, I say, "Please don't pity me." I've had enough of that in my life. Always pity, never a better outcome.

And it's like he gets it. Because the moment he says, "I don't," and still opens his arms wide for me, I can't stop myself anymore.

I rush into his arms and break down in a puddle of tears.

Sobs rack my chest as Aaron holds me tight, keeping all the pieces of me from shattering all over the ground.

"I just—" Hiccup. "I just can't seem to get a goddamn break."

I don't like complaining about my fate. As I already told Aaron, it is what it is. No one's life is perfect.

But in the past decade, I've only allowed myself to open my heart twice, to each of my dogs. They were the ones no one wanted to adopt at the shelter, yet they became my biggest blessings. And now, for some reason, life is trying to take one away from me.

He doesn't say anything because he knows me enough to understand it wouldn't help. The only thing he can do is what he's already doing.

I don't know how much time passes as I hold the back of his coat like it's my lifeline, nose buried in his woodsy-scented neck. But eventually, I get my breathing to calm down and am able to step away from him.

"I'm so sorry, I—"

"Hey, it's all right." Aaron doesn't seem bothered one bit by my tears and snot on his coat. He only watches me like he wishes he could do something more. As if he hasn't already done more than anyone could.

"No, it's not. Friends-with-benefits don't have to help each other during breakdowns." I wipe my face with the palms of my hands. "Don't worry, though. It won't happen again."

"Wren, stop it. I *want* to be there for you."

My jaw clenches. What does that even mean?

Fortunately, I don't have time to think about this any longer because the front door of the hospital opens right then, Martina coming out, dark circles under her eyes.

"They're out of surgery." She gives me a shaky smile. "She's not strong, but they think she should be okay."

Tears spring to my eyes, but this time for a whole other reason.

"Thank you," I mouth to Martina, not trusting my voice. Then I run inside, not thinking about the implications of what just happened. My mind needs to be focused on my girl right now, and if it can keep it away from Aaron, it'll be for the best.

CHAPTER 26

Aaron

"YOU'RE SO ANNOYING."

"I am not!" Wren laughs as I wriggle out of her way. "Just let me do this one, *pleaseee*."

I move out of her way again, focusing on styling my hair in the mirror. Jesus, this woman is relentless.

"Forget it," I groan.

"But it's so big and ready to pop!" She even has the audacity to pout as she mimics popping the blackhead she found on my back earlier when she was giving me a massage. I glance down at her nails. These things are fucking weapons. Killers.

"I'm not letting you try again," I deadpan. She almost tore my skin in half the first time she attempted to remove it.

"But it's part of the friends-with-benefits arrangement!"

I turn to her with a dumbfounded look. "And who's it benefiting?"

"Me!"

I bark out a laugh before wrapping her in my arms and giving the crown of her hair a kiss. Not moving, I glance at the mirror, where Wren is cuddling her face against my naked chest like a kitten. I'll never stop craving this.

She moves away too fast, looking at the time. "Guess we need to get ready if we want to make it to the party." She's so monotonous while she says it, she could be falling asleep.

"Please try not to look too enthusiastic," I tease.

"It's your fault I'm going there, so you better let me pop that blackhead when we get back."

I guess she does have a point. I almost harassed her to say yes to her cousin's invitation. She has barely any family, and it breaks my heart. I have no idea what I would do without my mine, as crazy as they can sometimes be. If there's one chance she could have someone like that by her side, she needs to take the opportunity.

"Deal," I end up saying.

With a smirk, she says, "Okay, go get ready, then."

With a salute, I exit the bathroom where we showered together minutes before and go put on a white dress shirt and black slacks. Knowing Wren takes forever to get ready, I head to her living room so I can feed the dogs and watch some TV while waiting for her.

Molly comes running toward me the second she hears the click of a kibble falling inside her metal bowl. Maybelle is slower behind, but she still comes. It took her a few days to get back on her feet after her surgery, but she eventually did. She's in even worse shape than before, though. With her age and all her health problems, she probably doesn't have long. I'm not sure whether Wren realizes this, but I know I'll never bring it up with her, knowing how much she loves this dog. It would break my heart.

I know I'll be there for her when she'll need it, though. Every step of the way.

Once the dogs are done eating, I take them out for them to do their business, and when I come back inside, Wren is standing in the living room.

Jesus Christ.

She's glowing.

I've always thought she was beautiful, but now? Now she's a fucking goddess. Her hair is falling over her shoulders in loose waves, dark makeup lining the top of her eyelids, while she's wearing a tight black dress that makes my dick hard just at the sight of it.

Wren starts smiling shyly before I even say a word, as if she can read my mind. In a way, I think she often can.

"God, how do you always take my breath away?" I whisper over her lips before kissing her, my hands trailing down to cup her ass.

"You're not so bad yourself."

I kiss her again, my tongue tangling with hers as I palm her. "What are you wearing under there?" I whisper as I pull back slightly.

She smirks. "What makes you think I'm wearing anything?"

Eyes closed, I let my forehead drop on her shoulder. "You're killing me, Wren. Fucking killing me." Telling me this before we have to leave, knowing I'll be dreaming about this the whole night.

She chuckles, then gives my back two little taps before going to crate the dogs. "Come on. I hate being late."

With a look that I hope conveys *you'll pay for this,* I help her put her coat on, then grab mine and head outside.

* * *

The party is great.

Nothing is inherently wrong with it. There's tasty food and great music and nice people. Sure, it's very extra for a wedding anniversary, but no one could objectively say the party isn't a success.

Yet Wren doesn't seem to be having a good time. At all.

When Aqidah came to her and said, "Oh my God, Wren, I'm so happy you came!" while hugging her, Wren's smile smelled fake from a mile away.

"Yeah," she answered simply, giving her cousin a distant pat on the shoulder.

Aqidah tried to make small talk after that, and while Wren was pleasant, she wasn't the woman I know. Nothing like the burst of energy and life she is when we're alone. Even once Aqidah left, when Wren spoke with her nephews and nieces, it was clear something was wrong with her.

Case in point: she agreed to dance with me without any argument. However, no part of her was in it. It didn't matter how much I teased her about her two left feet; she never laughed honestly.

"What's going on with you?" I ask her over a piece of cake once we've left the dance floor.

"What?" she asks as if she'd been lost in thoughts and I took her out of them.

"I asked what's up with you?"

"Oh. Nothing," she answers too fast before bringing her gaze to Aqidah's two sons, who are still dancing the YMCA on the dance floor. She pinches her lips between her teeth.

It doesn't make sense. Wren's great with kids. I've seen her with Callie, never blaming my sister for mistakes she might've made, and organizing insane activities to make her happy. So why would she be so tense while watching her own family?

They certainly didn't seem close. Aqidah had to remind her children of Wren's name.

Nothing about it makes sense.

I'm about to question her about it again when the sound of metal clinking against glass comes from the center of the dance floor, where Aqidah and Jerome, her husband, are standing. Wren's cousin has long dark hair, light-brown skin, and is wearing a long, sparkly red dress. Her husband's blond hair contrasts with hers, while his loving smile mirrors the one she's giving him.

The room hushes before the clinking stops.

"First of all, we want to say thank you to everyone who came here to celebrate our love today," Aqidah says while looking around the crowd. "We're so grateful to have all of you in our lives."

I throw a side glance at Wren, who's standing even stiffer than before.

"The past ten years haven't always been easy," she continues, turning to her husband, "with the death of my dad and your career reorientation and the arrival of our three little monsters." She waves at her sons and daughter who are now sitting cross-legged in front of them. "But through it all, we've never left each other's side, and I can say without a doubt that this is how it's always going to be. Through thick and thin, I know you'll always be with me, ready to support me and care for me, and that's the most beautiful gift you could've given me."

Wren looks behind her, at the back of the room. Following her gaze, the only thing I find there is the emergency exit. When she returns her attention to the scene going on in front of us, she's blinking fast.

Somehow, I doubt it's because she's touched by Aqidah's speech.

Jerome delivers a similar message, returning Aqidah's compliments tenfold, and then they kiss and the crowd erupts in cheers.

While clapping, I feel a hand on my bicep.

"Come on," Wren says. "I'm ready to go."

"You sure?" We stayed long enough for it not to be considered impolite if we left, but already, the music is turning up, an obviously great night ahead.

She nods.

"All right," I say as I put a hand on her lower back and lead her to the coat check, where we bundle up before going back into the cold.

The moment we get out, Wren takes in a deep breath before exhaling loudly. Her walk to my car is hurried.

"Are you okay?" I ask.

"Yeah."

Hurrying to match her gait, I grasp her hand softly. "So why does it look like you're running away?"

Lips pinched tightly, she shakes her head.

"Wren, come on," I say, squeezing her cold hand and making her slow down. "Tell me what's going on."

"It's just…" The sigh she lets out is not impatient. More like a popped balloon. "It's hard to see them, is all."

My brows furrow. "Why?"

"Because Aqidah has all the things I might have wanted and none of the guilt."

Her words are a kick to the gut.

"She has the husband and the children and no worry whatsoever," she adds before biting her lip. "You know she never got tested? She said she'd rather not know. As if being in the dark will keep Alzheimer's away."

The last part of what she says is a blur. I'm still focused on the fact that she is *jealous* of Aqidah's life.

"But…" I start, the right words escaping me. "Why does it make you sad? It should be encouraging to see her get all of this, no?"

Kids. Friends. Someone she could fall in love with and marry.

Someone like *me*.

A vigorous shake of her head makes the morsel of hope I had shrivel away.

"I could never. What she's chosen for her life makes no sense to me, after what happened with our respective parents." She quickly glances back at the venue. "I told you, I wouldn't put someone through the process of watching me disappear, and I wouldn't have kids. Even if I could go through IVF to have embryos that don't carry my eFAD genes, I would never put children through what I've lived with my mother."

I stare at her, stunned, as she shrugs. "It always makes me sad to see her with her family, which is why I avoid it. I don't need to be reminded of what I could never have."

I don't even realize I've stopped walking until Wren turns around and looks at me quizzically.

"Is that..." I swallow forcefully. "Is that really what you believe? That you could *never* have what she has?"

She frowns. "Of course it is."

There was never any doubt that Wren has some huge biases about things, but until this precise moment, I'd never realized just how deep they ran. She doesn't simply think that a relationship with me is a bad idea. She's constructed her life around the mindset that anyone in her position should be a martyr and keep everyone at bay.

And here I am. The bastard who fell for her anyway.

She did warn me, but I never realized how much she believed in this until now. Saying she doesn't agree with Aqidah for getting married and living a life she wanted... Where does that leave me?

My chest is burning, acid running up my throat. It's like she's just thrust a knife through my skin and bones without even realizing she was holding a weapon. And worse than that, I can't blame her for it, because she warned me to wear an armor in the first place.

"Right," I say, trying to keep the hurt out of my voice.

Whatever. It doesn't change anything. I can ignore this. Act like tonight didn't happen. Maybe I can erase it from my mind the moment we get home. It would be burying my head in the sand, but who wouldn't want to when being blind to the situation means continuing to play house with Wren? To kiss, and make love, and laugh.

I get back to walking, leading Wren toward the car. When we get to my SUV, I open the passenger door for her, then get in the driver's seat.

As long as I can put tonight behind us, everything will be fine.

CHAPTER 27

Wren

Something's wrong with Aaron.

He's been acting weird ever since we left the party. His hands are holding the steering wheel so tight, his fingers might break soon. And worst of all, he's silent.

Aaron is never silent.

Maybe in the beginning, when he didn't know me, he wasn't the most talkative, but ever since we started our arrangement, he's never stopped talking. Even when we tell each other goodnight and I close my eyes before going to sleep, he'll break the silence fifteen seconds later to tell me one thing he forgot to share. And every time, I'll open my eyes and listen to him attentively. It's like he can't tell me everything he needs to in a single day, and that always makes me feel warm inside.

But ever since we got into the car, the only sound between us has been the engine working and the soft music playing from the radio.

"Is something wrong?" I ask tentatively.

He shakes his head, but doesn't turn to look at me or throw me one of his seductive smiles, which confirms something truly is wrong.

I don't push it, instead leaning my head back and gazing out the window. If he doesn't want to talk to me about something, it's his right. There are certainly things I prefer to keep to myself too.

We continue the rest of the way in silence, tension still emanating out of Aaron's every pore. Must've been this party.

I still can't believe I brought him there. He's probably still thinking about the fact that all these people we saw, but most importantly, Aqidah's husband and children, will lose her sooner rather than later, and not in a beautiful, peaceful way. It's scary—horrifying, even—to be faced with this reality.

I've always known Aqidah didn't want the disease to affect her life, but tonight showed me just how much she's ignored her genetics. Does it not bother her to know she will break the hearts of everyone who was there tonight when she forgets them? Does it not tear her apart when she thinks about the fact that her husband will need to take care of a wife who will be nothing like the woman he met? Sure, when people get married, they say for better or for worse, but that's when the worse is not expected, isn't it? Not when they know with almost complete certainty that the worse will come, and fast.

My entire being *ached* while looking at them and their happiness, something so close yet so far.

Of course, we'd all rather live a nice, happy life like hers, but I don't see how I could live with myself if I did this to someone like Aaron. Vivid are the memories of the countless times my mother shouted at me to leave her alone, of her telling me she didn't know who I was and needed me to get out, or of the time she almost burned our house down by waking up at 3:00 a.m. with the urge to make grilled cheeses, then going back to bed without turning the stove off, forgetting all about her craving and the toast burning. I was so scared that night, the moment I made sure the flames were all under control, I ran to the bathroom and emptied my stomach multiple times in the toilet.

Alzheimer's isn't a cute disease. It isn't only forgetting about your first elementary school crush's name or the place you visited with your parents when you were five or the meal you ate for dinner yesterday. It's agitation and aggressiveness and bursts of sadness that break the hearts of everyone around you. It's not remembering how to braid your hair while looking at yourself in the mirror, and not realizing that when it is snowing outside, it means it's winter. It's looking at your husband but seeing a stranger. It's forgetting how to speak, but weirdly remembering the lyrics to a song you knew decades ago. It's shattered souls and broken hearts and sniffles hidden behind smiles.

So I can see why Aaron's in a bad mood. I was in a bad mood too. It's better now that I'm getting far away from it, at least. Going back to my place, where Aaron and I can be as close as we want and call it a friendship.

Once he parks in the back of my building, I unbuckle my seatbelt, then turn to him. He's not exactly scowling, but there's no sign of his casual, ever-present smile.

I poke him in the ribs. "If it makes you feel any better, I don't think I'll go back to a party of Aqidah's anytime soon, so you won't have to watch something like this ag—"

"Stop!" he shouts, his arms going flying around him. "Just fucking stop, will you?"

I retreat back. "What?" My voice is squeaky, small. I've never seen him like this before. It isn't like him to be this angry.

"Can't you just at least pretend not to find this so terrible?" he says, jaw square.

"I don't… I don't understand."

Aaron drags a hand through his mussed hair before letting it drop to the steering wheel with a bang. "Don't you see how upsetting this is? You talking about loving and committing to someone like it's the worst thing in the world?"

No. This can't be happening. My head starts shaking left and right as I watch the invisible castle we've built, made of secret confessions and stolen moments of happiness, crumble around us.

With a soft voice, I say, "I set rules, Aaron."

"Well, guess what?" he says, his dark gaze cloudy. "I didn't follow them."

I close my eyes. My gut is being torn in a million little pieces, heart beating out of my chest. In an instant, I see it all. Our entire history, all the moments of joy we shared, destroyed with a short set of words. And it hurts. It hurts so damn much, yet I can't do a thing to stop this moving train.

"You can't mean..." I whisper.

"Of course, that's what I mean, Wren!" He hisses, as if in pain. "God, how can you not see I'm so in love with you I can hardly breathe?"

"Aaron, please," I beg, pressure building behind my eyes. By saying this, he's making me a villain. Telling me I've set him up for pain.

And yet, for a millisecond, I can't help the flash of fireworks that light my chest, because this kind, incredible man loves *me*. My feelings aren't one-sided.

But this feeling quickly bursts, panic returning to me faster than a boomerang.

The air is thick in the car. Too thick. I can't breathe. Things were never supposed to turn out this way. I was supposed to hope for him in secret and wish for him in another life while he was supposed to keep his heart guarded. Not love. Never love. Stars start blinding my vision, not enough oxygen filling my lungs. We messed up. *I* messed up. I hurt the one person in the world I wished to protect with everything I had. The one who deserves everything I can't give. I was too selfish to see how he couldn't stop himself from learning to care for me. He's that kind of person. He couldn't not follow his heart, and I let my own happiness blind me from it. But now I see it all. His pain-filled eyes. The stark lines of shock on his face. The bob of his throat, tight from stretched tendons.

He must see what I'm about to do because he says, "Don't."

I don't listen. The only thing I can see right now is my need to escape. Without hesitation, I open my door and run outside. Icy rain falls on me, the droplets immediately freezing in my hair and on my skin. I don't feel them.

A second later, another door opens and closes.

"What do you want me to say, Wren? That I'm sorry for loving you? Because I'm not."

I squeeze my eyes shut. How can he say that when he knows the truth? Spinning on my heels, I shout, "You should be!" *Don't cry, Wren.* "Don't you see? There's no future with me."

I want it, Aaron, I want it so bad, but I can't.

"Why? Why are you doing this?" he yells, face pulled tight. "You act like you're already dead when you're so fucking alive!"

I feel my lips whiten from the pressure with which I press them together. Why now? I needed more time. *Wanted* more time.

Ignoring what he's just said, I tell him, "I'm not doing this to you."

"That's not your choice to make," he says, his dark hair glinting from the rain. Droplets run over his sharp cheekbones, his plump lips. It's as if the Universe is crying for us. Doomed from the start.

As I watch him stare at me, my thoughts blank for an instant, and his words bounce back in my head. They've hit me so abruptly, they tore a piece of my steel walls down. What if he has a point? What if I'm ruining my life, wasting the little time I have?

He looks at me with hope, eyes glistening, mouth half open. So damn perfect.

A perfection I would ruin, and I can't do it. Not to him.

"Yes, it is," I say, voice strained. "And I'm making it now."

His face falls, breaking my heart, my chest, all of me.

"This," I say, gesticulating between the two of us, "is over."

"Don't do this." His words are barely more than a whisper. Fatigue makes his whole body shrivel in front of me, shoulders heavy, neck slumped. I've never hated myself so much.

"Thank you for everything, Aaron." My voice is shaky as I succeed in getting those five words out.

I don't remain there to see the look on his face as I end the one good thing in my life. Instead, I run inside my building and take the stairs two by two to reach my apartment. Once I'm inside, I lock the door behind me. Aaron's the type of person who'd try to come up and get in to talk more about this.

A loud bark makes me look up. I open Molly's crate, and right away her large muzzle nudges my thigh. She's as close to me as my own clothes, as if sensing I need her. Without a second thought, I sink to my knees to hug her.

And then I let out all the tears I have in my body.

CHAPTER 28

Aaron

WHEN I WAS NINE, I BROKE MY ARM WHILE I WAS VISiting family in the Dominican Republic.

Tio Manuel had brought me and my cousins on a hike to a huge waterfall close to their house. It was all the way into the humid, thick forest, and I was so excited I was practically skipping around. Without my parents for once, I felt like a real grown-up. It was the best day of my life.

Until I slid on a rock and fell right onto my left arm.

For a second, the pain was so sharp, it overtook everything in me, like it replaced the blood in my veins and the thoughts in my brain. There was nothing but this. I couldn't even breathe. I thought I could never experience anything nearly as painful as that.

And yet the pain from that day doesn't even come close to what I'm feeling now. I'd break a thousand arms in order not to feel this kind of hurt.

My windshield wipers are working at full capacity against the icy rain to allow me to see the road in front of me. I've been in the car for thirty minutes, but for all I know, I might have been driving in circles. I'm so out of it, I can't think of a destination. The only thing I need to do is keep myself busy if I don't want to fall to the ground and never get back up.

I should've expected it. She told me word-for-word that I couldn't go ahead and develop feelings for her. Going against her request was my choice—if I can consider that a choice. Wren came into my life like a fucking bulldozer. Actually, that's not right. She came into my life like a warm spring wind. One that makes you realize what you've been missing for months. You think you're okay with the winter temperatures until you step outside and are hit with the hint of warmth that spring and summer will bring, and you think, *I didn't realize I could feel this good until now.*

And she wants nothing to do with me.

Maybe if she'd have told me that she had feelings for me too, I'd have fought harder. No way would I have accepted her bullshit excuse of trying to protect me. I'm a grown man who can decide what kind of risks I want to take, not that growing old with her could be considered a risk. If eventual disease comes in her baggage, then so be it. I don't love her with conditions.

But her face was made of stone as she told me I'd made a mistake. At some point, I was sure I'd caught her facade slipping, but I blinked and it was back on. As if she couldn't care less whether we weren't in each other's lives anymore.

Our connection was not one I imagined, that I know. She can pretend all she wants that she doesn't appreciate me, but I know she does. And I've seen the way she looks at me and touches me. The physical aspect of our relationship was not a problem. In fact, it was more incredible than anything I could've ever experienced with anyone else, and I'm convinced it was the same for her.

But she was closed off right from the start. Convinced herself that us feeling things for each other was a bad thing. I thought I could change her mind by becoming involved with her, but clearly, that was a naïve thought. She's always blocked any possibility of falling for me, so I can't hold it against her if she doesn't love me the way I love her. It's my damn fault.

Still, that doesn't ease the fracturing happening in my chest right now, tearing me in two. This isn't a natural pain. I feel like I'm having a heart attack, like I'm bursting at the seams.

On the passenger seat, my phone rings. I glance at it quickly, *Mamá* written on the screen. I told her I'd be coming home tomorrow morning to work on some papers the farm's part-time accountant sent us, but right now, I can't even imagine going there. It's only going to remind me of Wren. I let the call go to voicemail. She'll call again if it's something important. *Please, don't be something important.* I need a break, just this once.

I've now been driving around Boston for the past forty-five minutes, still no destination in mind. I can't go to my parents' place, but I can't go to mine either. If my childhood home holds too many memories of our relationship, then my place is a literal shrine to her. There's the toothbrush she left in my bathroom, and the smell of her lilac shampoo on my pillows, and the box of Oreos she bought me as a joke last week after I ate all of hers at her place.

I could go to Finn's, but he told me this morning that he'd be going on a date tonight, which obviously means I don't want to be at his place right about now.

Fatigue is pressing down on me. I never expected tonight to go this way. It feels like days ago when we were getting ready in Wren's bathroom.

At the first sign of a place I can walk in and have a drink, I put my blinker on and turn into the driveway. It looks like some kind of pub.

The smell as I walk inside reminds me of a beer barrel, but at least it's warm and it's a space that is Wren-free.

I make my way to the bar, where I ask the long-haired barman for a shot of tequila, then another.

God, how have I gotten here? Drinking alone in a bar with literally nothing in my life going right. It's pathetic. Back where I was six months ago.

"Aaron?"

I don't need to turn around to know who called my name, but I still do, just to confirm I didn't dream it.

Nope. Very real.

Amber is as different from Wren as could be. Blonde, petite

but curvy, smiling. She hasn't changed a bit since the day she turned down my proposal.

"Wow. Amber. Hi."

"I thought that was you." She grins. "How are you doing? It's been a while."

"Yeah." I drag a hand through my hair. Did I really need this tonight? "I'm...fine. What about you?"

"I'm good!" And she *does* look good. Much happier than when she was with me. "Are you here with someone?"

"Uh, no."

"Oh." Her cheeks become pink, letting me know it's not the case for her. I'm assuming the bald man sitting at the back of the pub who's currently pinning me with his stare is the person in question.

And that's the moment I realize I feel no jealousy toward him. None. In fact, if he makes Amber happier, then I'm glad he's in her life. She's a great person and deserves nothing less, no matter what happened in our past.

It's also the moment I realize I didn't love Amber as much as I loved the idea of her. I loved her like you love a gift that wasn't exactly the one you asked for. You wanted this cologne, but your loved one gave you this other one instead. And while it's not the one you initially wanted, it was a gift, so you *want* to love it. You want to think this is the perfect cologne, and after a while, you end up believing it. You wear it every day, love the way you smell, share the name proudly to your colleagues. But one day, you walk across the street and smell someone who wears the one you initially wanted, and you realize that you never actually loved your gift. You just convinced yourself that you did. And that doesn't mean it wasn't a great one. It simply wasn't yours.

I loved being with Amber. I loved thinking about our future, about growing old together. But I never loved the exact timbre of her laugh when her dog jumped on her bed or the view of her drowning in my old winter coat or the way I would feel with only her, like I matter as much as everyone around me. I loved the idea of her, but I didn't love *her*.

It only required me to fall head over heels in love with someone else to realize that.

"Look," she says, twirling a blond strand between her fingers. "I just wanted to make sure that we were okay. I'd understand if you hate me after what I did, but—"

"I don't hate you, Amber. You did the right thing." She didn't think we had a future together, and while I didn't see it at first, I can only be grateful she made the decision she did back then.

"Oh, thank God," she blurts, a hand on her chest. "It had nothing to do with you. I hope you know that."

"I do." It's not a lie.

"Okay, well, I won't bother you longer than necessary. Just wanted to say hi." After a quick smile, she walks back to her table.

"Hey, Amber?"

She turns around.

"I'm glad I got to see you today."

"Me too."

Twisting back to face the bar, I sigh and drop my head between my hands. I should feel better after realizing that what happened between Amber and me was truly the right thing. Instead, it only makes me think about what I've just lost. Not someone I love the idea of, but someone I've fought not to love and still lost. Wren is it for me.

And she made it clear there's no future there.

When the bartender passes me, I lift a hand and say, "Another, please."

CHAPTER 29

Wren

PEOPLE ALWAYS SAY TO DO THE RIGHT THING.

However, they never mention that doing the right thing can also mean feeling like the world is crashing down on your shoulders and burying you six feet under.

CHAPTER 30

Aaron

WITH A GRUNT, I SLAM MY HATCHET INTO THE LOG of wood. Every time I do, I hope the movement will rid me of the emotions rotting inside me, and every time it fails.

The week that just passed has been filled with cutting down the trees that had been damaged by the few storms we got in December and early January, plus the ones chewed down by the squirrels that Finn and I caught and released far, far, away from here. Working on the farm has been okay. Good, even. It's done wonders for keeping me busy, enough so that I don't spend the entirety of my time thinking about her.

It's been eight days since she told me she didn't want me, not that I'm counting. In fact, I've gotten numb to it. To everything.

The Monday after Aqidah's party, I went to the Arcade Games headquarters and gave my two weeks' notice. Craig had been expecting it for a while, although he'd thought I'd wait until I was finished with the design project I was halfway done with. I'd thought so too, in a childish, hopeful way. I'm not the type of person to leave things unfinished, and I hated disappointing my boss like this, but Wren's dismissal was a wake-up call for me. Dreaming of things that were impossible was useless. My parents would never *not* need me to handle the farm that's been in our family for generations, just like Wren would never fall in love with me. It was stupid of me to even keep hope.

Craig was great about it. At first, he threw out two or three curses because that left him with a very short timeframe to find someone to complete my designs before the presentation to the new investors, but he was still understanding. He knew about my family's situation from the start and was aware that I had huge responsibilities at home, so he didn't ask me for those two weeks, which gave me all the time in the world to work on the farm this week. I've used it to my advantage. Would I have preferred burying myself in my creative work? Of course. But that's life, isn't it? You don't always get what you want.

After chopping down another batch of logs, I roll them in the back of the farm's pickup.

Bend. Lift up. Throw in the cab. Repeat.

And don't you dare think about the fact that you'll be sleeping alone in your bed yet again tonight, or the fact that you'll never see her or hear her soft laughter again.

Once all the logs have been loaded, I hop in the truck and drive it the short way home. We're about to run out of fuel for the wood stove. Parking in front of the house, I pick up a batch in my arms and bring them inside.

"Aaron?" Ma calls from the kitchen the moment I step inside.

"Yeah?"

"Why are you still working?" she says as she steps in my way. Looking up to the grandfather clock next to us, I see it's almost 9:00 p.m.

"Hadn't noticed the sun set so long ago." Winter has this way of messing up your inner schedule. A broken heart can do that too.

I continue my walk toward the stove, but Ma follows me. After dropping the logs in the trunk next to it, I turn to find her there, watching me.

"What?" I ask cautiously.

"No estàs feliz." She doesn't phrase it as a question, but a fact. As if she knows I haven't been happy.

I don't answer. I can't. Not if it means I need to talk to her about Wren. She thankfully hasn't brought it up in the past week, and I don't need her to start now. Anyway, she's for sure aware whatever had started is now over. I don't pride myself in being that good of an actor.

To my silence, she sighs and says, "Come on."

"What? Where?"

"Your father has been trying to speak with you for weeks, but I think now it's more important than ever that you hear what he has to say," she says in Spanish.

She makes no sense. However, before I can ask her to explain herself, she starts toward their bedroom, forcing me to follow her.

My father is sitting in his reading chair when we walk into the room. In his hands is a piece of paper he seems to be reading. The moment he sees us, he opens his mouth, but the sounds that come out don't form a word.

"It's okay, Dad. Don't force yourself to—"

"Sit," Ma says before taking a seat next to my father. This seems strangely similar to an intervention.

"All right..." I sit on the corner of their queen-size bed, facing them. "What did you want to talk to me about?"

They look at each other before Dad offers Ma a small nod.

"You're not happy," she repeats, her dark gaze now on me.

I sigh. Talking about Wren is the last thing I want to do. I've stayed away from it as much as I could. I've even been avoiding Finn since last Saturday because I knew he'd ask me about what had happened.

"Ma, I'm not in the mood to—"

"You don't like managing Evermore, do you?" she interrupts, her accent familiar while her words aren't.

I stare at her with my jaw hanging. A talk about the farm was the last thing I was expecting. And while it's better than bringing up Wren, I can't see this going well.

"I don't mind it," I say, my back straight as a rod.

Dad tilts his head, his stare telling me he doesn't believe my bullshit.

"You never wanted it before," Ma says.

My shoulders lift in a shrug. "Things change."

"Do they?"

Teeth clenched, I stare at them. What the hell is this?

As she grabs my father's hand, Ma takes a sharp breath, then says, "We'll sell the farm."

"I'm sorry, what?"

"Càlmate." *Calm down.* She points to the bed, making me realize that, in my indignation, I'd gotten up. But what the fuck is she talking about?

"No, you're not," I say after I sit back down.

"Yes, we are."

I get back up again because fuck this. "It's been in our family for three generations, and you just want to throw it away?"

"Aarón, it's not like that. It's okay to let go of things that aren't working anymore."

"And what if Callie wants it?"

Ma's lips curl up. "Your sister wants to become a doctor. She's never shown interest in wanting to run this place, and—"

"But what if—"

"And neither have you," Ma finishes, making my throat close up. "We're not going to force something on you that makes you unhappy. What kind of parents would that make us?"

"But… But it's Dad's legacy." The one thing that has made me unable to let it go.

Ma turns to Dad, and they both exchange a knowing grin.

Then, Dad hands me with a shaky hand the paper he's been holding all this time.

The moment I look at what's on it, it feels like I've been punched in the solar plexus.

On the white sheet of paper is my dad's handwriting, barely legible.

What a lot of people don't know about Broca's aphasia, which is the type Dad has, is that it doesn't just affect the muscles you need to speak. It can also impair the movements responsible for written language or even sign language, making it difficult or sometimes impossible to write down a sentence.

Yet here it is, clear as day. My dad's shaky letters. I look at them all one by one, not even getting to the meaning of the sentences. The fact that my father has been able to write this is a miracle of its own. It must've taken him days to do this. I've seen him try in the past, and drawing a letter is a tedious process for him. It's so amazing, I can't keep myself from smiling.

That is, until I read what he actually wrote.

Don't keep doing this for me. Evermore is not my legacy.

You and Callie are.

It isn't until Dad uses his cane to help himself up and wraps his thin arms around me that I realize I'm crying.

No, not just crying. Sobbing.

Like a little boy, I wrap myself in my father's embrace and weep about his stroke. His aphasia. The loss of his old life. The fact that I might never hear him say my name again. And despite all of those hardships, his pure, undying love for me.

"I'm sorry, Dad," I cry as I grip his shirt. "I'm sorry I couldn't be the right person for this."

With surprising strength, he lifts my head and looks me straight in the eye. His hands grip my face, preventing me from looking away.

He doesn't need to speak. His shiny gaze tells me everything I need to know.

I hug him even tighter for it.

After a minute, Ma joins our embrace, her tears wetting my shoulder.

And while I never thought I would come to that conclusion, maybe letting go of the farm isn't the worst thing that could happen.

* * *

I walk out to grab the rest of the logs an hour later, feeling lighter than I have in months. Maybe not everything is right, but at least it's on the right path.

Tomorrow, first thing, I'll call Craig. We've always had a good relationship, and I know he likes my work, so I'm hoping he'll let me turn my resignation into a leave of absence and have me back once the farm isn't ours anymore.

Just as I'm about to head inside with my arms full of wood, headlights coming my way make me squint. At first, my throat closes up, but once it's close enough, I recognize Finn's truck.

"Hey," I say with only mild disappointment, dropping the wood to the bed of the truck as he steps out of his car. "What's up?"

Finn doesn't answer, instead rubbing his hands down his jeans, which is so unlike him, I almost feel like laughing.

"What's going on with you?" I ask, frowning.

I fully expect him to start joking around or tell me his nervous act is all a joke, but instead, he blurts out, "I've come to make you an offer."

With a lift of my brow, I ask, "An offer?"

"Yes." He dips his head sternly, to me or himself, I'm not sure, before saying, "I want to manage this place."

"I'm sorry, what?" Did they all tell each other to make me pass out from shock tonight?

"You don't like it, but you also want it to stay in your family. And if you and I aren't family, then I don't know what is."

I wait a moment, then say, "You're serious about this?"

"Dead serious."

"But what about traveling? You've never wanted to stay home before."

He shrugs. "Maybe I've found reasons to enjoy staying in one place after all."

With narrow eyes, I study my lifelong best friend. With his slightly shaky hands and his clean dress shirt, he looks as serious as he ever has.

"I don't understand where this is coming from."

"Wren, of all people."

I bite my tongue at the sound of her name.

"What do you mean?" I ask.

"She approached me with the idea a few days ago. I thought about it, and it actually makes so much sense. I love this place, and you need someone to run it."

Wren arranged this. After she told me she didn't want me. What is this? Some kind of pity move?

Even if it is, I can't help but want to kiss her feet in thanks. She's just solved everything. It shouldn't surprise me, even though I wasn't expecting it. That's her talent. Finding things that are wrong in my life and making them all right.

If only she could do the same for her and I.

I clear my throat. "We actually just talked about selling it, but—"

"You what?" Forehead wrinkled, he walks toward the front door. "No, no, you can't—"

I roll my eyes and stop him in his tracks. "Will you let me finish? I was about to say I think this is even better than selling."

"Damn right it is."

"Then go sell them the idea." I let him go, and with a determined walk, he reaches the front door.

"Hey, Finn?"

His head twists my way.

"Thank you for this. I couldn't imagine anyone better to take care of this place."

My best friend throws me a grateful smile, then knocks at the door.

CHAPTER 31

Wren

MY EYES ARE DROOPING CLOSED WHEN A PING MAKES me jerk up.

There's a new email in my inbox, and I feel too drained to actually open it. I let my head fall onto my desk in my office, letting out my thousandth sigh of the day.

That's how it's been for two weeks. I've tried to put my all into my work—one of the only things I still have—yet my focus and energy hasn't been there. I still like what I do, but it's like I've forgotten how to function.

Returning to my usual routine should've brought me peace, but it somehow hasn't. In the past months, I'd gotten used to not finding all my things right where I'd left them, or not always knowing where I'd be during each hour of the day. The anxiety linked to the smallest changes in my habits had dimmed, hence the lack of relief that returning to my normal life has brought me. I don't care about life as it used to be. I'd rather have the spontaneity I lost.

Burying myself in work has been more or less the same. While I'm trying to focus on a new client's case, I always find my mind wandering to what's happening at Evermore, or to what Aaron is doing. It's almost like a disease. I can't get rid of these thoughts. They're invasive, and each one of them is sharp as a knife, creating tiny cuts all over my body until it feels like I'm bleeding all over.

It's strange, really, how I never thought to protect myself.

Before, I'd wrapped my life around my diagnosis, but now that I've experienced living for something *more,* I don't think I can appreciate my old way of existing any longer. If all my life is focused on my memory and I one day lose it, then what will I be left with? Who will I be, when I don't know who I am and no one else does either?

That still doesn't mean I regret what I did. Aaron is an independent variable in this. It's not because I don't like my life any longer that he deserves to be put back in it. That man seems to have no self-preservation instinct.

He says he wants me, but that's because he doesn't know what it's like to lose someone to Alzheimer's. He doesn't know what being with me would entail. How could he?

I don't doubt it hurt him when I broke things off. He said he loved me, after all, as crazy as that sounds. But it was a necessary evil. His love will go away. He'll find someone who can love him for a lifetime, and in the end, the hurt he felt when I left will be a ripple of turmoil in the ocean of his life. Nothing like what he could've felt if we'd stayed together and he'd watched me slowly deteriorate.

Things will not be as simple for me, though. I know I'll never get over him. Simple as that. He's been the only person I've ever let myself develop feelings for—let's be honest, let myself *love*—and he'll be the last. I've tried sex. It was wonderful, and I'm never doing it again. Not after the way being with Aaron and having to let him go has broken me.

Aaron once asked me if I resented my life, and my answer was a lie. Or maybe it wasn't one at the time, but things have changed. How could I not resent something that dangled the epitome of happiness in my face, only to force me to give it back?

I can't.

As sad as it sounds, my life has been a series of hurdles, and the track never seems to end, new obstacles only getting added one after the other. Aaron was a quick reprieve, but I'm back to it. And maybe before, I thought those hurdles were fine, but now that I've experienced being able to run without them, I can't not be angry at life.

My inbox dings again, but I don't even bother looking up. This will have to wait until tomorrow. I don't even know how I'll find the energy to get home.

Pushing myself slowly off the desk, I lean down to grab my purse. Being home might make me nostalgic for the times I wasn't the only human inhabiting the place, but at least the girls will be there to cheer me up. The fact that I still have my Maybelle here is one of the few blessings I have to be thankful for. I don't know how I would've coped with losing her too. I probably wouldn't have been able to.

In my purse, something vibrates. I grab my phone, and the moment I see the text written on the screen, I feel like laughing and crying at the same time.

And I do.

> **Finn: Hey! Just wanted to let you know you're now looking at the official new manager of Evermore! Never would've been able to do it without you :)**

Goodness, finally, a good thing happening.

The day after I let Aaron go, I was wallowing at home—no fancy way to put it—and I couldn't stop seeing his grief-stricken face. I'd been witness to it a few times in the past months, like when Dennis had to go to the hospital, or when he'd been given the news that we wouldn't be going to trial. The last time I'd seen it was the night before, when I'd told him we were over. And while it kept flashing again and again in my head, I could only try to think of ways for him to never look like that again. I didn't have magical solutions to make his father's aphasia suddenly go away, or to make his tasks at home less of a burden, but I did think of one thing I could work on: him having to manage the farm. It made no sense for him to abandon his dream job only to do something he doesn't enjoy. I had to think through different scenarios, and it took me days of hitting dead ends. Until one night, as I was trying but failing to fall asleep, it hit me: Finn. I remembered the way he'd spoken about working on the farm, like it was his perfect job. He seemed happy in Sonder Hill. Plus, he was a perfect fit. I know Aaron, and he probably wouldn't have trusted anyone else to handle Evermore. So I took a leap and reached out to Finn.

Eyes brimming with tears, I hug my phone to my chest. This is the best outcome that could've happened. I hope having this weight lifted off his shoulders has made Aaron happy. No one deserves it more than him. He should have everything and more. Even if I can't be the one to directly give it to him.

A knock comes from my office door, making me jump. Quickly, I wipe my thankfully makeup-free eyes, then say, "Yes?"

The door opens, and in comes Selina, a warm smile on her lips. However, the moment she sees me, her happy expression is replaced by a worried one. "Are you okay?"

"Sure, yeah," I say, nodding.

Her head tilts to the left, but she doesn't push me on it.

"The girls and I are going out for a drink. Wanna come?"

For the first time in my life, I feel the urge to tell her yes.

It's easy to find comfort in being alone when you've done it your whole life. Humans are creatures of habit, after all.

But my habits were turned upside down the moment I turned my car onto the gravel pathway leading to a charming Christmas tree farm. Maybe even before then. Maybe my routine was actually jeopardized that summer night I walked into a bar I'd never been to and met a stranger who seemed to already know me despite us never having met.

And now that I've been surrounded by people almost nonstop for weeks on end, I don't quite enjoy my solitude the way I previously did. I miss Martina's loud laugh and Callie's eye rolls at Aaron and Dennis's warm looks. Of course, I don't miss any of that as much as I miss having Aaron by my side.

Selina lifts a brow.

I wince. "I'm sorry, but I have to go feed my dogs." Not a lie, but also a very obvious excuse. That's a good thing, though. I've tried being social. I made connections, and it's only brought me pain, just as it did for everyone who got in my path. I've always seen myself as a ticking time bomb, but apparently I didn't need to get sick to explode.

"You sure?"

"Yeah," I say. "Thanks for thinking of me, though."

"All right. See you tomorrow, then," she says before turning around. At the end of the hallway, I spot Jenny, the receptionist, and Sabrina, our paralegal, waiting for my boss with big smiles on their faces.

I wouldn't have fit anyway.

The idea of going out for a drink wasn't a bad one, though. While I usually stay away from alcohol, I wouldn't say no to it tonight. Just to help me numb it all for a few hours. It's obviously not a healthy coping mechanism, but being healthy is the last thing on my mind right now.

I leave the office and get into my car. The drive home is filled with loud music; I'm hoping it'll drown my thoughts.

It doesn't.

Once I get inside the apartment and feed Molly and Maybelle, I try to sit down to read a book, but my gaze strays to the one personal thing hung on my wall. The drawing Aaron made of the girls, which I had framed weeks ago. My eyes fill with water automatically.

I can't stay here.

Grabbing my keys, I crate the dogs and return outside.

The bar it is.

CHAPTER 32

Aaron

"YOU'RE GETTING SLOW!" FINN SHOUTS AS HE PASSES me, his hockey stick almost making me trip.

"Am not," I lie, pushing to gain speed. It's not like I've had much time to practice my skating technique while I was working two jobs and handling stuff at home.

All that should hopefully be getting better soon. Finn officially became the farm's manager today, which means I'm off the hook.

Thankfully, the day I decided to leave the farm, I emailed Craig, and he gladly took me back. I'm going back next Monday.

All in all, things are...good. Which feels so strange to say since, inside, I don't feel nearly as good as I should. I have the job I love and will actually have time to work on projects I'm passionate about, all the while having found a way to keep the farm in my family.

But all this still feels like assembling a puzzle, only to realize you lost one piece and will never actually be able to complete it. I have all my pieces except the most important one.

With one last stroke of my skates, I shift my stick to steal the puck from Finn. The moment he loses it, he groans.

"Okay, I think that's enough for tonight," he says, panting.

I slow down, realizing I'm drenched in sweat. Nothing like a good skating session to blow off some steam.

"You're just saying that because you're pissed I'm getting better than you."

"In your dreams," Finn answers before throwing my water bottle at me. I catch it, gulping down half of its contents. Then I join Finn on the outside bench where we left our bags and start untying the laces on my skates.

"Seriously, though," I say, "I hope you know how grateful I am for what you're doing."

Finn grins. "It's no biggie. It actually makes me really happy, on top of the fact that I'm helping."

I stare at my best friend as he removes his large gloves. A person who so many would dismiss as childish or ignorant because he's decided to spend a good part of his twenties discovering the world and sleeping around instead of settling down. Yet to me, he's anything but. He's generous and kind and adventurous. He's our Finn.

"You're a good man, you know?" I say.

"Oh, so this is sappy time?"

I roll my eyes, which makes him laugh.

"Just accept it and shut—"

My phone starts ringing in my bag.

I look through the dirty laundry and blade protectors until I find it in a pocket. The ring is almost up, so I take the call without looking at the ID. Probably just Ma, wondering if I'll be able to bring Callie to school tomorrow or something.

"Hey, I'm almost—"

"Aaron?"

My heart stops beating at the sound of the voice I never thought I'd hear again.

"Wren? W-what's going on?" There must be something wrong. She said she was done, and Wren's a woman of her word. She'd never call me again to change her mind or toy with me. Once she's done, she's done.

Beside me, Finn twists on his seat and stares as if he's waiting for me to explain. I shake my head.

"Oh, nothing," she says. "I just wanted to hear your voice." Something like a hiccup comes out of her mouth, and then she giggles.

Wren. Giggles.

"Are you drunk?"

"Uh…" She laughs again.

I throw my skates in my bag, then push my feet into my boots. "Where are you?"

"Nowhere important. Actually, I don't even know why I called, so I—"

"No, please don't go," I rush out, not sure why. It's not going to help me in any way to keep listening to her voice, but it's as if I couldn't resist asking for a little more. She's a drug, and what can an addict to but ask for his next fix?

There's noise in the background, like people chattering. She must be at a restaurant or a store, then. Or maybe a bar.

The idea of her drunk and alone makes goose bumps rise on my arms.

"I don't think this was a good idea," she whispers.

"Sure it was." Better her being on the phone with me than talking to some creep.

A sigh reaches my ears through the phone, soft and warm. "How are you doing, Aaron? Are you…seeing someone?" Hiccup.

"What? Of course not." I can't believe she could even think that. Did she believe that moving on from her would be easy? That what I felt for her was just some idiotic childhood crush? Was that why it was so easy for her to let me go?

Wren lets out a breath, and while I can't see her, I'd swear I hear relief in it.

"I wouldn't do that," I add, my voice low.

"You should."

"What?"

Beside me, Finn does some hand gestures, but I ignore him. This feels like a make-or-break moment.

"I said you should. See someone new, I mean. You deserve it."

My jaw ticks. "I don't want someone else."

In a low voice, she says, "Don't say things like that."

"Why not? It's the truth."

Deflecting, she says, "I wish I was more selfish, Aaron, but I'm not."

My fingers dig through my hair, pulling at the roots. "What does that even mean?" She's drunker than I'd initially thought. "Can you just tell me where you are? I'm getting worried."

"You know I can't do that," she says.

"Why?"

"Because then I'd see you again, and I don't think I have the strength to push you away twice."

A punch to my stomach.

"Then don't." *Please, please don't.*

At the same time, if she sees me and doesn't push me away, but also can't love me the way I love her, then maybe she's right to stay away. I can only get my heart broken so many times.

"You don't understand," she says, sounding tired.

"Then explain it to me," I plead, getting up to my feet and pacing around the ice, keys in hand, ready. This girl is so hard to understand. I wish I could just crack her like an egg and read all the thoughts in her head.

I hear something that sounds a lot like a sniffle before she says, "Aaron, I could only be with you if I loved you less."

Time stands still. Snow stops falling. Wind stops howling. I stop breathing.

"Repeat that?" I get out.

"I…I'm sorry." Then, the line cuts.

"Wren? Wren?"

Nothing.

I try calling her again, but she sends me straight to voicemail.

"Fuck!"

"What's happening?" Finn says as he gets up from the bench and walks to me.

Unable to move my gaze away from my phone, I whisper, "She loves me." I didn't dream it, did I? No, she definitely said the words.

Finn snickers. "Dude, are you serious? Of course she does. That was never the question."

"Well, it was for me!" She'd never said the words. Never even said anything remotely close to it.

"Are you blind, or what? That girl looks at you like you're made of gold," he says, eyebrows high.

"And you didn't want to tell me that before?"

"Didn't think I needed to."

She loves me, I repeat to myself. She actually loves me.

This changes everything.

I was willing to accept whatever she threw at me. Letting her go was something I'd come to wrap my head around, but that was when I thought she didn't love me. I would never push something on someone who doesn't want to be with me. Now I know love isn't the problem. And that was the only thing I'd be willing to let come in the way of me and her.

"I need to get her back," I state.

"I thought that was another given."

Eyes narrowed, I say, "You're not being helpful, you know that?"

"Don't care. You just said I was a good man."

"A mistake."

"Keep telling yourself that." He gives my shoulder a brotherly pat. "Now just go get her, will you?"

"Right." I finish packing my bag in a hurry, then throw it over my shoulder. "Wish me luck."

He smirks. "Don't think you need it."

Oh, how I wish that were the case.

Without wasting a minute, I leave Finn and start toward my car. Time to think of a plan.

CHAPTER 33

Wren

I'VE NEVER STRUGGLED DURING A RUN AS MUCH AS I DID THIS morning.

If that isn't a sign I went overboard on Friday night, I don't know what is. Still being hungover two days later isn't normal.

A shudder runs through my body at the thought of what happened when I was at that bar, getting drunk out of my mind. It wasn't the goal, at first. I started with only one glass of wine, but then it made me feel a little better, so I ordered another one. The more alcohol I ingested, the less it hurt thinking about Aaron. At some point, all I could feel was love and nostalgia while reminiscing about our time together, instead of regret and pain. Which is precisely when I had the brilliant idea to call him up.

I run a hand down my face as I give Molly and Maybelle their breakfast, the sweat from my run icing over my thawing body. What in the world was I thinking?

I wasn't thinking, that's the problem.

But in that moment, missing him had become an entire entity, like a second person living inside me. I didn't want to hear his voice; I needed to. And the moment I did, thoughts that I hadn't even let myself acknowledge came out of my mouth without me even realizing it.

I told him I loved him.

It's not like it was a surprise. From the way I acted, letting myself spend all my time with him and sleep in his bed before we parted ways, I'm sure it was obvious how I felt. But I never intended to say the words to him. Not when it could be a reason for him to want to stay with me.

Point proven by the fact that after I hung up on Friday, he called again, and yesterday, he called me twice. I let it go to voicemail each time.

Stupid. I was so stupid. He'd finally been able to get a clean break from me, and I messed it all up by telling him things he never should've heard.

Finished eating, Molly starts spinning in circles in the apartment. I watch her with shoulders slumped, removing my gloves and hat. How can she have that much energy? We just ran three miles. Sure, I wasn't as fast as I usually am, but still. Meanwhile, Maybelle is still chewing her food slowly. Not in top shape, but alive. That's all that matters.

Picking my phone up, I look at the screen with one eye closed.

No calls.

That's good. Maybe Aaron understood what I said Friday night was a mistake and I'm not going to change my mind, no matter how much I wish we would be in an alternate reality so I could.

Just as I put the phone down, though, three knocks come from my front door.

My heart stutters.

I don't need to go look to know it's him. First because no one knows where I live, and second because I can feel him, somehow. Like chemicals in my blood are altered when he's around.

Still, my heart skips a beat when I open the door and find Aaron standing on the other side, clad in a plaid shirt under his winter coat and jeans. He's not smiling, which again is so unnatural for Aaron. I don't like seeing him not as happy as can be.

"Hi," he says, his voice more unsure than it once was.

"Hey." I force myself to swallow. "What…what are you doing here?"

His shoulders straighten, as if he just remembered he's a confident man.

"I'm here to take you somewhere."

My eyes close. "Aaron..."

"Please. It won't take long." His dark gaze is pleading. Then, "You owe me this, at least."

His words are worse than a physical blow, mostly because he's right. I infiltrated myself into his life, in his bed, and got out once he developed feelings. Yes, I'd asked him not to fall for me, but I'd still taken the risk by letting myself get close to him. And then, to make things worse, I called him and told him things I shouldn't have after I broke things off. I don't know what part of our story he had in mind when he said I owed him, but whichever it is, he's right.

That doesn't mean I'm not terrified. We're supposed to be going our separate ways. The more time we spend together, and the worse it'll get when we need to part again.

As if seeing the concern in my eyes, Aaron takes my hand and says, "Please, Wren."

The way he says my name feels like a prayer.

"All right." I look down at my sweaty self. "Give me five minutes."

* * *

The ride in Aaron's car is silent and tense. I don't know where he's taking me, and he hasn't made a peep. It's not like I'm worried about being alone with him, but I don't know what his intentions are, and that's scary. What if he misinterpreted my call on Friday and thinks I changed my mind? Or what if he's angry with me and wants to let me know I hurt him more than I'd thought? I don't know why he would need to take me somewhere to tell me that, but the fact that ever-talking Aaron is silent does nothing to reassure me.

After a twenty-minute ride, Aaron turns the car into the almost-empty parking lot of a...pet store?

Once he's put the car on park, he gets out of the car, still silent. I follow him outside. Without waiting for me, he walks toward the store, then opens the door and gives me a look, asking me to come in.

I do.

The front desk is empty, no employee in sight. However, what I'd thought was a pet store actually looks like a shelter. Dogs bark in metal cages behind the front desk, some loud and deep, others sharp and shriek-like.

"I want you to do something for me," Aaron finally utters as he turns to face me, hands in his coat's pockets, jaw lined with short stubble. His gaze is warm, something I don't deserve. He should be pissed at me. He should hate me. There's no reason for him to look at me like I'm not the bane of his existence.

"Yes?" I croak.

"I want you to act as if you were going to pick a dog and choose the one you'd get."

I frown. "Why?"

"Humor me."

This is the strangest Sunday morning I have experienced in my life. I don't even get where this request is coming from. I'm not in a place to refuse, though. He says I owe him, so I will do whatever he asks, no matter how weird.

Without a word, I start walking toward the kennels. A dozen or so dogs watch me as I look into each of the metal crates. One has a large golden Labrador, barking loudly. Another has a white puppy that looks so much like a young Maybelle, with a similar slow energy, it makes me grin. I pass rows of angry dogs snarling and energetic puppies yapping, until I reach the final crate at the end of the hallway. In it sits an old, cappuccino-colored male. He must be a mix because I can't pinpoint the breed. Probably has some terrier in him, maybe coupled with some boxer. His ears are floppy, covered with white strands all over.

But it's not his color or his scraggly, unkempt fur that gets to me. It's his eyes. All the dogs I've seen before have looked at me like they wanted me to take them home with me. He looks at me like he doesn't deserve to be taken home by anyone. Everything about him screams that he's old and has gone through a lot. He doesn't look aggressive or particularly cuddly. Just tired.

"This one," I say. When I turn to where Aaron was standing, I actually find him much closer to me than he initially was, as if he followed me from a distance while I made my choice. I try to ignore the way he's looking at me, the same way he did that morning we woke up in the cabin together. The moment he opened his eyes, they shone bright, as if I was exactly what he'd wanted to see first thing in the day. "He's the one I would pick, if I had to."

Before Aaron can answer, a middle-aged Black woman appears at the other end of the hallway and beams at us. "Mr. Scott-Perez, hi! Woody's almost ready to go, I'm just finishing up the papers."

"That's great," he tells her. "Take your time."

What the heck? I look around, my gaze landing on the old dog's crate, *Woody* written in bold letters at the top of the crate's door.

"What's going on?" I ask.

"Well, you're almost ready to be the new owner of a cute dog."

"What? But... But I can't own another one." I always told myself that after Molly and Maybelle, there wouldn't be any others. Not when my situation is so precarious. It's not like I don't want more dogs, especially one like Woody, who melts my heart with a simple look and who I'm sure could bring me a short lifetime of infinite love, but it's not that easy. What if one day I forget to take care of them properly and they're left to their own means? What if I die before them?

Reading my thoughts like only he can, Aaron says, "If ever you couldn't take care of him anymore, I'd be there, Wren. I'll always be there."

I ignore the last part of his sentence and shake my head. "I don't understand. How did you know…"

"That you would pick him?"

Biting the inside of my cheek, I nod.

As he leans against the cement wall, he says, "Oh, that was the easiest part. You always choose to help the ones who need it the most. Woody was the oldest one and the one who seemed to be the frailest. A clear choice for you."

It's in this moment I realize how well Aaron has gotten to know me. Not just the parts I shared with him, but also the parts I tried to keep hidden. He's opened all my hidden closets, no matter how hard I worked to keep them locked.

Aaron takes a step toward me and parts the fingers I'm wringing together, taking each hand in his own.

"Now, cariño, I only want to ask you for one thing."

I blink, my heart beating lightning-fast.

"That you extend that same beautiful compassion toward yourself."

My breath stays stuck in my throat. I can't speak. It feels like he always finds the way to make me speechless.

"You don't care that Woody has a limited amount of years to give you love," Aaron continues. "You see his love as being just as worthwhile, if not more. You've understood the truth. That the depth of one's love does not equal to the time it will last. And that's exactly how I feel about you."

Not again. Please, not again. He needs to let me go. I'm not strong enough to keep pushing him away. I take a step back, but he only follows me.

"If you didn't care for me, I would let you go. But Wren, I know you're in love with me, and guess what? I'm so fucking in love with you too. So no, I'm not letting you go. You run away, I'm right behind you."

A tear falls from my eye, my lips quivering.

"Aaron, I can't..." I don't complete my sentence. It's too painful. He's saying all the right things, and the only thing I want to do is believe them and dive right into him.

Aaron licks his lips, never relenting. Instead, he steps even closer so I have to tip my head up to meet his eyes. His smell is everywhere.

"You can let me go all you want in the hope it'll convince me to move on, but you'd be wrong to do that, because I can tell you I'll never be able to love anyone the way I love you. Letting you go would not bring me any happiness, cariño." He brushes the back of his knuckles against my cheek, making my eyelids flutter. "Quite frankly, it would kill me, and I would *never* get over it. That, I can promise."

"But..." My thoughts are scrambled, a big mess of everything and nothing. He's picking at my defenses, one by one. Grasping at straws, I hang on to one of the strongest, most obvious barrier. "You want kids, and I can't give you that."

"I never said I wanted kids. I said I didn't know." He licks his lips. "And what I'm sure of is that I'd much rather have the certainty of you than the possibility of something I might never want."

I deflate.

"I'm so tired, Aaron."

Letting my forehead fall to his shoulder, I let myself go and cry. And for the first time in a long while, I let him comfort me without any reticence. He's where I want to be, and everything he's telling me makes me feel like no matter how much I've convinced myself we can't be together, maybe, just maybe, he has a point.

However, it doesn't erase all the doubt engraved in my soul, which makes me sob even harder. I've built my whole person around keeping people away from me, and suddenly, I'm supposed to let in the one I love the most, even if it means hurting him? It makes no sense.

And yet, I don't see myself walking away from him. Not again.

I've done it once, and it took everything in me. And with all his confident words, I feel my resolve fall brick by brick.

"I know, sweetheart. I know."

Aaron rubs my back and plays with my hair as I hold on to his shirt for dear life. It smells like his detergent mixed with something that is so him. This scent alone could make me feel less lonely.

With a hiccup, I whisper, "You deserve more than the future I can offer you." The simplest sentence that explains everything. He should run as fast as he can. It's his last chance.

He hugs me harder, leaning his bearded cheek on top of my head. "I don't care that you don't love yourself enough to believe I'd be lucky to be with you." A kiss is pressed to the crown of my hair. "We'll work on that, and in the meantime, I'll love you enough for the both of us."

A whole new set of tears stream down my cheeks. He's strong. He's so strong. Fighting for me, for *us*, when all I've done is run.

My gaze drifts to my left, where Woody is watching us intently. His soft ears are perked up, tail wagging. Aaron was right, once again. The time I would—or will—get with this dog could never affect my love for him, and the fact that he might not have long would never make me walk away. Same goes for Maybelle. I picked her up despite her old age. It never once occurred to me to protect myself from the pain of losing her sooner rather than later. I made the conscious decision to love her because she was worth it.

Maybe not all love stories need to last a lifetime. Maybe the most beautiful ones are the ones that develop *despite* the fact that they won't.

And maybe that's exactly what Aaron realized too.

I think I was wrong before, when I said Aaron doesn't know what he'd be getting himself into. By bringing me here today, he showed me he understands perfectly, yet he's still here.

I don't know what I did to merit this kind of love, but somehow, it happened. And while he's done so much for me, all I've done is push him away. If I'm to accept his love, things need to change. I need to give him more.

So, ignoring the pounding in my chest and the tightening in my lungs, I pull away to look at him when I say, "I do love you, Aaron. More than I could ever love anyone. You're everything." Everything I know. Everything I want. Everything I need.

Enough with fighting it. I'm not strong enough to continue.

If being with me is truly his choice, then I'll respect it and cherish him with all that I have. I meant it when I said he didn't deserve the pain I will bring him one day, but if he wants me despite it, then how stupid would I be to say no?

The smile Aaron gives me in return makes me regret not telling him sooner. He needs to be this happy all the time. And from now on, ensuring this will be my mission.

Leaning forward, he whispers above my lips, "You have no idea how much I needed to hear that."

It breaks my heart yet another time, to see how much he's been craving something I could've given him so easily. But at the same time, it gives me hope, because I can see in his lips that maybe, just maybe, I am truly what he needs.

"Then I'll repeat it every day," I say, a promise I intend to keep with everything I have in me. If there's one thing I can offer him, it's all the love I have in me.

Abruptly, I climb on my tiptoes and kiss him like I've wanted to kiss him for months. Like he's mine.

Because he is.

CHAPTER 34

Aaron

THE FACILITY IS LARGE AND SPARSE.

It's obviously been designed to house people who could be at risk of tripping in a cluttered space or of hurting themselves with objects that aren't essential.

Even then, it feels warm. Like a true home for the residents.

Beside me, Wren is chewing her bottom lip so hard she'll probably draw blood soon. I grab her hand, running a finger over her thumb.

Attention returned, she turns to me and gives me a tight smile.

"It's going to be fine," I tell her.

"You can't know that."

Leaning down to kiss her scalp, I say, "Yes, I do. Because even if she doesn't react well to me, I know it doesn't mean anything."

"It's a harsh thing to see." She blinks repeatedly.

"I'm sure." I squeeze her hand tighter as we walk toward her mother's room. "But I also know that it'll be the disease speaking if things go south."

"They will go south. They always do."

"Then they do." She needs to see this is not a problem for me. With her by my side, nothing could be.

With pursed lips, she says, "How can you always be so casual about things?"

Stopping in the hallway, I turn and hold her by the shoulders. "It's your mom, Wren. Even if she isn't the person she used to be, she's still the person who raised *my* person, and I'm honored to have the chance to meet her."

The moment her eyes start filling with tears, I look away and start walking again. This is not the time for a breakdown from the both of us. I'm not sure whether she believes me, but I certainly do.

Wren's fingers are tight around mine as we reach her mother's room.

"Want me to go in first?" I ask.

She shakes her head, then exhales sharply before opening the door.

"Hi, Mom," she says in a low voice, walking in slowly. I follow behind her, never letting go of her hand.

Melissa Lawson slowly shifts her gaze from the window at the end of her room to her daughter. A small frown overtakes her face as she examines her. The two of them look so alike, with similar upturned noses and dark hair.

"I-I brought someone I'd like you to meet," Wren says, pulling me closer.

"Hello," I say with a small voice. After clearing my throat, I add, "I'm Aaron. It's very nice to finally meet you."

Melissa's gaze drifts from Wren to me, a little empty, but her eyes narrow when they land on me. As if she recognizes I'm someone she hasn't met before.

Wren's Mom hasn't uttered a word yet, and I want to say something before she does. If Wren is right and she does get angry soon, I want my message to be delivered beforehand.

Taking a few steps forward, I crouch next to Melissa, careful to keep space between us. I haven't forgotten what Wren told me about physical touch triggering her.

"I'm Wren's partner."

It still feels surreal to be able to say this. It's been a month, and I haven't come down my cloud. As if I'm living a dream, but every morning when I wake up, it's still there.

Wren is tense behind me. I can feel it.

"I wanted to thank you for raising your daughter the way you did, and I also wanted to reassure you that she's in good hands." I swallow. "She isn't alone anymore, and I'll take care of her for as long as I can." Not a simple reassurance, but a promise I intend on keeping.

Wren's hand lands on my shoulder, warm and anchoring.

Melissa stays still. Not a single twitch occurs in her face.

That is, until she tilts her head and moves her gaze from me to Wren, and back again.

My breaths are short, stuttering. Something is about to happen. I wrap a hand around Wren's shaking wrist, letting her know whatever happens, it'll be fine. I'm not going anywhere.

But the thing that occurs next has me taken aback.

As she fixes her gaze on us, Melissa's expression changes. Muscles are finally used. I feel it's something out of the ordinary when I hear Wren's soft gasp.

Melissa stays silent, but she doesn't need to speak.

Her smile says everything.

* * *

"Can you come here? I want to show you something."

"Coming!" Wren calls from the kitchen, where she's supposedly cooking the best pasta I'll ever taste. Apparently, I needed to be thanked after this morning's visit, which exceeded all our expectations.

I've eaten some of Wren's meals in the past, and to say I'm the cook in this couple would be an understatement. I'll still eat every damn bite off my plate.

At my feet, Woody shifts, slowly spinning three times before lying down in the exact same position as before. With a snort, I scratch his head with one of my feet. Beside him, Maybelle sleeps soundly. The two of them have become the best of friends the moment we brought him home weeks ago. They haven't slept by themselves once.

Molly, though, is another story.

Every time Woody is playing with a toy, she'll rush to take it away from him. It's like a game for her. It annoys him to no end, but thankfully, he isn't aggressive, so he'll just huff, go pick up another one, and restart the game with her all over again.

"What's going on?" Wren asks as she walks into the room, her hair piled in a bun on top of her head, strands falling over her forehead and framing her face.

I tip my head. "Come here."

She follows my lead and joins me in the makeshift office I created for myself in her bedroom. Sometimes, when I'm not done with work but don't want to come home too late, I'll bring my work with me. I very well could've gone to work at my place after our visit to her mom, but one thing we realized since we officially got together was that if we have the choice, we'd rather spend the least amount of time apart, hence the desk in the only bedroom of the apartment.

With a gentle movement, Wren sits in my lap and wraps her arms around my neck, watching me. A beautiful smile adorns her lips. Not to sound like a conceited prick, but I've never seen her as happy as she's been these past four weeks.

It's been the most rewarding and encouraging thing I've seen in my life.

Leaning forward, I start pressing kisses all the way from her collarbone to her ear. "Has anyone ever told you how beautiful you are?"

"Maybe. Maybe not."

She laughs as I groan before pressing my lips against hers, then whisper, "*cariño mio.*"

Her head tilts. "You never did tell me what that means."

"What do you think it means?"

Her shoulders lift then drop.

"It means sweetheart," I say.

Her eyes narrow before bulging out. "But you've been calling me like that for...a long time."

I grin. "Yes. Because you were mine way before you even knew it."

I expect her to call me smug, or to roll her eyes, but she doesn't. Instead, she presses her nose to my temple and says, "I really was, wasn't I?"

My answer is to kiss the shit out of her.

When we come back for air, both our chests rising and falling fast, Wren clears her throat, her cheeks tinted pink. "So what did you want to show me?"

"Oh, right, sorry. You're quite the distraction."

Now, she rolls her eyes.

God. I'll marry this woman someday.

Going around Wren, I open my computer back up, then load the program onto it.

"So," I start, "you know I've been working on this new game for a while, right?" Ever since I've returned full time to Arcade Games, I've dedicated all my time to this project, with a renewed inspiration and energy. It's like the moment I left the farm and knew that I had the chance of making my dream career my reality without letting anyone down, I was able to jump into it without restraint. It's been tiresome, but mostly a great time.

"Yes, I know."

"More specifically, I work on—"

"Backgrounds," she finishes, a twinkle in her eye. "Contrary to what you might think, I do listen when you speak."

"Right," I say, hiding my grin. She's such a smart-ass sometimes, but most importantly, she's my smart-ass. "Well, I've finished the first draft of the design."

She gasps, then shakes my shoulders. "Aaron! That's wonderful! I want to see."

"Yes, yes, okay." I laugh. I've never seen someone so excited to see one of my projects. Not even my bosses, who'll make quite a good dime with this if it does well.

After selecting the right file on my laptop, I tell Wren to turn.

The moment her gaze lands on the screen and her eyes fill with tears, I know this is a success.

"Oh, Aaron..."

I follow the same path her gaze does. The snowy trail leading to the forest. The wooden cabin, next to a bigger, but just as rustic, house. The pine trees going on for miles and miles.

"I might have left Evermore on paper, but I realized when I gave Finn the job that I might've been even more attached to the place than I thought. After that, I couldn't think of a design I wanted to work on more." The game is still based in the Scottish countryside, but I was still able to transform one of the villages to look like Evermore, the game now reminding me of a faraway place and of home, all at once.

"Obviously, there'll be different buildings and structures for quests added on top of it, but—"

"It's perfect," she says as she continues studying it. "Absolutely perfect." When she finally turns to me, her eyes are glistening. "*You're* perfect."

I can't hide the feeling of rightness that goes through my body as I hear those words. For a time, I thought a moment like this one would never happen. And now here we are. With her in my arms, showing me her love is real. Every day, she tells me, and every day, it makes my heart soar.

"So I take it you think this will go well with my boss?"

With a straight face I've come to know so well over the past months, she says, "If he doesn't like it, I think I'll go there and tell him just what I think of his opinion."

"Am I dreaming, or are you getting confrontational?" I squeeze her hips.

"Only for you."

The muscles in my cheeks hurt from how much I've been smiling lately.

Wren's attention returns to the computer, where I show her some Easter eggs I've planted throughout the game for only my loved ones to recognize and understand. After half an hour, the dogs leave the room, probably annoyed with our excited chatter.

Once we've finally gone over everything game related, I close the computer and bring her to our bed.

"So," she says as she plays with a strand of my overly long hair. "What's next?"

Lips pursed, I take a moment to think. What's next? I didn't even ask myself that question. I've been so overworked for the past year that I never took the time to think about what I'd want to do after finishing this project. Obviously, I'm still helping my family as much as I can when they need it, but with the farm taken care of and this design draft done, I have some time on my hands.

Without thinking about it, I say the first thing that pops into my head. "How about a vacation?"

Wren lifts her brows.

"Yes," I say, more confidently. "A vacation. Away from here."

Her eyes bulge. It brings me back to that time at the pub when we went out with Finn and he asked her whether she liked to travel. At the time, she said no, but I have a feeling this might've been related to everything I'm trying to make her see about herself and the world.

"I don't know…" she starts.

"Come on," I say as I roll closer to her and prop myself on my elbow. "Let's go somewhere new. Let's go see the koalas. I'll wait for you to pet them all fucking day, if you want." She laughs, although the terrified look in her eyes doesn't disappear. "Let's jump in the ocean and swim with sharks and make love all over the place. Let's make memories, no matter how long they'll last." Her throat bobs, telling me I've hit just the spot. "Let's *live,* cariño."

I never thought about all of those things, but now that they're out of my mouth, I see they're exactly what I want. She's spent all her life making it as beige as possible.

I want her to experience the world's entire palette, always.

She watches me for a long moment. So long, in fact, that I start thinking this might've scared her. Too much, too soon.

Until, with a small voice, she interrupts the silence with, "Okay."

"Okay?" I say, incredulous. This is a lot to take in for her all at once.

"Yes, okay." Her lips quirking up, she puts a soft hand on my cheek. "You got me with the koalas."

Letting out a roar of laughter, I roll on top of her and kiss her, my tongue pressing against hers as the sounds of our happiness mingle around us.

This is actually happening. The true beginning of our lives.

We have no idea what the future holds. Maybe we have months or years or decades. It might be filled with all sorts of things, and no one knows what's ahead.

But what I do know is the present is really, really beautiful.

EPILOGUE

Wren
18 months later

"DIOS MIO, LOOK AT YOU!" MARTINA CALLS FROM where she's standing in my hotel suite.

I grin as I look down at my white, floor-length dress, willing my hands to stop shaking. When Aqidah recommended I try it on, I wasn't sure about it, with its silky material and tight corset, but she was right. It looked perfect on me.

And now that I'm here, in the Dominican Republic, I'm even more thankful I didn't pick a dress made of a heavier material.

"Thank you," I answer, wiping my clammy hands down my dress. "And thank you for being here with me."

Our wedding was never supposed to be something big. When Aaron proposed eight months ago by kneeling in the middle of the Christmas tree farm where I got to know the love of my life, our fur babies by our side, I said yes in a heartbeat.

The next thing I said was that I wanted something small.

Aaron, however, wanted to have a wedding with approximately eight-thousand guests. So we compromised and decided to get married in the Dominican Republic, on a beach close to where Martina grew up, with our closest family and friends.

But right now, even thinking of our fifty-something guests is making me nervous.

"Of course, mi amor," Martina says with a pat of the skin under her eyes. "I can't start crying now."

Just then, a knock comes from the door.

"It's time," my almost mother-in-law says as she gets up and claps her hands. "You are going to be wonderful. I'm sure Aaron will die when he sees you."

Fighting to keep my giddiness from coming out of my every pore, I hug her and accept her kiss on my cheek. Then I wait as she opens the door to leave, letting Dennis in.

Aaron's father never fully recovered from his stroke. He can say or write a few words from time to time, but overall, our communication has been limited. Still, I feel like he's one of the members of this family who understands me the most.

We exchange a glance, and the smile he gives me makes me take in a deep breath. It's time.

I nod, then start out the room with him. Our walk to where the ceremony takes place is short, the thick humidity already making the hairs curl at the nape of my neck. Thank goodness we waited for the sun to start setting before the ceremony. Above us, exotic birds sing while large palm trees surround the alley that leads us to the alcove where our guests are sitting.

When I start to see water and white chairs on the horizon, I stop, then turn to Dennis. His hair has grayed a lot since I met him, yet he looks younger somehow. Most importantly, he looks so much happier.

"I never thought I'd get married, but even in my wildest dreams, I didn't think I'd have anyone by my side to walk me down the aisle if it happened. So… Thank you. I'm so grateful to have you in my life."

Dennis's gaze becomes watery before he opens his mouth. A few sounds come out, but none what he wants to say. I wait patiently until the word he was looking for comes out.

"Honor."

Keep it together, Wren.

He must be having the same thought as I am because we

simultaneously turn toward the beach. Then, without another word, we start walking.

The music soon reaches our ears, a bridal march played by a string trio, so beautiful. And when we get close enough, everyone rises.

To my right stands Aaron's Dominican family, who I finally got to meet on a trip last year, each of them kinder than then last. On my left, Aqidah is holding her husband's hand while her two sons wave at me. I wave back. I know Josslyn, her daughter, walked in before me as our flower girl. Behind her stands Finn, Aaron's cousin Will, and his wife, Violet, who I've gotten close to in the past year. We text every few days, and she's always there to remind me of my worth in her life, and Aaron's too, just like I do when her anxiety and depression rear their ugly heads and she starts pulling away. A few other friends of Aaron are here to celebrate with us. All the people we need.

Well, minus one.

My mother passed away six months ago. It was peaceful, in her sleep. She simply stopped breathing. It was the one thing that brought me joy, that she died in a dignified, calm way.

Her death itself, though, was hard to take in. It wasn't a relief like I'd expected. Despite all the struggles of her life with Alzheimer's, there seemed to be happiness to be found in her own little world. Nurses would tell me how big her smile got when they gave her plastic dolls to care for or laundry to fold. Even though it wasn't the life she'd known, it was *her* life, and losing her caused a deep, bittersweet grief. Thankfully, my fiancé and his family were there for me to help me through it all.

Only once I've looked at everyone around me do I lift my head to the front, and my heart stops.

Aaron stands in front of a white flower arch, his dark hair styled the way I love, a few strands falling onto his face. He wears the white shirt and beige pants we picked together, nothing too formal for a wedding that was meant to be intimate. He looks too handsome for life.

But what strikes me the most is the smile he's sporting. In the past two years, I've seen my optimistic, full-of-life boyfriend grin on so many occasions, I've lost count, yet today takes the cake. I've overcome a lot of the doubt I had in the past about our relationship being good for him—thanks to online support groups for people with eFAD, self-reflection on my warped vision of life, love, and worth, and endless discussions with the people surrounding me and my therapist—but this smile truly makes me see that I can make him happy. So happy.

When we reach the end of aisle, I turn to hug Dennis, thanking him again with a tight squeeze. Aaron does too, and then it's just us.

"You look stunning, cariño," he whispers as he takes my hands and kisses the knuckles.

I don't think I could ever tire of hearing those words. Of feeling this way.

"You're not so bad yourself," I answer, making him smirk.

"Everyone, please be seated," the officiant says. With the sounds of seats cracking, I assume people listen to his instruction, but I couldn't know for sure. My gaze is stuck to my lover's.

The officiant starts talking about the importance of marriage. About love and duty and a life shared between two people. It's all beautiful, but my attention is split. I'm still halfway stuck on wrapping my head around the fact that I'm actually here, marrying the love of my life.

"And now, our bride and groom will share their vows."

Aaron squeezes my hands and winks. We decided I'd go first, considering I was nervous about sharing my feelings in front of everyone, and I'd rather not go after him when he'll obviously have the best vows ever written. I still agreed to write and read our own vows because this is not exactly a typical marriage, and I wanted our ceremony to reflect that.

I didn't write anything down. It's all there, in my head. Exhaling through pursed lips, I keep my eyes on Aaron and Aaron alone.

"When we met, I honestly didn't know what to think."

He lifts an eyebrow, lips quirked up.

"You were there, so ready to talk freely to anyone who would listen. So open to all things. Life had given you a lot of struggles—I could see it, even then—yet you had never lost that part of you that makes you so wonderful. And I found that both extremely strange and so, so impressive. I couldn't imagine being brave enough to never lose faith in life and love. The time we've spent together since then has only proved what I already knew that first night in the bar, and it inspires me so much. The way you live your life has quite literally changed everything I thought I knew about the world."

My throat closes up, but Aaron's thumb caressing my hand keeps me grounded enough to continue.

"You told me once that I didn't believe I could make you happy, and you were right." Everyone here now knows about my genetic susceptibility for Alzheimer's, so there's no need to hide anything. "I didn't think you or anyone here with us today could benefit from having me in their life. But by loving you and being loved by you, I learned to love myself too."

Aaron isn't simply holding my hands now. His fingers are intertwined with mine and squeezing hard, as if holding on for dear life. His eyes are shiny. Mine probably are too.

I lick my lips. "I also learned that time didn't have to be my enemy. Before, I was constantly wishing I could live in a world where time would stop. But I came to realize that the clock is not as scary when you're by my side."

I only realize I've started tearing up when I feel Aaron's

thumb on my cheek. For the last part of my vows, I step even closer so that I can wrap my arms around his neck. I don't know if this is considered appropriate for a wedding, but right now, I couldn't care less. This is a moment I need to share with him, as close as can be.

"I will always wish I could have more time with you, Aaron. No amount of years will ever be enough." I swallow. "But even though our time will likely be cut short, I'll cherish it with all I have. Because it was, and still is, *everything*."

Aaron leans his forehead to mine, sniffling.

"I told you years ago that I wasn't bitter about what life gave me, and I still believe that. Because it gave me you. And for a minute or a lifetime, it will always have been worth it."

The moment I finish, Aaron's lips are on mine, the kiss salty and bursting with love. He pulls away too fast for my liking.

"Too soon, I know," he tells the officiant. "Sorry."

The man only laughs knowingly.

Pulling away from me, Aaron rolls his shoulders back and exhales sharply. Then, he turns to the crowd and says, "Wow, tough act to follow."

Our audience laughs as I smile at him.

When his attention comes back to me, all the seriousness returns to his face.

"Wren," he starts, making me shiver with a single word. To my left, the sun is creating a warm, pink glow over the water, reflecting in Aaron's whiskey-colored eyes. "I won't be long, because if I started to say everything I love about you, we would be here until next week."

I grin.

"I could also promise to love and cherish you until death do us part, but I assume this is a given. So, instead, I'll make you another promise I think you need to hear." He takes a step forward, our bodies two magnets.

Hands in mine, he murmurs, "I promise to remember everything."

I close my eyes to prevent an avalanche of tears from falling.

"I'll remember the Sunday mornings we spend in bed with the dogs barking for us to get up and come feed them. I'll remember the way you take your coffee, and the feel of our kisses, and the hugs we share before falling asleep, with our legs intertwined. I'll remember how it felt when we jumped from that waterfall in Belize, you shrieking and me laughing. I'll remember the moment we met in that preppy bar in Boston. I'll remember our first kiss after a New Year's Eve countdown, and our second kiss in the cabin, and all the ones that followed."

I'm sobbing now. There's no other way to put it. Tears are sliding down Aaron's cheeks too, although much more elegantly.

"I'll fill my mind to the brim with all the moments we have spent and will spend together, big or small. And when I become old and dusty one day and feel like they're starting to slip away, then I'll write them all down. I won't let any moment go."

Aaron's hands cling to my face, soft yet reassuring.

"I know forgetting scares you, and I get it. I get it so much. But don't worry about our memories, cariño. They're safe with me."

Leaning more deeply into his hand, I nod vigorously. He couldn't have made me feel more seen or understood if he'd tried.

"I love you," I murmur to him.

"And I love you."

The officiant to my left sniffles, the sky now a burning red behind him. "By the power vested in me, I now declare you husband and wife. You may kiss the bride." He clears his throat. "For real, this time."

The man who owns my heart—my *husband*—beams grandly, then says, "With pleasure."

And he does.

***

Many, many years later

It starts whisper-like, as the dusk settling in after a long and warm summer day.

I sit down on the steps of our porch one morning to tie my running shoes, and something happens. A blank, as I hold the ends of the two laces. In a blink, it's gone.

But it still happened.

My heart starts racing, my thoughts blurring as I look around, forgetting all about the shoes or the run.

And then, I see him. He's walking back from the mailbox, his hair streaked with gray, face just as lovely as the day we met. My body instantly relaxes.

And when our eyes meet and he smiles at me, I know that whatever happens, it will be all right.

ACKNOWLEDGEMENTS

It always feels surreal to get to this part. Three books in, and I still cannot believe the luck I have to be doing this. So first of all, I need to thank you, my dearest readers. I never in my wildest dreams would've imagined having such supportive, wonderful, and kind readers. Interacting with you always makes my day. All of this is because of you, and I promise I will never take it for granted.

Obviously, the people I need to thank next are my wonderful critique partners. Rebecca, Darienne, Jessica, you have made this book infinitely better and it honestly wouldn't be half as good without your input. I'm so lucky to have you in my life.

To Gab, Émilie, Michelle, Raph, and Marie, my early readers, friends, and sisters, who have supported me from day one. I love you girls so much.

To my sensitivity readers, who have allowed me to tell a story that is hopefully respectful and accurate. Krystal, Jackie, Crystal, Romina, Zeineb, Nikitha, thank you from the bottom of my heart for your time and kindness.

To Murphy, who again outdid herself with this cover. You always find a way to bring my books to life, and I am in awe of your talent.

To Jackie, whose sharp eye and meticulousness is unparalleled. This book would be filled with inconsistencies (and very weird preposition choices, lol) were it not for you!

To my parents, brothers, and in-laws, who have read my romance novels despite having no interest in the genre because they wanted to show their support. I'm incredibly grateful—and only a tiny bit embarrassed!

To Louis, who never complains when I say, "Just one more

chapter!" You are the most amazing partner a person could ask for. I love you.

And finally, to the bloggers, Booktokers, and Bookstagramers who have quite literally built my career from the ground up. If you hadn't shared your love for my first two books, this one would not exist. I don't think I will ever be able to thank you enough for everything you have done for me. Your aesthetic videos, reviews, reels, posts, and annotations make me so incredibly happy. I couldn't possibly name all of you, but I need to offer special thanks to Tish, Pauline, Lola, Brittany, Anna-Marie, Demi, Tina, Dom, Larissa, Kimmy, Candace, Taliyah, Clara, Jess, Lil, Monica, Elle, Julie, Elsa, Kenna, Sophia, Gray, Rana, Lianna, Jean, Nikki, Eliz, Kody, Isabella, Rose, Sirine, Emily, Anna, Olivia, Sarah, Taylor, Aya, Ashley, Shelli, Lindsay, Kristina, Cassie, Bri, Brenna, Haley. You made it all come true.

ABOUT THE AUTHOR

N.S. Perkins lives the best of both worlds, being a medical student by day and a romance author by night. When she's not writing, reading, or studying, you can probably find her trying new restaurants, dreaming about the next beach she'll be visiting, or creeping the cutest dogs in the parks near her house. She lives in Montreal with her partner.

Find her on:
Twitter: @nsperkinsauthor
Instagram: @nsperkinsauthor
TikTok: @nsperkinsauthor
Website: www.nsperkins.com

ALSO FROM THE AUTHOR

A RISK ON FOREVER

THE INFINITY BETWEEN US

CPSIA information can be obtained
at www.ICGtesting.com
Printed in the USA
BVHW092322181122
652274BV00036B/980